WOMAN ON TOP

WOMAN ON TOP

Deborah Schwartz

For my children

CONTENTS

FALL 1994

CHAPTER 1

October

Leonard told me that it was his mother's fault, a result of the fact that she smoked throughout her pregnancy with him, that he would grow to a mere five feet five inches. Since I never saw a picture of her, I never knew if it was also her fault, although hardly preventable, that no woman on the streets of New York would ever turn her head if he walked by.

He had married a beautiful woman, his high school sweetheart, and considered their union as one of "Beauty and the Beast". He had all the trappings of the little man, the Napoleon, who was to succeed grandly and existed to control those around him.

His wife had died after twenty-four years of marriage, although her cancer allowed her to linger for the final eighteen torturous months. But Leonard was not one to linger over anybody. Two months after her death he was reading the personal ads in *New York* magazine. It was there that he found mine.

Beautiful lawyer, 40 year old winsome widow in
Ct. with two kids looking for love and laughter
with a kind, professional man. Photo available.

Over the course of three weeks, I received forty letters in
response to my ad. I threw away thirty-nine. The man who
sent a picture of himself in a Speedo bathing suit with his
muscular hairy chest bursting left nothing to my imagination.
Several women failed to realize that a beautiful widow is a
woman and sent me pictures of their cleavage. And, of
course, the man incarcerated in Alabama who read *New York*
magazine and sent a salacious letter was not what I had in
mind when I placed the ad. Leonard's letter arrived last, just
when I had nearly given up all hope that a widow living in a
small town in central Connecticut could ever find her next
love.

The envelope was marked with the insignia from the Ritz
Carlton Hotel.

Dear Young Widow in Ct.

*I read your ad on the plane going to a business meeting
in Arizona. I am a young 50-year-old widower who lives
in New Jersey. I am a very personable, warm, kind, very
intelligent, loyal, romantic, energetic, very athletic, emotionally and financially secure person with a great sense
of humor and a high degree of integrity. Women general-
ly describe me as 'very cute'.*

*I love kids and enjoy family, friends, travel, sports, mu-
sic, and theater. I have never responded to an ad before
but I was struck by your being a widow and a lawyer
(describing yourself as beautiful also helped). I am a
real estate investment banker with a large U.S. based
company. I have three great children, a son who is in*

medical school, a daughter who is a teacher and a son at Cornell.

I am interested in meeting a person who is refined, very sweet, warm, intelligent, articulate and very attractive – a woman who I can admire and who is comfortable in jeans or black tie.

While you will meet men who are better looking (and who have better handwriting) you will not meet anyone who is more personable, or a nicer, higher quality person.

Since I have not responded to ads I do not have stock pictures to send. I therefore am sending a passport photo type picture I had taken – which honestly does not do me justice even though I do not claim to be Robert Redford.

If my letter merits your interest call me at the following number. The best time to reach me is between 9 p.m. and 11:30 p.m. during the week – anytime on the weekends (although I frequently travel to watch my son play college football). I am an early riser so you may call me after 6:30 a.m. – if I do not answer I am either traveling on business or out jogging.

I am a non-smoker. I hope to hear from you.

Sincerely,

Leonard

The picture had fallen out of the envelope and fluttered to the ground. As I picked it up, one look at the black and white photo revealed a man who could have claimed to resemble a blondish version of Edward G. Robinson but should have been flattered to have his name merely mentioned in the same sentence as Robert Redford. Yet, I was determined to press on because I had two precious children who needed me to do just that. After all, cancer had made me a widow at the age of thirty-five and it had been a long uphill climb since then.

Cancer ended Jake's life; along the way it had ravaged mine. The fifteen months of Jake's illness I had spent caring for him, having abandoned all other roles, and then I had lost that job too.

When I thought of Jake, I could only envision him sick, his body devastated. It was at least a year before I could picture his thick black hair, straight aquiline nose, large brown eyes, and full lips smiling. And then one night I had a wonderful dream of making love to a healthy Jake.

Jake seemed like an island of tranquility in this world, and once I landed on that island I couldn't imagine life anywhere else. Jake and I were married the following May, for better or for worse. Our marriage lasted twelve years, deprived of the next forty years we craved.

■ ■ ■

I called Leonard at 9:30 the night I received his letter.

"Hi, this is the winsome widow in Connecticut you wrote to."

The phone went quiet.

"Oh, hi. So you got my letter," he finally said.

"Yes. I really liked it. My name is Kate."

"I liked your ad. You said you're a lawyer. What area do you practice in? Oh, and you can call me Len."

"Healthcare. I'm a healthcare lawyer."

"And your kids, how old are they?"

"Chloe is thirteen and Ben is ten. They're genuinely great kids, " I promised.

"Mine are great too. I'm very close to them. Very close."

"How old are yours?" I asked.

"Jennifer is twenty-six, Dale is twenty-four and Peter is twenty-one."

My mind wandered. Why had he answered a personal ad if he was truly the man he portrayed in his letter? Countless people told me not to bother with personal ads, usually considered mating grounds for the desperate with nowhere else to turn. New York men portrayed as gobbled up like turkey at Thanksgiving within minutes of exiting a marriage by hordes of starving women. None of this would stop me. I wanted to know the man described in that letter.

"When did your husband die?" he asked using the softened tone I had learned to expect whenever anyone inquired about Jake's death.

"Five years ago."

I looked up at the white stucco ceiling and then at the equally white walls, as they seemed to close in around the bed that I was laying on, the bed that Jake and I used to share. The phone became a tape recorder as I repeated, for what seemed like the hundredth time, a quick rundown of my past. The same speech that I had delivered numerous times to strangers with whom I ventured out on dates, to see if they could be my match.

"After Jake's death I had to take the Bar because I needed to get a job. My kids were so young at the time. I had graduated from law school eight years earlier and for those eight years I never opened a law book."

The sigh that Len emitted felt so predictable it led to me releasing one of my own.

"That must have been difficult," he replied.

I figured "No shit," would lessen my chances of ever meeting him, so I continued on with my speech. I breathed in.

"I've dated a lot but I don't know. This one guy, a lawyer, I dated for two months turned out not to be such a nice guy and the guy after that was too weak. What I'm honestly looking for is what I had with my husband. I wan—need to have that again."

Len remained silent. I took the time to count the pictures on my walls. What was he thinking? Had he hung up the phone?

"Listen," he said, "we should meet. You live in Connecticut, right? We should meet somewhere halfway."

Breathe out. Other men from New York, blind dates through friends, had told me that we should meet the next time I came to town. New York talk for "see you…maybe."

Len and I made plans to meet the following week at a restaurant that I found in the Connecticut edition of *Zagat*. After we hung up, I lay in the comfort of my dark room in the loving arms of my bed. Listening to the silence of the night in my small town, I read his letter over and over again, not quite believing my good fortune.

On the Wednesday night that followed, wearing my lucky Donna Karan navy blue boucle suit with navy heels, I pulled into the gravel parking lot of the restaurant. I had last worn the suit to interview for my current job. Quickly remembering to check my hair in the mirror at roughly the same time that I found a parking space, I nearly caused an accident in the midst of this sudden impulse.

A few seconds later, with the car in a safe position, the mirror reflected the sophisticated New Yorker that I used to be and was now desperately trying to portray. I smiled in relief. Len was not about to meet a woman cloistered in Connecticut after the death of her husband.

The walk toward the restaurant seemed to take an eternity. A man passed by me and in the dark of the parking lot I could see only that he appeared tall, good looking. It probably wasn't him. The restaurant's small wooden façade stood as the marker of a land far away, and a land into which I was not eager to venture.

With every step that I took, the dread that I felt about meeting Len increased. My expectations were high and for that one moment, I simply did not feel like I had the guts to go through with it. There have been many times in my life where the bad events and feelings lost their foul veneer. This could be one of them. Being single was not as bad as they say.

He was pacing around the small alcove of the restaurant when I walked through the door. I timed myself to be five minutes late—I just didn't know that Len did not expect to be kept waiting. Ever. His movements were abrupt, his impatience directing his steps. His back faced me as I walked over to introduce myself.

He turned around and under the dim lights of the old restaurant we sized each other up. I don't remember what I expected him to look like, as the photo he had sent had left me anything but optimistic. A face-to-face inspection showed that the photo had been kind. I looked at him with dismay.

Blondish hair covered what seemed to me to be an unusually large head. Long lips and a large nose rested beneath eyes that were set far apart. If Robert Redford was not available for the next screenplay offered to him, Len should not have waited by the phone.

It took me a second to realize the worst of it. A closer inspection led me to the discovery that I was looking down at this man who seemed to be sporting a decent sized belly. Granted, I stood only at five-feet-five-inches, but I had chosen a pair of two-inch heels. It would be a long night twisting my ankles to appear shorter.

"Kate?"

"Len, hi," I answered back, half wondering what he thought of my appearance and how to inconspicuously walk on my ankles without tripping.

"Nice to meet you," he said. "Let's go in."

Following Len in, I wondered if I would ever be able to sleep with him.

One look around the restaurant revealed what physically at least looked to be a hidden gem of southern Connecticut. Old wooden walls lit up by the glow of candlelight, skylights glistening with the images of lustrous stars above us, and simple white linen created a romantic setting. We were seated in a quiet corner of the restaurant.

Len seemed agitated as he fidgeted with his glasses in his hand. He wore a suit that would generously be described as not-quite navy and sheen. Not quite the outfit I envisioned for a partner at a major New York investment bank.

We sat in the wooden spindle chairs and looked at each other. After our phone conversation the past week, I felt that I knew a modest amount of information about this man, and yet I knew nothing. We were so far along in our lives that our histories could be conveniently revised. If I told him at that moment that I once played violin for The New York Philharmonic, he would have no choice but to believe me.

"How was your ride here? Any traffic out of New York?" I said.

"No, no traffic."

Len put on his dark brown glasses and picked up his menu. He wore the glasses low on his long nose and peered at me over the top of the menu.

"Do you know what you want?" he asked.

Quick with the waiter, Len took off the glasses and looked at me.

"Where are your kids tonight?"

"I'm really lucky. The town I live in is very close knit. My kids spend a lot of time at their friends' houses and their friends camp out at ours. And I have au pair from Germany, Myra. She's just wonderful. Young enough to be playful but extremely responsible with them," I said.

"My wife Judy stayed home with my children. I could work as much as I wanted."

Len looked unconcerned how I might react to his words.

"Guess I don't have that luxury. But having grown up in New York, I now get what a gift living in a small town has been to my kids and to me."

I sat there counting my blessings to not be on a date with another bitter divorced man. But I intended to be serious, and ask him lots of questions. After having gone on so many dates, I became determined to unearth as much as I could the first night and sniff out the defects quickly.

"Do you like your work?" I asked.

"Absolutely. Everything about it including my company, Duke Heller, and a very large corner office on Wall Street."

"You're a lucky man."

And then he blurted out, "I'm the safest partner in the company."

Were all the other partners stealing the clients' money?

"One of our partners has had affairs with some secretaries and junior women," he continued, "Not me. No one could ever accuse me of that. I'm the safest partner."

"You're the safest partner? What an interesting way to look at your colleagues."

Len now sat stiffly in his chair. He appeared in complete control as if anything short of this would be evidence to me of some inherent weakness.

"You wouldn't believe the things I do because of the people I meet through work. Opening night at the theatre, dinners with movie stars at the next table, travel around the world. I went to the Grammys last year," he said.

I imagined being swept out of the restaurant, out of the awkwardness of blind dates and Connecticut suburbia and launched directly onto the red carpet in between the shadows of Mariah Carey and Kenny G. My life as I knew it would be far, far away.

Interrupted by the arrival of our dinner. Len went back to his stories and I pushed the food around my plate. The meal tasted mediocre at best but neither of us seemed to care. We both knew our way around the world class restaurants in New York. The night was not about being dazzled by the cuisine, but by the company.

The conversation was flowing easily but neither of us flirted and for the moment I felt hardly any chemistry for Len. One friend had advised me to put on my game face when out to dinner with a man but I had no intention of playing with this man – yet.

All too soon, the waiter arrived with the check. Len put on his glasses again, peered at the bill and calculated the tip.

"Let's go," he said.

We walked out to my car, a white Volvo sedan, and stood next to it in the cold night air, under a sky filled with glimmering stars and black landscape.

"I'll call you, if you don't mind?" he asked.

The night seemed a pleasant success. He wasn't quite what I had pictured after reading his letter but for the first time in many dates I didn't think being alone felt less painful than being with a man. There were possibilities here. The very good-looking men I'd encountered since Jake hadn't looked so good when I got to know their character. So for once, a man's looks were going on the back burner in my priorities.

"I'd like that."

I stood still, bending awkwardly downward, hoping that a good night kiss was on its way. No luck. As he walked away toward his Mercedes, I wondered what Len thought of our evening. I would have to wait and see if he would call.

Len drove away and I sat motionless in my car. The stalemate between the punishing details of the past and the possibilities of my future constantly filled my head. The familiarity of the past often won after an evening with another new man provoked new fears. As the memories settled into the car, I surrendered to reliving them once again.

The first time I noticed Jake, in my freshman year of college, he was walking across the college green. One look at his handsome face, six foot five, two hundred twenty-five pound body and unassuming walk and it was love at first sight. But the thought didn't last long when I noticed his girlfriend, a beautiful tall Swedish blonde, by his side.

"Forget it," I thought and kept going.

Four years later Jake happened into the bar in Harvard Square where I was waitressing for the summer and strode right over to me.

"You went to Brown, didn't you? I remember seeing you on campus," he said.

He stuck to me like glue that night as I worked.

"Here's my phone number, give me a call," he said as he headed to the door around midnight.

I looked at the slip of paper and knew it wasn't in me to phone a guy.

Ten minutes later Jake reappeared in the bar.

"I walked around the block and realized you wouldn't call. Please give me your number," he said.

Our first date was on a Friday night in August of 1975. I had just graduated from college. Jake, now a fourth year medical student, picked me up in his decrepit 1965 Buick. We sat in a local restaurant, and then my apartment, talking until four in the morning. By Sunday night, our second date, we had decided to live together.

It felt so easy to fall in love with Jake. His gentle, soft-spoken manner was disarmingly at odds with his large body, a big teddy bear of a man, and rugged good looks. Having grown up with very little money, he loved to tell stories about his dogged transition from a blue-collar future to what he called the halls of the Mecca of medicine.

During the three months after Jake died, I went to his grave at least once a day and begged him to come back. For six months I cried myself to sleep. Sometimes as I shut my eyes, I thought of Jake trying not to close his for the last time. I opened my eyes and shut them, over and over again.

Each night at eight I crawled into bed, as soon as my children, seven-year-old Chloe and four-year-old Ben, were asleep. Not able to face evenings without Jake, sleep was my escape. But it was nightmarish that they might feel they had lost both parents.

Bedtime was often hell for Chloe and Ben. After we finished our nightly ritual of reading before trying to sleep, Jake's absence took hold.

"How could there be a God? How could He take Daddy away?" Chloe screamed one night. "Daddy was so good. I want him back. What if you die and I have no parents?"

I hugged her tightly and after she calmed down a bit, I repeated to her the words that Rabbi Shapiro had said to me shortly after Jake died.

"You will never know if there is a God, you will never know why Daddy died. But tomorrow morning you will get out of bed and have a wonderful day because that is what Daddy would want you to do."

Chloe seemed to find consolation in these words. She put her head down on the colorful Strawberry Shortcake pillowcase and fell asleep quickly. Then alone in my room, I cried wondering how long I'd have the strength to comfort my children.

Ben was full of fear. He cried for his Daddy but also for himself.

"I'm scared of dying. What if there is no after-life?" my precocious four-year-old son asked one evening.

Ben became hysterical one night missing his Daddy. For the first time I consoled him with a new message.

"One day I will remarry and you will have a father again."

"When? How soon?"

"Well, first I'll have to find someone to love, and he'll have to love me too."

Chloe, sitting on her brother's bed listening, rolled her eyes up as if that could never happen.

"Do it while I'm still young," Ben said.

After school one afternoon, while emptying Chloe's backpack, I found a paper on which the teacher asked her students to make a list of wishes. Chloe had two: I wish I had a father, I wish I won't die young. My children lost their innocence so early in their lives. Only time would put enough distance between Jake's death and a life for Chloe and Ben and me. I had to pay my dues in time, to serve time in a grief cell.

As the months went on, I stopped going to the cemetery so often. The grave was covered with snow and I wondered if Jake felt cold. But he was buried near the main street of my small town and I drove past there several times a day. His arms seemed to reach out to me as I drove past begging me to visit. I began to resist.

I found a therapist and lived for that one hour a week appointment. And then I tried a widow's support group for a while. It was easy to identify with these women and the experience felt beneficial for a short time. But it appeared most useful in showing me what I didn't want to be – a professional widow.

At Christmas time an invitation arrived for a party for many of the doctors from the hospital where Jake had worked. Walking into a large room where couples stood laughing, holding hands, and sharing stories of their latest vacation or purchases, I floated around, trying to fit in but regretted accepting the invitation.

There were days when I even expected Jake to show up, to ring the doorbell or call on the phone. Maybe God would give him a special dispensation to make one call or Jake would just sneak one in. I felt desperate for that one contact. Jake's eyes gazing at me. Just one more long embrace in his arms. But I knew if I found myself one day thinking Jake was back, alive, I'd have lost my sanity. The price tag was too high. Chloe and Ben needed me.

We began to travel. To pay for our trip to St. Lucia, I sold Jake's car. Terrified of going on this trip, I dreaded feeling alone once we were there, but when we arrived, I was lulled at first by the beauty of the island and the Caribbean. It felt wonderful to be thousands of miles away from my nightmare, but how foolish of me to think my suitcase of memories had not traveled with us.

This trip meant a break with the past and, Lord knows, I might even have fun, but I felt so jealous of the couples there. They couldn't possibly have a past like mine, not with the abandon with which they seemed to enjoy themselves. Each evening at dinner I watched as the couples around me appeared to relish each other while I sank into my chair with envy.

Chloe, Ben and I also learned to cope with the fact that one adult and two children on vacation are a family.

"I asked your son where his father was, and he told me your husband is in Africa hunting wild animals," one woman informed me.

Ben was in the room.

"She asked me where my Dad was. I just wanted her to leave me alone. If I told her the truth she would have asked me a thousand questions."

"But you don't really believe that's where Daddy is, do you?"

"No!"

The first anniversary of Jake's death approached, a whole year without Jake's love permeating everything I did. Now determined to build a core of strength within so that no matter how low I might sink, no matter how much I missed Jake, I knew I would make it. What went down, must come up.

Laying in bed that night, while staring at the holes in the wall that had been made to hold intravenous lines for Jake, I decided to plug them and reclaim my bedroom. With the wall painted and a new pink flowered duvet, the room appeared revived and the chains of cancer removed at last.

It took me a year and a half to take Jake's clothes out of my closet, and then I kissed and hugged his shirts goodbye. It took me two years to take off my wedding ring. First I put it on my other hand and then began practicing taking it on and off. I even put Jake's desk in the basement and threw away his radiology journals.

Breaking out of my shell felt terrifying and fear pervaded every step of learning to live all over again. I created a comfortable place for myself where I wasn't crying myself to sleep anymore, but it was such a cold place. Living in a world with tunnel vision, taking care of two young children, I denied myself the many experiences and pleasures the couples around me seemed to enjoy.

Secure in my widow's walk I took no risks. I did not date. When any man showed interest in me, I only was reminded I had lost my match. Not running away from a marriage lost in divorce, I was not consumed with anger at an ex-spouse. But I feared spending the next forty years alone. No men, no sex, no love.

And yet the kids' energy and resilience pulled me into their world. Chloe and Ben would lead the way back into life. I would lose them if I didn't make a life for them; they had suffered enough.

"Is Daddy in the same heaven as Babe Ruth and Lou Gehrig?" Ben asked after Little League one day.

"Sure he is."

"Then he must be very happy."

"I never thought of it that way. I bet he is."

For two years after Jake died we lived on money he had left us and I felt grateful for that time to be with Chloe and Ben. Now I needed a job and money and passing the Bar that summer removed one major hurdle in the way.

A friend suggested I call the law department of a large insurance company in central Connecticut. He said the

General Counsel at the company, a woman, was paving the way for female lawyers. Since Ben would be starting first grade in the fall and I desperately wanted to be there to put him on the bus in the morning and when he arrived home, I asked about a part-time job.

"The only part-time jobs we have are obtained through a temp agency," the woman informed me.

"Why?"

"Well, that is how we've always done it. It is essentially the policy of our department," she responded.

"Why?"

An hour later, after we had discussed over and over again the logic of how "we've always done it", she caved and offered me an interview. I was hired immediately after the meeting.

My friends repeatedly assured me the sun would sneak into my hobbled world again. I no longer doubted them as a certain lightness returned when the denial and anger died.

Then, no longer feeling sorry for Jake but for myself, I wanted to live again. It was not the highs that I craved, but the lows I feared. Just feeling okay sufficed.

Re-entering the world of my neighbors, my friends, no longer did I draw them into the darkness of my life. It was time to live in the compelling light of theirs and move forward. I started the car and headed home aching for Len to call again.

CHAPTER 2

November

For our second date, Len surprised me in a number of ways. First, he drove to Montwood, the small town where I lived, a two-hour plus from his home in New Jersey. Second, he looked dramatically better dressed in a black sports jacket, grey slacks and a light grey button down shirt. We were off to a good start.

We decided to meet at Mia's, a favorite Italian restaurant of the area, a favorite mostly by default with only one other good restaurant in the area. Len was waiting, once again, when I walked through the door. Sitting on a stool at the bar, he scanned my tight velvet pants and turtleneck as I walked up to him. I had just spent the past hour trying on every outfit in my closet.

When we were seated, he ordered two glasses of Chardonnay.

"So, why were you reading the personals?" I asked.

He was slow to answer.

"About a month after my wife died, I received a book in

the mail. It was sent anonymously. It was all about dating and said that the best place to meet quality people was through the personals in *New York* magazine. All of my friends encouraged me to move on. They said that I suffered enough through her illness."

Was there really a book? Why had I never seen it?

"Didn't your friends try to fix you up?" I asked.

"Well," he hesitated, "I just didn't feel ready for that. What would that say about my marriage?"

He continued, "I've responded to a number of women but they've all been awful. They profess their beauty in the ad and turn out just the opposite. I was married to a beautiful woman."

I had described myself as beautiful but cute, and yet pretty made for a more accurate description. The word beautiful had been used to describe me, but I knew it was with a great deal of affection and largesse. Nevertheless, men had told me that they wouldn't respond to an ad if a woman didn't describe herself as "beautiful". And I was, after all, competing with pages of:

> Sexy long legged beauty. Strawberry blond,
> voluptuous, successful and waiting
> to meet her Prince Charming.

I thought about his letter. He had written that he had never responded to an ad before and I had thought that his letter to me was his first.

"I worried that one of my letters would go to someone who knew me. Can you imagine?" he said.

"Can't imagine that."

He seemed anxious to reveal himself to me and I attributed this to a lack of experience in dating, a desire to connect, albeit with a stranger.

"Have you gone out with other men who responded to your ad?" Len asked.

"No, your letter resonated with me. I found it warm and thoughtful."

"So why did you place the ad?"

"Two months before I did it, I was flying on a business trip with a colleague. I told him that I had broken up with Phil, a physician and my boyfriend of three months, the night before. Phil often acted more like a child. He seemed like an extremely needy guy. I actually felt sorry for him."

Len's eyes registered that comment. They radiated a clear message of anything but weakness.

"Phil wasn't going to be hard to get over. I just didn't know how difficult he would be to replace. My colleague suggested I put an ad in the personals, and he wrote the ad. I figured any failure of this venture could be blamed on him," I said.

Len, as he had on our first date, sat upright in his chair. How could he remain motionless for so long displaying no tics, no nervous habits, no energy leaking anywhere?

"And your family? Do you come from a large family?" I asked.

"I come from an incredibly screwed up family. My mother was a bitch. My brother's an alcoholic and my sister committed suicide. Only Judy knew that."

As he shared this with me, his eyes felt imprisoning.

"They found my sister dead in her car in the garage."

"How'd you know it wasn't murder?"

"It was suicide. Her first husband died and her second husband was a nightmare. He drove her to it."

"You must have been devastated," I said.

"I cried. I told everyone she had a stroke. I miss her, I really miss her."

Tears came to his eyes.

"I've never dealt with my feelings about the past very

well, particularly strong feelings. I've built some strong walls and solve problems in a different way than you do. I can tell that already. You seem to wear your heart on your sleeve. It's part of your warmth and attractiveness, I must say," he said.

The headwaiter approached the table and interrupted us.

"Excuse me sir, but we need to seat the table next to you. Would you move your chair?"

Len glared at the man and didn't move an inch.

"If the tables weren't so close together, there wouldn't be a problem," he finally said.

"I'm sorry sir," the headwaiter, standing erect, said.

Len glanced at me and moved his chair.

"He needs to learn the word 'please'."

Len leaned his elbows on the table and bent towards me.

"So what was it like growing up as Kate?" Len asked

"I felt kind of invisible. My mother focused on her career and everyone always told me about the importance of her work since she was the Dean of a Pharmacy College. I got the message that my needs weren't that important so I felt kind of helpless. Like I had to compete with her job. She's a wonderful woman and her colleagues and friends adore her. And in her retirement and because of Jake's cancer she became a devoted mother. She's been incredible with my kids."

"But doesn't she mind leaving her New York life when she's in Connecticut with your kids?"

"Ben told me that she took him to McDonald's once near our house and I guess she'd never been to one before. So this sophisticated, urbane woman went up to one of the McDonald's employees and asked where she could check her coat."

Len gave a smug, approving look.

"My mother has acknowledged that her great sense of purpose and pride during my childhood was her career, not her kids," I said.

"And how has that played out in your life?"

"I got lucky. Jake was very loving and giving and he seemed to anticipate my needs, probably better than I did or do now," I responded.

"So does the next guy in your life have to compete with memories of Jake?"

If it were possible for Len to hold himself any more rigid, he had just managed to do so.

"Jake wouldn't recognize me now. I relied on him so much. But since his death I've become so strong because I had to for the sake of my children. And I'm working full time as a lawyer. He never saw that part of me," I said.

"I'm not sure you answered the question. But that's ok."

I glanced up and looked around the restaurant. It appeared packed with diners but Len and I had retreated into our own little world. The entire evening he kept his eyes focused on me despite the buzz of the restaurant around us. They were certainly the one attractive part of his face. All of my life, I had been told that my best feature were my large hazel eyes, that they sparkled and laughed. Len's eyes appeared serious, old, wise, and always calculating.

"You know, it's funny. Yesterday we had a meeting of the Law Department at the insurance company where I work and our General Counsel told us that we should all have a 'five-year plan'. I sat there thinking that I'm not sure I have a 'five-minute plan'," I said.

"Oh, I have a five-year plan."

"I bet you do. I'm just not that ambitious. My mother was the prototype of the ambitious woman. My plan has always been for Chloe and Ben to have a wonderful childhood, a sense of optimism, everything missing from mine. And Jake's death hasn't stopped me."

At last, Len's face revealed a warmth seeping through a

crack in the machine like workings of his mind. What had I said that resonated?

"Although, even if I'm not ambitious, my plan is to keep my job so we have some money," I said.

"I don't think women need to work. Judy never did."

"I haven't heard a comment like that from a man in my entire adult life."

Len picked up his glass of wine.

"I'm not your typical man," he said as he took a long drink of the wine.

I took a deep breath to stifle any laugh that might emerge.

"With your mom working, you probably weren't sheltered as a girl growing up in the City."

I told Len how in retrospect, I couldn't believe how little supervision I had growing up in Manhattan. From second grade on, my parents allowed me to walk home from school alone. And those were the pre-Giuliani streets of New York. But my father repeatedly told me not to talk to strangers. One day when I was in second grade a car pulled up next to me as I walked along First Avenue and asked me to get in. They opened the car door and offered me candy. I was about to get in when I heard my father's voice in my head and ran away. I never told my parents about that.

When I finished Len looked ready to pounce. I just wasn't sure at whom.

"In high school, my best friend Sarah and I walked to school together and each morning a man stood in his second floor window naked as we went by. We used to giggle at him. We never told anyone."

"You seem to have turned out pretty normal. None of this frightened you?" Len said.

"Yes, but my father was a wonderful, loving man. Guess I looked to him as my touchstone for men. Any other guys were aberrations. At summer camp, the mail arrived every day with a new handwritten love poem from my father. I still have all of them."

"That will be hard to compete with." Len chuckled.

"I hate to tell you but I've received some pretty good love letters and poems since my father."

Len stared at me with his competitive, calculating eyes.

As soon as dinner ended, Len paid the check and we went out into the cold night. I found myself in the same position as after the first date, waiting for the kiss, although this time I had worn ballet flats.

"I'm going away for two weeks over the holidays with my kids. It will be our first vacation as a family without Judy. I'll call you when I get back," Len said.

He didn't kiss me goodnight. Again.

It was lunchtime at The Oasis, a small but very crowded and noisy diner near my office in Hartford.

"No kiss on the second date. Maybe he's gay," I shrugged, almost desperately.

This caused a ripple of laughter at the table. My friends, who were also colleagues, and I met there almost every day for lunch. It provided us a welcome retreat from the confines of the office and a chance to do something that we did almost as well as practice law – gossip. They were three smart, witty, loving women – all lawyers. I adored them. We were professionals in a competitive environment and yet the best of friends.

"He's not gay. Maybe he's showing you some respect," Bonnie said. Bonnie was my rational friend, always a source of good level advice. Bonnie married for the first time just two years before and seemed very pleased with her choice after waiting so long for a good man to come along.

"Kate, we all make the same mistake. We find a man and clearly don't know the guy, but we think he's special and hop into bed with him too quickly and get emotionally attached too soon. We don't sleep around so we think it's okay," Zoë began.

"We're confused, believing that the intimacy of sex is more than it is and then we wake up six months later and find out who this guy we slept with really is. And then the relationship ends and we're hurt. Take your time. Don't sleep with this man for at least three months." Zoë said.

"I think men will show more of themselves if there's more at stake. They tend to take the path of least resistance. So if you want to force a conversation and see if there is a relationship worth having, just say no to having sex for a while," Bonnie said.

"But what if he doesn't call? What if he meets someone while he's away? I liked him," I asked.

"What did you like?" Rachel said. Our offices abutted each other, and I often overheard her drill a point into opposing counsel in her quiet tone. She had mastered keeping a soft-spoken even cadence in a world of shrill litigators. Already on her third marriage, she would never dare to offer advice about relationships with her track record.

"He's a widower, loves his three kids, is a partner at a major New York company and seems relatively normal. He's not great looking – kind of an Edward G. Robinson type. But is it too much to ask for a kiss? How long can this go on? I'm used to men slobbering all over me. This is just so weird. And think of the men I've dated. I told you about the Cockroach Man, didn't I?"

"Remember, we're eating," Zoe said.

"Before I met Len I was fixed up on a blind date with a very wealthy New York real estate developer. He was a tall, attractive man who had been married twice. We met for a drink at Crystals's. Within an hour, he gulped down three scotches while I sipped a Chardonnay.

"First he asked me four questions: Did I work for the money? Did I own or rent my apartment? What did my father do for a living? How many bedrooms were there in the apartment where I grew up?"

"I can't believe it. And they say that women are always trying to find out how much money men have," Rachel said.

"He was trying to see if I was worthy of him. But then he began relating his psychiatrist's take on his second marriage to a much younger woman when I noticed an enormous cockroach crawling up the wall between us. I couldn't listen to another word he was saying and sat there wondering when he'd notice the insect. I just sat there and stared at the wall. But he didn't notice and kept talking. And talking.

"Finally I motioned to the bug. He glanced at it smiled and then went on to describe his first marriage. At this point I took off my shoe, whacked that cockroach as hard as I could with it, put my shoe back on and left."

"Only in New York," Bonnie said.

But Zoe wasn't paying attention to my story.

"I bet Len makes a lot of money. I bet he makes ten million dollars a year," Zoë said.

A rare silence engulfed the table for a moment as we digested that possibility.

"But he's a partner at that place and they're usually such bastards. Be careful Kate. Do you think he'd be making that kind of money if he didn't have something of the bastard in him?" Bonnie declared.

Zoë looked at her watch and interrupted.

"We need to get back to the office. Lunch tomorrow. Analysis of Len, part two."

Bonnie looked at me, almost with pity.

"Something tells me we'll be dissecting this man for a long time to come."

WINTER 1995

CHAPTER 3

January

Len called the night he returned from his holiday vacation. Snuggled under a thick duvet and reading the *New York Times Magazine*, the ring of the phone startled me. His voice sounded sweet and eased the frigidness of the cold night outside where beautifully untarnished snow laced the ground. I sank further into the sanctuary of my brass bed.

"How was your trip?"

"Good, but I'm glad to be back. I can't wait to get to the office. And actually I did quite a lot of work while away. I need my work, my routines," he said.

"Then we're polar opposites. I dread the end of vacations and am miserable for days after I go back to work. I actually hate routines. They feel like heavy chains waiting to be broken. Routines mean boredom and predictability to me."

"I wouldn't have gotten to where I am unless I was willing to be the workhorse on the farm. So you're the wild horse that makes a great ride but needs to be tamed?" Len asked.

"'The Taming of the Shrew'? Not likely."

We arranged our third date at Max's Grill, in Litchfield, Connecticut. *Zagat* said that we'd like the contemporary ambiance. This time I made sure to be early and stood waiting in the crowded entrance at the door. Every time a patron came in, I was blasted with the cold night air. Len finally walked in, and kissed me on the cheek. Just a little peck on the cheek, but a little peck could be a kiss and a kiss was a kiss. I felt a small victory.

Dressed so casually this time, Len no longer resembled the uber Wall Street man. The sense of power that had infused his appearance on our previous dates disappeared in the corduroys and flannel shirt he had chosen.

We were guided through the crowd to our small table on the side. The restaurant decorated in black and gray tones looked filled with New Yorkers on their weekend out in Litchfield. Even the waiters had an air about them.

When we were seated, the waiter handed us our menus and I looked Len over. He had a slight tan but not much for having just spent two weeks in the sun.

"Do you always order fish?" he asked.

My eating habits were predictably the subject of discussion. Obsessed with exercise, health and maintaining a size six figure, the food I ate was perhaps the one area where routine and a sense of control gave me comfort.

"How was your vacation?" I said.

"Vacation felt good. When word got out I'm a widower, people on the beach were constantly offering me women's phone numbers."

"Did you take the numbers?"

And why the hell did he have to tell me this?

"No, it wouldn't look right. It's too soon after Judy's death."

Len caught me staring at the odd yellowish cast of his hair.

"I dye my hair," he said.

"I realized that on our first date. It looks kind of unreal."

"No you didn't," Len said as he frowned at me.

Then he put on a sheepish look and displayed the tiniest of smiles.

"Did you? When Judy was dying, she asked me to dye my hair to get rid of the gray so I'd look young again for her."

"I thought you colored it after Judy died so you'd look younger. For dating purposes."

"No. And I hate doing it. I feel like such a phony. I'm not doing it any more."

Len's face resembled that of the Everyman – a large non-descript look that could be found on hundreds of men walking the streets of Jersey City where he had grown up. But his eyes revealed an overwhelming intensity. I wasn't sure if they scared me outright or if he used them as a warning signal "Don't mess with me".

"Why do you work as in-house counsel and not at a law firm? You know the only things that matter are money and power," Len said.

"That's such a cliché, isn't it?" I asked. "I've never experienced either. My relatives have always worked in public service, universities, hospitals."

His money and power had been impotent against cancer, unable to halt the suffering, unable to prevent Judy's death.

"When Jake died, I had to get a job. I couldn't bear to leave my children for any length of time so I started part-time in-house. The people I work with are really smart, they've just chosen to go in-house for quality of life reasons. We don't have to work nights or weekends," I said.

"I've been working non-stop for twenty-five years. I understand your predicament but those Harvard and Yale educated friends of yours. Why would they give up the money of a law firm to work in-house? What are they earning? A hundred thousand a year?"

Probably Len's weekly income. For him to acknowledge the choices of my friends would be to abrogate all that he had worked for.

"Your kids are pretty lucky to have you," he said.

"I'd do anything for my kids. I remember growing up, my father would look me straight in the eye and say 'I'd die for you'. I thought it was a bit extreme at the time and never understood why he would say something like that. Now I do since I feel the same way about my kids."

"My father was weak, just another victim of my mother," Len said.

"So who loved you? What got you through all this? You were a child."

"I have my mother's strength. I used it."

I was about to ask if he was like her in other ways but held my tongue for the moment just as the waiter brought our desserts. I thanked the waiter. Len barely nodded at him.

"You know, I didn't shed a tear when my mother died. I felt relieved," Len snarled.

Relief when his mother died? I remembered what they said in all those dating tips about how a man feels about his mother are clues to how he'll treat you.

"I can't imagine how that feels. The night before my father died his doctor told me that my dad would be gone in the next twenty-four hours. The doctor said later I didn't even register what he told me that night. I had 'disassociated' from the whole experience. Guess I didn't want to hear what I didn't want to hear," I said.

"Did you do that with Jake?" Len asked.

"I've been known to tune out what I don't want to know or hear more often than I'd like to think."

Len remained quiet, visibly computing what I had just said. Uh oh, I shouldn't have told him that.

When dinner was over, I watched as Len scurried across the restaurant to get his oversized tan sheepskin coat. The coat, clearly the wrong size, drooped over his body and the color washed out his face. The small, quick steps he took radiated inexhaustible energy.

Wearing baggy greenish corduroy pants and a plaid flannel shirt, he appeared dressed for dinner possibly in Juneau, not Litchfield. His bulging pocket stuffed with his wallet and keys looked comical. What was he thinking when he dressed for our date? That I should see his casual side?

The bitterly cold wind slashed over our faces as we left the restaurant. The streets of the small Connecticut village looked deserted. Len put his arms around me and leaned in for the kiss. We placed ourselves to the left of the restaurant door as he held my face and very tenderly stroked my lips with his fingertips.

The kisses felt gentle at first but then he wrapped his arms around me and began to kiss me with swelling hunger. His breath kept getting faster, and suddenly, he began to wobble. He latched onto the signpost in order to continue kissing me.

I could only guess that he felt nervous, I laughed to myself, as the shaking didn't stop.

"I ran a lot today and my leg is giving out from under me," he said.

I preferred to think that he was apprehensive about kissing a woman other than his wife, the first new kiss in twenty-four years.

"It's freezing. Let's get in my car," he offered.

We climbed into the front seat of his car and immediately began again. The kisses were long and deep. He began to open my coat and put his hand under my sweater on my breast. After several minutes he pulled my sweater up and began to suck on the nipple.

. . .

"He's not gay," I declared triumphantly.

My friends and I had escaped to the Oasis once again. And once more Len's behavior was under scrutiny similar to what we applied in legal analysis. An interpretation.

"Not only is he not gay, but he's a great kisser. Very tender, very passionate."

"Interesting," Zoë said, "I've always wondered if those ultra-successful macho types are good in bed or not. When a man has money and power, you'd think that he would just take a woman, like doing a deal."

"I haven't slept with him yet, but I can't picture that sex would be like that with him."

"Please don't sleep with him right now," Zoë begged.

"That's actually what's so attractive about these rich, successful men," Rachel chimed in. "They have this aggressive, macho, dynamic veneer and underneath, what you hope for, is a soft and tender man."

"But do you get nice? A man who will treat you well?" Bonnie, ever vigilant, asked.

"The likelihood of us figuring out what makes Len tick is very low. He's just not like any man we've had to deal with," Rachel said as we paid the bill and headed out the door back to work.

. . .

"Would you like to spend the weekend with me in New York?" Len asked one night during a call three weeks later.

"We could go to a show, "Phantom of the Opera", spend the night in a hotel?" he added.

I hesitated.

"I'll make reservations at The Madisons. I'm concerned that one of my out of town partners will see us if we stay at The Four Seasons," Len said.

The following Saturday night, we were sitting in the crowded theater during intermission when Len began to talk about Judy.

"She suffered from depression and took anti-depressants for the last ten years of her life. The doctor said it had been a biological imbalance in her body," Len said.

She was dead. Dead meant letting Jake rest in peace without a negative word ever being said about him.

"But she was a great mother to the kids. A perfect mother," he added. "It's funny but we were happiest in the early years of our marriage. We fought like animals the first year and then we rarely fought."

"When did you meet Judy?"

"In high school. We dated during college and then married after we both graduated."

"Was Judy the first woman you ever slept with?" I asked.

He paused.

"No. I had sex once before with some girl in high school."

Not your typical guy.

"What about you?" he said.

"What about me?"

"How old were you when you first had sex?"

"Sixteen. It was Martin Luther King Day. We had no school that day so I told my parents I was going ice-skating. I came back that night with my ice skates over my shoulder, no longer a virgin, and told them how much fun I had ice skating."

"Who was the lucky guy?" Len asked.

"Tommy, my high school boyfriend, captain of the basketball team. I was the captain of the cheerleaders."

Len looked around the theatre for a moment.

"So how many men have you slept with since Jake died?"

"Two." I said. "And you? How many women have you slept with since Judy died?"

"One." He looked at me to see my reaction. "Judy and I never had sex from the day she was diagnosed. I couldn't take it anymore. My best friend gave me the name of a woman in Birmingham I could sleep with about a month after Judy died."

"You flew to Birmingham to have sex?"

Sex in Birmingham meant that no one in New York or New Jersey, other than his best friend, would know that Len had sex with another woman one month after the funeral.

"Her husband had prostate cancer and is impotent. She hadn't had sex in years. We stayed in a hotel for the weekend."

I was trying to digest the news when Len interrupted.

"Seems like you had a good marriage. Is Jake on a pedestal?" he asked.

"We did have a good marriage but I don't think he's on a pedestal. He was just a good guy. Only once in all of the time I knew him, I heard him lose it. A month after we met he asked me to marry him and after I finally agreed, he called his mother. She argued against it and I heard him tell her 'Then fuck you. Don't come to the wedding.' I was stunned and I never heard him swear again after that."

"You must have been worth it to him," Len chuckled.

The room at The Madisons seemed hardly fitting for the romantic evening ahead. It was not small but decorated in forest green. The forest green rug, bedspread, pillow shams and curtains had witnessed far too many years and looked tired and worn after servicing so many guests. The room felt so dreary that when Len drew the curtains, we left the glistening lights and excitement of Manhattan at night behind.

Our first attempts at intimacy seemed terribly awkward. Len had brought his pajamas.

"You won't be needing those," I said and proceeded to undress him.

He was wearing white baggy Jockey underwear, the kind Ben had stopped using at six years old, and on Len's short legs it looked like a diaper. Boxers would have to be discussed. He seemed embarrassed.

"Judy and I only made love a handful of times each year," he said.

Some women might have found his inexperience in seducing a woman charming. Len was almost virginal.

His legs looked short and exceedingly muscular, a vestige of the years of playing catcher in college baseball. His belly protruded like the typical middle-aged man, but his arms had some definition. This was a body you had to learn to love.

If Len had approached me wearing shorts and a t-shirt at my gym, I would have taken one look at him and run the other way. But something about him had me in a hotel room naked. Either I wasn't so shallow as to care about Len's looks, or the seductive charms of his world now blinded me to this man's unappealing appearance.

We rolled around in the bed for the longest time, kissing and hugging and playing with each other but going nowhere. Obviously, he didn't have a clue. Finally, I took his rather erect penis and put it inside of me. He came quickly and that was it.

"I guess we should have used birth control," I said, completely unsatisfied.

"What for? We didn't have sex."

I looked at him.

"I wasn't inside you. What's the problem?" he asked.

"Of course you were. I put you in me. You can't tell the difference?"

"No, I thought I was between your legs."

"Thanks."

"You raped me," he laughed.

"Not one man on a jury at our rape trial would believe your testimony – you can't tell when you're inside a woman."

"Rape. That's it. You raped me," he said.

"It's impossible for a woman to rape a man."

What had I gotten myself into? I lay there wondering how a man with a corner office on Wall Street and three kids could be that clueless in bed.

CHAPTER 4

February

After that weekend, Len began to call more frequently to meet for dinner, and inevitably, we'd end up at some instantly forgettable motel near the restaurant and have sex. Our sexual relationship felt pretty lame at this point. While Len expressed how thrilled he was I could excite him, he didn't begin to know where to start to return the favor.

Soon he began to call almost every day and like all new lovers we would talk for hours. We continued to meet halfway on a weeknight at some motel, and fumbling around my body, he struggled to please me. We even skipped the pretense of having dinner together when we couldn't wait to get into bed.

"I want you to know that I'm dating other women," he told me one night, after we had sex. "I'm just out of a long marriage and feel entitled to play the field."

"You are still responding to ads? Do you tell them what you told me? And if you feel entitled to play the field, then I'll be heading home."

Lying on his back, covered with a white sheet and looking at the ceiling, a smug look filled his face.

"It's been good. I took one woman to Café des Artistes, one of the most romantic restaurants in New York. We should go there."

"What an idea."

"I always check these women out. I have a security agency investigate them. Can you imagine one woman told me she was forty years old and when I met her I was absolutely sure she looked at least fifty. The agency looked into and she was fifty-one. She was lying and I was right, " he said.

"Have you investigated me? Did they uncover my two speeding tickets, my three parking tickets?"

▪ ▪ ▪

"There's an inn in Connecticut, the Stony Field Inn…would you spend Friday night there with me?" Len asked on the phone Sunday evening.

"I'd like that," I responded knowing that Friday was Valentine's Day.

We met around eight that evening and Len seemed to be grossly uncomfortable about something.

"What's the matter? Why are you staring at that young woman?" I asked.

"She's from my office. Can't imagine what she's doing here."

The woman walked over to us and Len cringed.

"Hi Amanda. This is Kate. So nice to see you," he smiled and immediately ushered me to the table. I could not be part of his public persona yet. Dating, the sex, the intimacy were still under wraps. What would people think of him?

We had a quick, quiet dinner downstairs at the Inn. Since Len appeared so unnerved to have this woman just a table away, we rushed through the courses and headed up to a small room decorated in early New England. The room, although tiny and quaint, seemed a vast improvement over the motels we had been frequenting.

"Happy Valentine's Day," I said as I gave Len a pair of red silk boxers.

He opened the box, delivered a perfunctory smile and set the box on the bedside table. He offered nothing in return, not even one red rose.

We lay down side by side on the four-poster bed.

"Look, I am really uncomfortable continuing our sexual relationship as long as you are dating other women," I said.

He lay there, apparently structuring the deal.

"I guess we have four choices. One, we can stop seeing each other altogether. Two, we can stop having sex and keep dating. Three, I can sleep with other women and you. Four, I can stop seeing other women, " he said.

"Do you understand that I prefer being in a monogamous relationship?"

"You are. I'm not having sex with these other women."

"What're you doing?" I asked although not wanting to know.

"Kissing, touching their breasts. That's it."

He turned to me, looking embarrassed, to see how I was taking the news.

"That's enough for me. Who says you'll stop there? You're like a kid in a candy shop and that's fine for you, but I can't just be one of your many goodies," I said.

"I have to think about this. By the way," he added, "these women tell me I'm a great kisser."

Eighth grade all over again.

"I still want to make love with you tonight. Don't know

what you're thinking or will be thinking. But one more time?" he asked.

"Might be the last time."

"I'll call you tonight with my decision," he said the next morning.

What would the master negotiator, the brilliantly successful man who had been involved in scores of deals say? Len had told me he never backed down, the king of manipulation in any deal.

That night I lay sprawled out on the leather couch in the family room, enraptured by Gabriel Garcia Marquez's, *Love in the Time of Cholera*. The room was my cocoon, cozy and comforting, with a floor to ceiling brick fireplace, built-in oak bookcases and large windows looking out to a wooded knoll. The phone rang at ten.

"I thought about it and I think that there is only one option. I want to have one-night stands and sleep around. We can keep dating," Len said.

It didn't take me a second to respond.

"That's fine for you but it won't work for me. I'm not interested in a man if that's what he wants. If I'm not enough for you sexually, then I'm out," I said.

Dead silence.

"I need more time to think."

"I'm going to Atlanta for work on Monday and will be back on Thursday. Why don't you think about it and call me then?" I said and hung up the phone.

My colleagues and I were back at The Oasis on Monday for lunch with my flight scheduled to leave for Atlanta at four that afternoon.

"Would you feel awful if it's really over?" Rachel said.

"Well, the sex isn't very good. He doesn't have a clue yet how to please a woman."

My friends laughed.

"Is he teachable?" Zoë asked.

"I'm not sure. He's very tender when he kisses me but after that he wants me to please him. He could be a real project. Not a big loss at this point."

"I wonder if he had affairs during his marriage. Men don't have sex twice a year," Rachel declared.

"Maybe he sublimated all of that sexual energy into his work and that's why he's so successful," Bonnie said.

"He swears that he never cheated on Judy. He's always bragging about what a loyal guy he is."

"How could he have had affairs if he's so inexperienced in bed?" Bonnie asked.

"Because women serviced him. He's probably never had to please anyone outside of work," Zoë said.

"Can you believe that I thought I was in an exclusive relationship and sleeping with him while he's still reading and responding to the personals in *New York* magazine?"

Atlanta was rainy and miserable. The relationship appeared over. We'd had sex dozens of times and he said he had reveled in the intimacy. Although not the sex of which fantasies are born, I liked him. Maybe because he had that veneer of power and strength that had been absent from my life after Jake's death. But if he wanted other women's bodies, I knew it was the end for me.

He called promptly Thursday night.

"Hi," he said in a soft, sweet, maybe conciliatory voice.

"Hi."

"I want you to know that I sat down this week and made

a list. Since Judy died, I've thought about what I wanted in a woman in my next relationship and you have every quality on that list. You realize we're entirely compatible?"

He paused.

"And I don't want to sleep around, that's just what my guy friends told me I could do now that I'm single and, you know, in my position. But I do want to keep dating other women. This is all too new. So can we keep dating and not have sex?"

Reluctantly, I agreed to the deal. He said he wasn't sleeping with anyone else after all. And having experienced just a small taste of Len's world I wanted more.

The last two weeks of February I endured knowing that Len was out there fondling other women's breasts. But my life had taught me to be a master of endurance of far more painful events than whose nipples Len might be reaching for at that moment.

WINTER 1988

CHAPTER 5

February

It was the depth of winter in New England, snow on the ground, gray skies and bone-chilling temperatures. It had been dark for hours by the time my husband Jake got home from work. Sitting on the floor of the family room, wrapped in a blanket, I was watching the Detroit Pistons demolish the Boston Celtics. A diehard Celtic fan, I felt heartbroken.

When Jake walked in he sat down on the couch and looked sullen. Something seemed to be upsetting him, and not just the basketball game I assumed he'd listened to on his car radio.

"I have a lump on my shoulder."

It was all he said, but it was enough.

I felt my blood turn to ice. I turned off the television – worrying about the fate of the Boston Celtics suddenly seemed ludicrous.

This wasn't Jake's first lump. Nine years previously he had a fibrosarcoma removed surgically, a slow-growing solid tumor in the muscle of his abdominal wall. The doctors told us then that if he were tumor free for ten years he would be considered cured. Over those nine years we had two children, Jake had flourished in his career as a pediatric radiologist and I had gone to law school. We had lived our lives. Now, the other shoe might have dropped.

Jake removed his tie and then opened the collar of his shirt so that I could see and feel the enemy. It looked tiny, pea-sized. If this was cancer, it had been caught early. That is, if it was nowhere else in Jake's body.

I looked into his large brown eyes.

"It's very small and feels soft. I thought cancerous lumps were hard."

"Cancer can come in soft little packages too," Jake said.

We knew perfectly well that once you've had cancer, you're at a greater risk to get another cancer. The lump did not go away so Jake had it removed two days later.

Jake went to work as usual. Our six-year-old daughter Chloe was at school, our three-year-old son Ben napping when the call came.

"Bad news. The biopsy showed Non-Hodgkin's Lymphoma. I need chemotherapy."

His voice sounded calm, almost serene.

"WHAT?" I screamed.

"I'm with the oncologist," he said. "He wants to get started right away. It's a very aggressive tumor."

I began to cry. Nothing could hurt as much as this did.

Jake came home an hour later. I looked at him and tried to imagine what chemotherapy would do to him. As always when he came home from work, the tail of his shirt was hanging out of the back of his pants. I loved the way he could be so unassuming about his appearance, so absent-minded in his habits.

He lumbered into the house. As a child his nickname had

been Old Father Time. His brother would run up and down the hilly streets near their house in Lawrence, Massachusetts while Jake plodded along far behind.

We looked at each other for a long time

"After I got the results," Jake said, "the surgeon took me to Henry, one of the hospital-based oncologists. He's good but we'll get a second opinion anyway. He said I'll need to have a bone marrow biopsy."

Neither of us could sleep that night. There were hours of rolling around in the sheets trying to fall asleep, staring at the ceiling and then surrendering. There would be no sleep.

"I'm wondering what I did to deserve this? All those years struggling to get through college, medical school and training and now what?"

"You never did anything to deserve this. Let's see what happens with the CAT scan tomorrow. We'll do whatever it takes to get you well again."

In the morning we walked the halls of the Radiology Department where Jake worked. Some of the doctors and technicians Jake worked with looked at us but none of them said much of anything. What was there to say?

The CAT scan seemed to take forever but the news appeared good. The only evidence of tumor was the small pea Jake had found on his shoulder. So we went to talk with Henry in his office in the basement of the hospital. Henry looked slight, a short man. He didn't seem dynamic or on a crusade to cure cancer. A local doctor who took care of cancer patients to the best of his abilities.

Henry and any number of doctors told us to consult Dr. Davis, a world-class expert on lymphoma, at one of major cancer hospitals for our second opinion. Our next stop.

Dr. Davis, a man I assumed to be in his late fifties, looked his part: the prestigious, learned doctor complete with gray hair and chiseled features. Yet there was a reticence about him, an awkwardness with people.

"Jake, you're going to need a combination of chemotherapy drugs including Methotrexate and Adriamycin," Dr. Davis began.

"When I was an intern we called those 'the red death.'"

"Then you are aware that your urine will turn red, you'll probably experience severe nausea and there is the potential for disastrous effects on your immune system," Dr. Davis explained.

Jake did not respond.

"Jake, you'll get six doses over the course of four and a half months. We used to give many more doses, but the side effects outbalanced the effectiveness of the chemotherapy. In other words, it wasn't the cancer that killed you."

"What determines if I have a good prognosis or not?"

"You have an excellent prognosis, Jake," Dr. Davis said. "Your tumor is very small, it's localized and you discovered it very early."

"My local oncologist mentioned that I might need a bone marrow transplant. What do you think?"

"You don't need a bone marrow transplant. Definitely not. By the way, your local oncologist can treat you. You don't need to travel here for the chemotherapy."

Jake and I flew out of there. We could handle four and a half months. We had our marching orders and were ready to forge ahead to the front lines.

Time to tell our children.

Bedtime was special to Jake and Chloe. They would curl up on her bed and read until Chloe fell asleep rolled into her father's large body. Chloe usually took a long time to fall asleep, and often Jake fell sound asleep in her bed before her.

That night Jake tried to explain.

"Remember how Mommy and Daddy went to see the doctor? It turns out that I have a lump on my shoulder. The lump is made of cells called cancer. We want that lump to go away, and the only way to make it go away is with some very strong medicines. It will take a while, but once the lump goes away, I'll be fine."

"Why do you have to make the lump go away?" she asked. "What's so bad about cancer?"

"Cancer cells are bad cells, they're not good for the body. If you let the lump grow it will just keep getting bigger and bigger and hurt all the good cells."

So far, so good. Chloe seemed attentive but not upset.

"Chloe, this medicine I'm going to take will make a lot of my hair fall out. The medicine gets rid of cancer cells but it also hurts hair cells."

"It'll grow back, right?"

"Of course. And then everything will be okay again."

Jake looked at Chloe. She said nothing but looked bewildered, as if her life was about to change but she couldn't figure out how.

Jake hugged her and told her how much he loved her.

"I love you, Daddy." She hugged him back.

And that was enough for one night.

The much easier task of telling Ben fell to me.

"Ben, do you remember how Daddy and Mommy went to see the doctor?"

My three year old nodded.

"The doctor says Daddy has a bad lump on his shoulder called cancer. Daddy's going to take a strong medicine that will get rid of the lump but his hair will fall out for a little while because the medicine is very strong. Then Daddy will be fine. Okay?"

"Okay. Now can you read the book to me?"

"How'd it go?" I asked Jake when we were ready to go to sleep ourselves.

"You can never tell with Chloe"

"Ha! If that's not the pot calling the kettle black."

Chloe, at six, was Jake in miniature, as pretty as he was handsome and just as sweet and mellow. Calm, diplomatic, and gentle, both of them would avoid confrontation at all costs. Trying to get Jake or Chloe to talk about anything wrong felt just hopeless.

Chloe got away with a lot where her father was concerned. Jake was always on Chloe's side against the world and she knew it. They shared this special bond. There was magic in that voice of his, and he used it on his daughter when others would have long lost their patience. More than once I had to page Jake at work so he could talk to an inconsolable Chloe. Once, in the middle of a procedure, he had the tech hold the phone because his hands were gloved while he soothed his daughter until she calmed down.

Jake cherished this child who shared music and books and secrets with him, who looked at the world the way he did. She loved to follow him around, and sometimes he let her come with him to work on a Saturday. While at the hospital Jake wore a lead apron to protect himself from radiation when he performed procedures. One day Chloe asked one of the doctors, "Why's my daddy wearing an apron at work?" For a long time, she believed the answer: "Your Daddy is washing the hospital dishes."

Three-year-old Ben was as different from his sister as he was from Jake. An impulsive, impish, enthusiastic, stubborn little boy who had all of his feelings either written on his face or on the tip of his tongue. He could be aggressive, but in the same way a crocodile can be pacified by rubbing his belly, Ben could be tamed by Jake. Ben would lie on his back in his father's large lap while Jake rubbed his feet and soothed his wild child.

The Friday morning Jake was to receive his first treatment, we woke up to an enormous snowstorm. School was cancelled for the day, chemotherapy wasn't. We couldn't call up and say we'd like a snow day; the cancer was rapidly dividing in Jake's body. When we stepped outside to leave for the hospital the air felt crisp, the woods filled with snow.

I tried to imagine the fear the Jake must be experiencing. More than once I'd awaited in terror the results of a biopsy on a suspicious mole, a lump in my breast. While I sat there waiting for the doctor, I would close my eyes and pray. I played the same games everybody plays, promising God anything for a good result.

I'd been lucky up to now. But if a doctor told me the words Jake had been forced to hear? Would I faint or cry or scream? How lucky to never have to hear the "C" word applied to you because your life changes and the clock starts ticking a whole new way. You are now living on cancer time.

SPRING 1995

CHAPTER 6

April

Are you ready to stop dating other women?" I asked Len during another one of our marathon calls. We had not had sex in weeks but were always on the verge.

"I'm ready. Can you meet me on Friday night?" he responded.

He was waiting for me in the parking lot of a small motel about an hour from my house. He kissed me on the lips briefly and carrying a small bag he led me into our room.

"This is for you," he said as he handed me a large red Cartier box.

Inside lay a stunning woven gold necklace. Jake and I never had much money and jewelry was never on the list of things I desired.

"You're spoiling me."

"Do you like it?" he asked.

"I love it. I just can't believe it."

When we had sex that night, I discovered that Len was

possibly teachable after all, as he concentrated on pleasing me. But his learning curve had been so very steep, which left me wondering who else might be coaching him.

We met in motels all along the various highways between our homes and quickly learned the price and quality of each one. It wasn't long before I could easily have written a lover's guidebook to the motels of the Tri-State area. One night during the week and one night on the weekend we would meet for dinner and then tear each other's clothes off in a motel, while other nights we would pull over to the side of the road and do it.

It seemed like we were back in high school, only Len had never done this in high school. After dinner on a freezing cold night, we pulled into the parking lot of some dreary industrial park. The car windows were completely fogged from the heat generated.

"I wonder if they have surveillance cameras in these lots? We're going to get caught and my face will be on the front page of *The Daily News*," he said.

"The worst part will be when New Yorkers wonder why an investment banker couldn't spring for a cheap motel room."

"That's it. I'm not doing this in a car anymore."

And we didn't. We made love in every hotel and motel from his house to mine. The worst was The Cliffside about forty minutes from my house. No one ever stayed there overnight; the place was made for having sex and getting out. The rug and bedspread looked so dirty and the bathroom so grimy, we pulled off the covers, made love and left. We never used the bathroom or let our bare feet touch the floor.

"I'd like you to come to my house this weekend," he said late one night on the phone. "My friends don't think I should invite women to the house because they're worried about the gold diggers out there. It's a nine thousand square foot house so I haven't invited any women over. You'd be the first."

The house sat at the end of a long stone driveway, a sort of treasure at the end of a long hunt. Large and made entirely of imported Italian stone, it captivated those who dared to take the journey, and yet somehow managed to blend into its woodsy background.

It was obvious, even to the untrained eye, that much time and money was spent in its upkeep, as junipers and rose bushes danced in the whistling wind, and tall blades of perfect green grass stood at attention as Len drove by. A look around the back revealed a huge backyard, equipped with a kidney shaped swimming pool, Jacuzzi, and a small pond with a flowing waterfall stocked with red Koi fish.

Inside, the brick house opened up to a high ceilinged room that seemed to glisten with sunlight in every corner. Polished marble floors, the color of white pearls with overtones of cream and silver, covered a maze-like stream of endless rooms, each decorated in its own unique style. The style appeared eclectic with Len's antiques set amidst contemporary furniture and Leroy Neiman type paintings. In the basement, Len set up a private gym.

"I prefer not to exercise with other people," he explained.

Money had definitely been thrown down in his house, just not always well.

"This is my office and where I spend most of my time when I'm home," he said as he showed me around. "When I worked in my home office, Judy usually watched TV in the family room. I wasn't here that much anyway. But she went to bed early and I always went to sleep very late. I've never needed much rest.

"We were like two ships passing in the night except that I always saved Saturday nights and Sunday afternoons for Judy," he added.

I stood there trying to imagine what it would be like to live in a home like this. But not under the terms that Judy lived there.

. . .

If you asked Chloe to look back, she probably would have a hard time remembering the first time that she ever laid eyes on Len. Just fourteen at the time, her world revolved around not much more than herself, her social life, and how long it was possible to hide behind the closed doors of her room without needing food, money or a ride to one of her friends' houses. That Passover, the night that she first met Len, really had no importance to her at all.

Although we had never been religious, I relished the opportunity to demonstrate we were a real family. Not a second rate, single mother one. My mother and I had been preparing a feast featuring brisket, matzoh ball soup and flourless chocolate cake for four days.

The dining room was set to near perfection with our Royal Derby China, Tiffany silver and Waterford crystal for the adults, and a variety of Passover toys and books for the kids.

We were expecting twenty people, a collection of work friends and family, and of course, Len. This was Len's first time meeting the people most important to me. Having everyone encounter Len at once seemed a gentler way for Chloe and Ben to experience him. But I felt nervous about the impression that he would make. And yet, my worries once again took second place to his.

"I told my Jewish friends I had to work on a deal and would be not available for the first night of Passover, but could come the second night," he said when I invited him to my house.

"So your friends and family still don't know I exist?"

"Appearances mean everything to me," Len explained. "And please, don't ever tell them the date when we actually met."

"This might be good blackmail material one day. Well, you are about to meet my family and some of my closest friends," I replied.

"It'll be fine. I've been to a Seder before. I do have Jewish friends."

All of my guests arrived by five-thirty that night and proceeded to mingle in the family room until the food was finished being prepared. My friends brought bottles of wine and various desserts. Len arrived bearing a stunning silver plated Passover plate.

My colleagues and I had vowed to lay off of the office talk for the sake of their long-suffering spouses, but of course were unable to do so.

"The statute is clear in that any provider such as a doctor who chooses to join a network must accept the terms of participation offered. Its purpose is to keep the managed care organization's costs in control. The question of whether a statute like this is preempted by ERISA will have to be decided one day," Janet, my boss and mentor was explaining.

A brilliant woman who had clerked at the Supreme Court, first in her class at law school and a former partner in a firm, she personified women's accomplishments over the last decades. Len's world was not populated with women like this and he said little but kept a sweet, patronizing smile pasted on his face. Len seemed so out of his element since my female friends would never find it necessary to defer to Wall Street men. Never.

When everyone was seated around the table, I asked Chloe to help me get the salt water, parsley and other fixings we would need for the Seder.

"He's ugly. How could you possibly date him?" she whispered to me in the kitchen.

I peeked into the dining room to take another look at him. I cared for Len at this point and quite frankly no longer thought about what he looked like. 'It's her age,' I thought and shrugged it off.

No one else said a word to me regarding anything about Len, no gushing and no criticism. I assumed the jury was still deliberating.

Cleaning up, shuffling between the kitchen and the dining room, I felt so proud of the people in my world. A world where money and power were not the primary motivation for getting up in the morning.

Len walked into the kitchen and pulled me outside as he prepared to go home.

"Would you like to go the Caribbean for a long romantic weekend?"

Caught off guard, I had to pinch myself to see if the two glasses of Sauvignon Blanc were playing tricks on me.

"I'd love to," I told him and then ran back into the house before he could withdraw the offer.

We flew to Anguilla at the end of April. As we buckled our seat belts on the flight from New York to Puerto Rico, Len appeared fidgety.

"I hate takeoff and landing." he said when he noticed me watching him.

"But you fly all the time for work."

"I'm superstitious. So I have these rituals and they seem to guarantee the safety of my flights. Judy was terrified of flying and we both had grown used to our mutual panic each time we flew," he said. His eyes had a vulnerable look for once.

The plane from Puerto Rico to Anguilla was on an old tiny Cessna.

"I don't fly small planes. Ever," Len said. He held my hand tightly the entire flight.

We landed in Anguilla at night and the warm breezes enveloped us as we walked outside of the small airport. I took a deep breath of the Caribbean air and a longing look at the palm trees. This felt natural, like we'd done it many times before.

Len had made reservations at the Malliouhana, a posh resort, for four days. We checked in and as we casually walked along the stone paths to our room, a bellboy passed by. He stopped and smiled at Len.

"Welcome back sir."

The comment stopped Len in his tracks.

Len scowled at him and then inspected my face.

"I've never been here before," he said and continued walking.

If I said something, if we had an argument, would we have to leave this beautiful island? I didn't say a word.

The room, enormous and decorated in Moroccan furnishings, sat directly on the beach. In the bathroom, the size of my bedroom at home, a double Jacuzzi abutted a glass wall. I walked around the room nonchalantly as if accustomed to living a grand life and Montwood was a distant memory.

Len ordered a bottle of sparkling wine and then checked his voice mail at work. He seemed tightly wound at the moment and I wasn't sure how long it would take to relax him. Sex would be a good place to begin.

So we made love three times a day, tenderly and passion-ately. He was learning. We snorkeled off a fifty foot private boat he rented for the day, lay on the beach for hours and talked, swam in the warm Cerulean blue water, took baths together in the Jacuzzi, ate dinners around the island in romantic outdoor restaurants under the stars and danced in the moonlight.

"This is the first time in twenty years that I've been in the ocean or snorkeled," he said on our second day.

Each evening before dinner, Len arranged for us to have massages in our room. The first night two women arrived, set up their tables side by side, and Len and I lay naked on the tables, covered by small plush white towels.

After a few minutes of pressing her hands into my sun-drenched body, my masseuse stopped.

"You know, I just gave a massage to Claudia Schiffer. She's in the next room."

I giggled.

"You're kidding, aren't you? Is she gorgeous?" I asked.

This woman had just massaged the perfect body of one of the world's top supermodels.

"Will you please let Ms. Schiffer know tomorrow that you've massaged my body?" Len said.

That night at dinner I got my first glimpse of her as she dined with David Copperfield.

As we lay in bed on the last morning of our stay, I felt completely exhausted from so much passion.

"I can't handle any more," I said.

"Finally!"

He wrapped his arms around me and kissed me. He had mastered yet another discipline and was relishing yet anoth-er success.

"These have been the best four days of my life," Len whispered as he held me tightly.

I didn't respond as I made a mental list of the best days of my life. All of them had been spent with Jake, Chloe and Ben.

"There will be some surprises for you in this relationship. Good ones," he said as we road back to the airport.

"I hate surprises. Tell me now."

"I'm actually six feet tall. That's one of them."

He smiled at me, so pleased with himself.

WINTER 1988

CHAPTER 7

February

Treatment began with a routine that was to last us throughout the course of chemotherapy. After seeing Henry briefly, we walked down a long dreary gray cement underground tunnel in the basement of the hospital to a clinic where they administered the chemotherapy.

Jake was infused with the chemo at nine in the morning. The first time Jake looked helpless, as if he were surrendering himself. The two drugs most likely to cause nausea would kick in around seven p.m., then again about midnight. At six in the evening I would give Jake anti-nausea and sleeping pills. He would fall asleep quickly, wake up at eight or nine, vomit three times over the course of an hour, then feel relief for several hours.

Jake went back to work and looked fine. We wondered about the cumulative effect of chemotherapy but the only thing we felt truly fearful about at this point was whether one of the kids' friends would expose Jake to chicken pox which he never had as a child. Neither Chloe nor Ben had ever had it, and if Jake were exposed to it while his immune system compromised, he could die of complications.

After several treatments, Jake ran a high fever for days on end and was unable to swallow. The chemo had acted against not only the fast-growing cancer cells but also the fast growing cells of the lining of his esophagus. On a Sunday night around nine o'clock, the doctor finally wanted us to meet him in the Emergency Room. We left the kids with my mother who was staying with us.

The waiting room looked filled with people needing attention of every imaginable sort. Surrounded by so many sick or injured people and by the busy staff, I felt anonymous and abandoned. We were led into a small examining room where, over the course of the next few hours, we were to find out that the chemotherapy had wiped out Jake's immune system and he needed to be admitted to the hospital. He had no white blood cells to protect his body against infection. I started to cry. But Jake never said a word. The more he hurt, the more he battened down the hatches and braced himself for the coming storm. There would be no talking that night, just whatever comfort I provided simply by being there.

The noises of the Hartford Emergency Room buzzed around us. Not far from Jake, a man in his sixties who had been brought in with chest pains lay on a stretcher. Around midnight, while I stood near Jake's side, this man died. His wife became hysterical.

This was about all I could stand. I wanted to go home, get into my warm bed on this cold night and pretend none of this was happening. I didn't want to witness this woman's heartbreak, knowing well it could be me one day. Life was slipping completely out of my control.

Finally, around one in the morning, Jake was taken up to a room where he quickly fell asleep. Sitting in the chair next to his bed, I raged at God, at fate, at whatever caused Jake to suffer so much. I wanted to be with my children and have the kind of normal life my friends were having. I wanted their problems.

Watching Jake sleep in the hospital bed tormented me. He had already lost ten pounds and a lot of his hair. At five in the morning I left the hospital and headed home to see the kids before school. In the car, I screamed at God at the top of my lungs, "You'd better lay off Jake. This is it, he's suffered enough!"

That week with Jake in the hospital seemed endless. When I was with him I wanted to be home with the kids, when I was with the kids I wanted to be with Jake. But Jake's white count slowly returned to normal. He said he was fearful of the next round of chemo and rightly so as he lost more and more of his energy, and all of his hair.

Each time we walked from Henry's office into the bowels of the hospital, Jake looked weaker. He shuffled along the long walk and looked as gray as the walls we passed. And then on June 3, Jake received his last treatment. We were euphoric. We were promised a cure and we expected one. The pea-sized lump on Jakes' shoulder had melted with the first treatment, and there had been no evidence of tumor during subsequent treatments.

Soon Jake was working full time again and we were back to the life we had known before cancer. We were truly the most grateful people alive. My grandmother had a Yiddish expression, "Scare me God, but don't punish me." Well, we had been scared but we had not been punished. We picked up our lives as if we had just been married, with the same excitement and hopefulness. We made love as if we had just discovered each other. Jake said he felt so appreciative to be back at work, doing what others might consider the same old thing but Jake could never again take for granted.

SPRING 1995

CHAPTER 8

May

L en began inviting me to dinners with his friends, most of whom were investment bankers with whom he worked. One night we were to have dinner at a small but very exclusive French restaurant in New Jersey with Thomas, a tall and strikingly handsome man. Len would hint to me at the extent of Thomas' wealth but never give flat out figures.

"He donates millions every year to charity," Len declared.

Thomas was accompanied by Linda, his beautiful wife and former secretary, who showed up with the largest breasts and most jewelry, both very real, that any woman could possibly carry all at the same time. Joining us at dinner was Paul, a media mogul from Alpine, and his surprisingly very ordinary wife, Sandra.

"Paul might be hard to take. He's very full of himself," Len warned me on the way over.

The restaurant looked crowded with diners elegantly dressed for a suburban restaurant on a Saturday night. Our men surveyed the wine list and finally agreed on the appropriate bottles, each well over a hundred dollars. The women sat idly by, so conversation had to be made with Linda and Sandra.

"Do you have children?" I smiled politely at them.

"Two, both in boarding school," Linda replied.

"No, we don't have children," Sandra said quietly.

"Did you do any skiing this past winter?" Len asked Paul.

"Went heliskiing for a week in British Columbia. Spent a week skiing in Chamonix. We also went to Paris for ten days and did a week in Israel. I have to say, I love the French. Definitely prefer them to Americans," Paul said.

Nobody said a word.

"And more than the French? I certainly favor the Palestinians over the Israelis. The Israelis are just a bunch of terrorists," Paul continued.

Silence.

"I'm not sure how many people would agree with you that the Israelis are solely responsible for the troubles there and that they are a bunch of terrorists," I finally said.

"Are you kidding? Are you aware of what goes on there?" Paul asked.

"Yes, as much as anyone is. I don't think it's as black and white as you make it out to be. It's a very complicated situation," I responded.

Len asked the waiter for the bill and paid.

Dinner ended and I gathered it was not a success.

We said our very polite good-byes while the valet parking attendants retrieved our cars. Len opened my door for me and then quietly got in on his side of the car. We drove in silence until we emerged out of the long driveway of the restaurant. Len turned to me as he drove.

"If you ever do that again, ever argue with a client or at a dinner, I'll kick your chair right out from you at the table."

Len glared at me and with those icy, unforgiving eyes. I did not doubt his words.

I filled my friends in on the details of the dinner while we ate our salads at The Oasis.

"Those women just sat there, like they're not supposed to talk."

"Len didn't really say that to you? Did he?" Rachel said.

"Yeah, he did. These people live in another world. You wouldn't recognize the women I'm meeting. It's the fifties. They don't work. All they know how to do is play tennis, golf, exercise and shop. They're subservient to these rich, successful men. One of these women was laughing one night at dinner that she had just flown over to Paris for the weekend. She said she did the Louvre in fifteen minutes and checked it off her list. She said and I quote, 'Nothing in there'."

"But they can't be happy. Can they?" Zoë asked.

"Why not? They don't have to drag themselves out of bed to work when they don't want to. They have tons of money, spend weeks in Europe and at spas every year, and all they have to do is keep their mouth shut while their narcissistic rich husbands do their thing," I answered.

"But, it's not us. Can you imagine being so stifled? It's like being a prisoner in a marriage," Bonnie said.

"These women are not the 'social X-rays' that Tom Wolfe wrote about in *Bonfire*. They're a step below the sophisticated Manhattan socialites who are at least into charities and museum work," I said.

"Who are they?" Rachel asked.

"I don't know but what does this mean for our daughters?" I asked her.

Rachel had two ambitious daughters, an actress making it on Broadway, and a daughter in medical school. She couldn't be concerned.

"Do we teach them to be gold diggers so they can marry rich men and live soft lives?" I continued. "Or do we tell them to be like us, women who most of these rich men can't handle?"

A rare silence enveloped our table.

"Why'd you work so hard to get into Harvard and Harvard Law School? You could have just married a rich man and had a soft life," I asked Zoë.

"I love my work. Aren't you missing that point?"

"I do too. I can't picture living such empty lives. And imagine how bored their husbands must get with them," Rachel responded. We all knew that she had left her first husband after he refused to let her go to Yale Law School.

"What happens to these women when their fifty-five-year old husbands trade them in for thirty-year olds? They're nothing. At least we have our work," Bonnie said.

"One night we had dinner with a couple who just bought a huge mansion. The wife did nothing; the husband another big success in finance. Both of their kids were about to leave for college. I asked the wife why they'd bought such a big place at this time in their life and she actually said that she felt bored and this was her new project. Her husband was happy to comply."

"Would you want to be one of these women? Kate, you could be one, if you marry Len," Zoë said.

"I guess I can see why certain of these women would be seduced, they might not have other choices. But we are not those women. I feel so schizophrenic about my experiences in Len's world. I want to take the moral high ground and yet I'm not running away from Len and his friends. But I will always work. These are the Stepford wives," I answered.

"But what kind of compromises are you willing to make to be in that world? There is the security of a lot of money." Bonnie said.

"I care about Len and I don't think it's about the security of money," I said.

"Think about it, Kate. How far are you willing to go to be with Len?" Bonnie asked once more.

"I just don't know yet. I just don't know."

My friends and I had to pause the deliberations. Four very confident, successful lawyers appeared lost, lacking any experience navigating their way through Len's world.

The following week Len and I had dinner with one of his best friends, Brad and his wife, Catherine, an elegantly dressed woman and wearing much less jewelry than Linda. Brad had also made millions and was on an airplane five days a week traveling the globe for business.

We met at La Grenouille, a sumptuous little restaurant I had never been to before. Enormous vases of fresh flowers filled the small opulent room.

One could tell that Brad seemed pleased with himself by the smug smile he maintained on his face.

"I'll take the wine list" he told the waiter and then ordered two bottles of Cabernet at $150 a bottle.

"So Len, I was in Asia last week. Quite a trip. Hong Kong for two days, Singapore for two and back to Hong Kong for one. Very productive."

"Did you close the deal?" Len asked.

Catherine leaned over to me.

"I'm always home alone while Brad is off traveling. It gets lonely as you can imagine," Catherine whispered.

"Do you work?" I whispered back.

"No, I've never worked. And now I'm suffering from depression. The meds help but Brad seems to be enjoying the view from the top and I'm languishing in the basement."

Dinner was pleasant enough until Brad appeared to have reached his limit on alcohol.

"Somehow Brad and I seem to be going in different directions. He's traveling, happy, and we....we honestly only have sex like once every six months at most. I wonder..." she whispered to me in one ear which allowed me to overhear Brad telling Len what sounded like a joke when I heard him use the 'n' word.

Len, whom I had never known to be a racist, let it slide. But I just couldn't, could I? Would Len literally kick my chair out from under me at the table if I said something, even something simple like I didn't appreciate that kind of humor?

I squirmed and fidgeted, trying to gag myself wondering whether the two glasses of wine I consumed would dictate my behavior. Was I supposed to accept the comments, because Brad was one of Len's best friends, because I was becoming part of a world where women don't make waves, or because I was just plain scared of Len?

Struggling through dinner and wondering what to do. Picturing the possibilities and the consequences. How punitive could Len be? At least I was sitting on a banquette this time.

But the worst part of it all, in the end I never said a word. I went home disappointed in myself. Lonely and desperately trying to fit into Len's world, I began to wonder at what price that would be. Did I have the potential to be one of these women enjoying their husband's riches and silently enduring the rest? Was I envious of these women or did I abhor them? Was ignorance bliss? The one thing I knew for certain – I was not one of them.

Sarah flew in from California just in time for me to unload on her. We had agreed to meet for lunch and now hugged each other tightly.

We'd known each other since we were six. Sarah was all of five feet tall, short wavy hair, big blue eyes, and a large smile. Whenever I ran away from my family when I was growing up, it took about three hundred yards to get to Sarah's building. And my mother knew exactly where I had escaped to. But Sarah's apartment provided a refuge and Sarah did the same three hundred yards in reverse when she needed to run away. We lived in standard two bedroom apartments, each shared a bedroom with our brother, had parents who both worked, and we went to the same schools and summer camps.

Sarah became a social worker and married for the first time in her forties to a California man. She often returned to New York to see her family who still lived in her childhood apartment.

Now one of the people who knew me best was sitting across from me in a small crowded restaurant on Bleecker Street in the West Village.

"Hi sweetie. How are you?" Sarah said.

"I'm so happy you're here. Just looking at your face provides continuity in my life."

"Len's not behaving?"

"Well, maybe you can psychobabble this man for me."

Sarah sighed deeply and then let out a loud laugh.

"For you, and only you, my friend, I'm going to put on my demi-therapy hat and psychobabble both you and Len."

The look on Sarah's face changed. The girl I knew in elementary school assumed her professional profile.

"You know we were brought up in households where our brothers sucked all the air out of the room and we got no attention. Your mother worked all the time, her career was her world, your father was wonderful but had a serious heart condition from the time you were three, and your brother? A total mess. How old was he when he started seeing a psychiatrist, nine? So you used to go into your half of that divided bedroom, read books and tune out all of them," Sarah sighed.

"I definitely wasn't the center of the universe. I feel like my life began when I met Jake."

"The message to a kid is that they're not important. Ok, tell me why Jake married you?" Sarah asked.

"Why Jake married me? He loved me."

"Why did Jake love you?" Sarah persisted.

I paused.

"Hey, come on. I never thought about why he loved me. I never had a reason to. I just fell into Jake and stayed there."

"You just don't get how much you bring to a relationship. So Len can take advantage of you and be as selfish as he wants." Sarah frowned at me as she spoke.

I sat there feeling pretty damn angry with Len and myself. The only pure emotion I still knew was the unbound love for my children. My husband was dead. And who had come up with this ridiculous scheme of life anyway? Where love consumes you? Where that person dies?

The pensive look on Sarah's face made it clear she was in her element and not done with me yet.

"When we were in high school all of our friends had so much money, huge apartments on Fifth Avenue, the Upper East Side, terraces, doormen, vacations at every school break in the Caribbean and Mexico. Jeff Brody had a Porsche in high school. And we were worried about our apartments being burglarized," Sarah said as the waiter placed our food on the table. One could only imagine what he thought if he had heard any of our conversation.

"That might be part of your attraction to Len. You've never been shallow, the New York gold digger. So what's going on here? We were so envious. Remember when the Carlsons went to Mexico for spring vacation in seventh grade? We set up towels and beach umbrellas on your living room carpet and put on our bathing suits."

"Well, with Len I could easily live in a luxury doorman building on the Upper East Side. Everything I ever wanted, or so I thought, when I was fourteen," I responded.

Sarah sat busy eating her lunch while I didn't feel hungry anymore.

"One of Len's friends told me, while warning me that I had to keep this to myself, Len is insecure and worried that I'll run off with another guy. That's why he's glad I don't live in New York. He prefers having me cloistered in the suburbs. I find that hard to believe," I said.

"Believe it. Just because he's rich and powerful in his day job, doesn't mean he isn't making up for how inadequate he feels."

A calm came over me as some of the chaos of Len disappeared.

"Look," Sarah implored, "It's time to move on from the past, Jake's death. Spend the time now to focus on what kind of man you need and want to love. And then take pleasure in all the things he would love about you."

These words could only come from Sarah's heart and I took them to mine. I might have resented them from someone else but I trusted her completely.

But the task was daunting. Jake's love had come so easily. But why? How to find a love like that? Might as well ask me to figure out the cure to cancer.

CHAPTER 9

July

L et's go to Europe for two weeks. Your kids will be away then," Len asked.

"I haven't been to Europe in years. I'd love to."

"Where would you like to go?" he asked.

"Italy! I've never been."

"Then we'll go to Italy. I was there with Judy but that's where we'll go. I'm that kind of guy."

He made the plans. He was constantly making the plans and I just had to show up. And he said he loved how spontaneous I could be, ready to accompany him at a moment's notice. He was often invited to the parties of wealthy businessmen and benefit dinners attended by socialites and movie stars. Just that week we had been to a benefit for Lincoln Center where I tried to act like having Alec Baldwin and Kim Basinger at the next table was how I always spent my time in Montwood.

"Sometimes when I'm sitting in a board room, I laugh that this little guy from Jersey City is telling these multimillionaires what to do with their money," Len had told me.

We flew first class to Rome over the July 4th weekend. Len would not travel any other way and once I was used to it, I understood why perfectly. When we landed, Len immediately called his voice mail at the office. There were always at least three or four messages from anxious clients waiting for his judgment, his expertise, Len made it clear to me that he was absolutely indispensable to them and that he wouldn't have it otherwise.

Len's son, Peter, who was spending two weeks in Europe had left a message.

"Hi Dad, just wanted to let you know I'm in Rome. The trip is just great. I'll leave you a message about my next stop. Hope you're good and not working too hard."

"You won't believe it. Peter's in Rome right now. I thought he would have left by now. He left a voice mail," Len told me.

"What does that mean for us?" I asked.

I had not met Len's children yet and he didn't want them to know that I accompanied him to Europe. He had insisted that I tell my kids that I was traveling with a group but he didn't have to know that I didn't comply with his instructions. We scheduled the trip to coincide when Ben would be on a three-week bike trip in Vermont and Chloe a six-week teen tour out West.

We arrived at our hotel, the opulent St. Regis Grand Hotel, and as we checked in Len let me know that the hotel provided butler service.

"And what will this butler be available to do?"

"Anything your heart desires. Other than what I do."

Len had secured reservations at La Pergola for our first

dinner. The elegant, expensive restaurant with gorgeous views of Rome served food that rivaled anything we had tasted in New York.

"This meal, this restaurant is dazzling. I don't know what to say but thank you."

Len leaned back in his chair. His mind seemed to be constantly churning. And yet, at this moment, he looked truly relaxed. The wheels slowing down for one evening.

As we lay in our enormous bed our first night, I kept thinking about the butler. Butler's had simply never been within my reach or desire.

"I can't think of a single thing I would need the butler for. What a waste," I said.

"Believe me, there are plenty of people in this hotel directing the butlers to run around for whatever suits their fancy at any moment."

"At this moment? I don't fancy anything the butler could do for me," I said as I slowly pressed my naked body against Len's.

"Then it would be my pleasure to take care of your needs. I prefer the woman on top, only in bed of course. Climb on top of me Signorina. You don't need a butler after all, do you?"

Our days in Rome proved to be comical. While I marveled at the masterpieces by Michelangelo and Bernini in St. Peter's, Len stood watch, an unlikely addition to the Swiss Guards, on the lookout for Peter. While I gawked at the Coliseum, Len, no less a Roman emperor in his own mind, gazed mightily over the crowds. Was his son walking where he, Len, would easily have ordered to have his enemies fed to the lions?

"Let's get out of Rome. I'm uncomfortable," Len said the day before we were scheduled to depart.

"I've never been to Florence. Of course."

That same day, Peter left another message,

"Hi Dad, I am leaving Rome and on my way to London today. Amazing time in Rome. Speak to you soon."

We ate and drank our way through Tuscany. Len had hired both a driver and a guide but we sat in the back seat of the Mercedes and necked for hours. We ate al fresco in small villages, stuffing ourselves with linguine primavera and sloshing down the local Frascati. We saw little of the ride to Florence and only surfaced as we began to climb the hill to our beautiful hotel, the Villa San Michele, once a monastery designed by Michelangelo.

The view of all of Florence from the balcony of the Villa was spectacular.

"Thank you for showing this to me. Florence is everything I've imagined. And it makes me realize how much I've been missing all of these years," I said at dinner that night.

"Did you travel when you were growing up?" he asked.

"We went to Miami once or twice. The one big trip was to London when I was eleven and my brother was thirteen. When we arrived my parents said they were tired and needed a nap. My brother and I were allowed to wander into London alone. We were New York kids and if we could survive there, well…."

"So we went walking around Piccadilly Circus and Covent Garden for about an hour. And then as usual, we had a fight and my brother took off. So there I was, eleven years old, my first day in London and all alone. Fortunately, I really was a New York kid. I got in a cab and told him to take me to the Intercontinental."

"There's not a chance in hell I would have allowed that with my kids," Len barked.

"Me either. But my brother and I were on our own a lot in those days."

"Did you travel in high school and college?" Len asked.

"Yes, but when I got married right after college Jake and I had very little money since he was in training. So we rarely went anywhere. And since Jake's death I've been so consumed with taking care of my kids and trying to do my job that my world has been so limited. This trip makes me feel like I'm waking up out of a long slumber."

Len leaned back in his chair and looked pleased with himself.

The next day we walked the streets for hours, in and out of the Uffizi, the Galleria dell' Accademia to see The Justin, the Duomo, until we couldn't walk another step. But there was one very big incentive that kept us going that day. Len was addicted to ice cream and uncontrollable in his desire for it. When we stopped for gelato he ordered six flavors, including his three favorites, pistacchio, cassata siciliana, and pera, and tried each one.

We roamed around Florence for an hour searching for a particular vendor. Once found, Len seemed compelled to indulge in every flavor he had never tasted before. He finally stopped at eleven. On several of them, he had asked for panna, a scandalous fresh whipped cream.

"Look at how big my belly is! How could I have eaten all of that gelato?" He sulked as we slowly made our way back to our hotel.

On our last night in Florence I took Len out to a five-course dinner at Bevo Vino as a small gesture to thank him for our trip. The restaurant was described as a local favorite in a guidebook. It was a small charming place hidden on a side street crowded with locals, wrought iron furniture and gaily-painted walls right out of a post card. We ate ourselves silly and drank a glass or two of wine with each of the courses.

Around midnight, stuffed and drunk, we staggered back

into our room and I slid into bed. While Len went into the bathroom, I called room service and asked them to deliver Len's three favorite flavors of gelato as quickly as possible.

Room service arrived immediately and as I hurriedly took the tray from the young man, I thanked him and ushered him back into the darkness of the night. Naked in bed, I covered my breasts with a thin layer of the gelato just as Len emerged from the bathroom to his great surprise and delight. He began to slowly lick off his second dessert. We made love and Len fell asleep within seconds, spread out on the bed face up, as content as a man could be.

. . .

Len's tuxedo looked snug as we walked into the wedding of his niece on Long Island. My tight sequin dress had a jewel neckline and multiple crisscrossed spaghetti straps. Len's eyes seemed to crisscross when he first saw me in it. Was he stifling his anger at my display or actually pleased for once?

I'd be meeting his children for the first time, all three of them in one shot. Three young adults whose mother had died less than a year ago. I wasn't sure how they'd react to me and I wasn't sure how I'd respond.

Len and I never discussed whether or not he wanted to take on Chloe and Ben. He knew that if he wanted to be with me, how he treated Chloe and Ben would be critical.

But his grown kids? Did they need me? Would they resent me? And Len made it clear he didn't want me infringing on his sole command of the control panel of the lives he needed to govern. Even his grown adult children fell into his domain.

For months, I'd wondered about Jennifer, Dale and Peter. Pictures of them lined the bookshelves of Len's office. Judy supposedly had a gentle spirit to balance the warrior in Len. It seemed a good omen that he even wanted me to meet them.

As soon as we walked into the large wedding hall, Jennifer rushed over and quickly kissed and embraced Len. She held out her hand to shake mine.

"Dale and Peter are inside," she said.

Jennifer appeared to have tried her best to transform Len's looks into a New York stylish, attractive woman. Her blondish hair streaked with highlights, her makeup attempting to accentuate her eyes, diamond stud earrings, her short trim body in a Dolce and Gabbana print silk dress.

Two hundred people were gathering for the wedding. Judy's brother, the father of the bride, stood at the door to the room set up for the ceremony. He graciously introduced himself to me as he held my hand.

"Congratulations on your daughter's wedding," I said as we exchanged pecks on the cheek.

"Thank you. It's such an emotional day for the father. But I'm so pleased to meet you," he said as he continued to hold onto my hand.

I couldn't ask for more from John, Judy's brother. Len had allowed me to enter Judy's world and I knew the eyes of her family and especially his kids would be carefully watching me, comparing me to Judy. Everything about me would be up for comment.

As we walked to the first row, Dale and Peter stood up and both shook my hand. Except Dale leaned in to exchange a kiss.

'You'd be surprised how often my dad speaks about you," he said.

"That's so sweet of you to say."

Dale, the medical student, seemed to exude a warmth that doctors could certainly use. And like so many of those male Hollywood stars, very short but very handsome, Dale's looks more than compensated for his stature. Len's genes must have simply skipped right by Dale, his middle child.

Peter, still at Cornell, appeared more reticent. He stood still, simply observing me. He had a melting pot appearance of Len and Judy. Some compelling Judy features interspersed with Len's.

Jennifer, maybe defending her mother's honor, stared at me with cold, angry eyes. That anger probably cloaked a great sadness lingering over her mother's death but I felt disappointed in the twenty-six year old teacher of young children. After all, I'd recently been down that road with death myself.

The evening was a blur of the routines of a wedding with any number of guests whom I assumed were invited for peripheral reasons, just like me. Some weddings are emotional highs for everyone there because the bride and groom pull off a kind of theatre and the whole event is pure entertainment. The story of the love affair, the journey together is told so beautifully, so differently, through toasts, dancing, body language, that the wedding could be staged on Broadway.

There had to be people who felt the stirring emotions of this day. Just not me, since I didn't know the bride and groom and the stagecraft was missing in action.

The room was decorated rather simply. I'd heard John didn't make much money at the men's shoe store he owned in a small Long Island town.

"I gave John $25,000 to help pay for the wedding," Len said as we drove to the ceremony.

"Judy would be so happy you did that."

"It's really nothing. When Jennifer gets married, I'm sure she'll spend at least several hundred thousand on the wedding."

Len strolled around talking to various relatives of Judy's.

Each time, I'd see a head turn and someone staring at me. I knew how hard it was for her relatives to see Len show up with a new woman, Judy's possible replacement.

The whole evening, Len appeared so out of his usual element. These were some of the people he had grown up with in Jersey City but had left behind long ago. There didn't appear to be a person in the room, other than Len, whose net worth was worth talking about. No eye-popping jewelry, designer handbags or shoes from Bergdorf's that cost $600.

Although my attendance at the wedding might have been compelling for gossip or curiosity purposes for others, I tried to remain as invisibly present as possible. As the evening passed enormous relief began to set in, especially after those awful looks Jennifer had thrown at me when we met. We might escape the night with no great drama.

As we were preparing to leave, I walked over to Jennifer.

"It was so nice to meet you since I'd heard such wonderful things about you from your dad."

"Don't get so comfortable with my father. My mother hasn't been dead even a year."

"You know that my husband died of cancer. And I lost my father when I was twenty-one. I know how much it hurts."

"Then why don't you give us some space?"

Jennifer obviously didn't have a clue what her father had been up to within a month of Judy's death. And it wasn't like I was some thirty-year old showing up on Len's arm.

"I'm sorry you feel that way. Your dad is interested in moving on in his life and I hope you will be too at some point."

"You expect to replace my dead mother?"

"Jennifer, no one can replace Judy. I've heard about what a loving mother and wife she was. And no one can replace my husband, the father of my children. We are simply living our lives."

Tears began to fall from her eyes.

"Can't you let my mother rest in peace for one year at least?" she said as she stormed out the door.

Len sauntered over a few minutes later. I hadn't moved an inch. When I relayed the conversation his smile faded and the tension that pervaded his body returned.

"I'll deal with this."

Good luck with that, I thought. Since Jennifer seemed to think I was some kind of seductress to her poor innocent father, he'd have quite a task ahead of him. How was he going to explain this one? Yet, I'd never underestimate Len's ability to get his way.

FALL 1988

CHAPTER 10

September

It was Rosh Hashanah, the Jewish New Year. Jake had been off chemotherapy for two and a half months. He looked like Jake again. His hair was growing back. He had filled out, weighing in at two hundred twenty pounds; he had color in his cheeks. Nausea, mouth sores, fevers and exhaustion disappeared into just bad memories.

We went to Temple to thank God for our special blessings, then to our friends Susan and James's house for a holiday dinner. Jake was full of talk and laughter, and I was full of gratitude.

Susan and I left James and Jake to their work stories and went into the kitchen.

"How're you doing?" Susan asked.

"I'm scared. Since you asked."

"Come on, Jake looks great."

"I know. But I'm scared it will come back again. After all we've been through, I couldn't take any more of this."

"Maybe you need to see someone. You're being awfully

hard on yourself."

"I saw a therapist after Jake's first tumor nine years ago. He told me there was no reason I should fear a recurrence, the likelihood of Jake's developing a second tumor was about the same as being hit by lightning. Now nine years later we know he was obviously wrong – dead wrong."

Several evenings later I was lying on our bed talking with a friend on the phone. Just past nine o'clock, and the kids had been asleep for the past hour. Jake closed the door downstairs and headed right up to our bedroom, which was unusual. Normally he would go through the mail and the refrigerator.

He walked into our room and said, "Hang up the phone." Jake never talked to me like that. I hung up. He sat down on the soft round chair in the corner of our bedroom.

"I found another lump on my shoulder. The lump is on the other side this time, the left shoulder. It's the exact same size."

This must be what it's like when you're sitting in the electric chair and they turn on the juice, I thought.

I went over and looked at it. It appeared as innocent looking as the last one. I felt it.

"I think it feels different this time," I said.

"Why?"

"It's not as soft."

We both touched the lump. Jake's hands were experienced at examining the human body, mine were just instruments of hope.

"If there are little changes from the last one, do you think that's a good sign?" I asked.

"I don't know. Anything. What do I do now?"

"Call Henry."

I felt sure that if I had looked out the window at that moment a dark cloud would be arriving to cover our house again.

Henry could not reassure Jake, only arrange another biopsy. Trying to comfort Jake, I didn't believe a word, and Jake probably didn't either.

CHAPTER 11

October

J ake, this is Henry. I'm in the pathology department. I looked at the slides myself. The biopsy shows Non-Hodgkin's lymphoma. The same as last time."

Silence.

"I'm afraid you'll need a bone marrow transplant. Your next step is to see Dr. Davis again."

I sobbed. Jake started to cry but then he looked at me and stopped. Jake called the hospital and was told that Dr. Davis was not available. His call was directed to a Dr. Martin Lee, responsible for transplants for lymphoma patients.

We would be seeing Martin on the day before Yom Kippur, the holiest day of the Jewish calendar. It is between Rosh Hashanah and Yom Kippur that God supposedly decides whether He will write your name in the Book of Life for the next year. On Yom Kippur God closes the book for another year.

On Tuesday we drove to the cancer center to meet Martin. Jake was also scheduled for tests to determine the extent of the recurrence. It helped when every now and then one of the technicians talked to us. Some of them did; some of them couldn't.

Time passed before a short, middle-aged man flew into the room, put his foot up on a chair, leaned his elbow to rest on his knee, and began to talk to Jake, who was still laying on a stretcher.

"I'm Martin. I know you're scared, Jake," Martin said as his eyes kept darting left and right. It was as if his mind was racing while his words slowed him down.

"We'll talk later. Don't worry about a thing."

And then he was gone. Jake and I looked at each other and smiled. Martin seemed confident, quick and smart. He had dropped into our lives just when we needed him.

Then we got good news. The scans showed no other signs of cancer in Jake's body. Once again, the only evidence of cancer was the pea-sized lump on his shoulder. He had endured four and a half months of chemotherapy to get rid of that tiny lump. Now the doctors were bringing on the really big guns, to get rid of that same enemy.

We found an empty room in a clinic and sat down to what turned out to be nearly three hours of getting to know Martin.

"I'm a very dedicated physician," he said. "I care about my patients and I do the best I can for them. I've had some famous people as patients, I've cared for the best of them. The fact that you're a doctor Jake won't make any difference at all. I've had many physicians with cancer as patients, even one who looked bound to win the Nobel Prize in Medicine, until he passed away."

Jake and I could only watch him. This was Martin's stage.

"Jake, you clearly should have had a bone marrow transplant to begin with instead of the chemotherapy Dr. Davis recommended."

Not sure how Jake was receiving this information, I felt blindsided. This was Davis' colleague saying this. Was this maverick saying that the great Dr. Davis had been wrong and Jake had not only received the wrong treatment but had gone through four months of hell for nothing?

"You just didn't receive a high enough dose of the drugs when you were on them," Martin said. "Only with a transplant can you get enough of a dose in to achieve the results we want. You could be cured with a transplant."

"Jake's tumor is fast growing. Is there any advantage to having a fast growing or slow growing tumor?" I asked.

"I'm always worried about patients with slow-growing tumors," he said. "They can appear to be in remission for a long period of time and then it's back, the tumor is just insidious. A fast-growing tumor isn't like that. It doesn't come back. You're either cured or dead in a year."

"Jake will be cured," I said.

Jake turned pale and froze in his chair. He looked ghastly. I sat upright and firm. He heard the other possibility while I refused to believe it.

We loved Martin. We loved his intense desire to cure his patients. His energy, his intelligence, his hope were our lifelines now.

FALL 1995

CHAPTER 12

September

On a hot, muggy Friday evening over Labor Day weekend Len and I headed for the first time together to his summer home a few blocks from the ocean in pristine Spring Lake, New Jersey. The house, with whitewashed board and batten siding, boasted a great room with huge windows facing the water and an enormous fireplace. It looked understated compared to the formality and abundance of art and antiques filling Len's house in Alpine.

When we awoke in the master suite early to bright sunshine and the sound of the waves, I knew that Len would not be so derelict as to miss his morning run. Len was almost as compulsive as I was when it came to exercise, especially since he seemed to keep putting on weight.

"You go first. I'll start in about fifteen minutes and catch up to you," he offered as we put on running shorts and t-shirts. Len never wore anything under his loose fitting nylon shorts.

Since he was much stronger and faster than me, I headed out, knowing he would easily catch up. It was only seven in the morning and there were few cars and few runners to interfere with the pristine blue sky and my run. Gloria Estefan was singing "Turn the Beat Around" through my earphones, the sun was not too strong, and at first my body felt timeless. But after running three miles, I began to lose steam and finally just sat down. Len would be coming along shortly and then we could run together for a few minutes before he'd leave me in the dust.

It was quiet as I sat there waiting for him feeling kind of foolish, wishing I had more stamina. Then he appeared far in the distance. Len's thighs were large and powerful and carried him along steadily. Watching him approach me, knowing that what drove him were not only those legs but his determination, I felt humbled and defenseless against him. As a man, he was a force that I had never encountered before, so unlike Jake, and yet his command felt irresistible. I wondered if that's why he seemed addicted to power.

He barely smiled when he saw me, obviously concentrating on the running. I joined him as we ran on the now flat road.

"I couldn't make it any further," I said.

"Then meet me back at the house," he said and ran on ahead.

So I turned around and jogged and walked my way back to his home.

. . .

For Len's fifty-first birthday I arranged a weekend at The Lakes Inn in Rhinebeck, New York. We drove up late on a Friday night and after wandering down a deserted dirt road, found the charming Inn set on a lake. In the room we discovered Nineteenth Century Empire Revival furniture, a canopied bed, a fireplace, antiques, countless books lining the bookshelves and French doors overlooking the lake.

"This is even better than I had expected," he admitted.

"I did well?"

It felt cozy and wonderful and Len started a fire. He began to take off his clothes and before long slipped into bed. He lay on the bed with his arms behind his head folded on the pillow watching me.

"Your turn," he said.

I slowly took off my sweater, my pants, my bra, my panties. He stared at me as I stood there naked.

"Come into bed. I want you," he ordered.

In the morning the innkeepers delivered an enormous homemade breakfast of sausages, muffins and pancakes to our room in a large wicker basket. Feeling more than satiated from sex and breakfast, I started putting on a new sheer black silk sweater with a low neckline, when Len looked at me and made a terrible face. He grabbed the sweater playfully and tried to hide it from me while I chased him around the small room. Our tug of war was very brief – he won. He had me pinned to the floor with the sweater in his hand.

Len needed me to dress modestly so he could avoid having to witness other men staring in my direction.

"I only wear what you like, so why won't you do the same for me?" he asked.

We were giggling while the sexual tension mounted.

"I surrender, I surrender. I won't wear the sweater!" I conceded.

That day we wandered around the quaint town and then ended up in a small bookstore. I took Len to the section on sexuality and picked up a copy of *Top Sexual Positions*.

"I'm buying this. We can try each position between now and tomorrow," I coyly offered.

"I can't pay for it. I'm too embarrassed," he whispered.

"I'm not."

I took the book up to the counter and paid while Len hid behind one of the rows of bookshelves. And when I left the store, he followed behind quickly.

"You're a fifty-one-year old man with the sexual soul of a sixteen-year old boy," I said as we headed for the car.

"Judy was a virgin when we married. We dated from the time we were sixteen but we wanted her to be a virgin."

"How did you survive so long without doing it?"

"I don't know but I thought when she died I'd get my chance to play around. And then I met you." Len responded.

I was about to ask him if that would be the fatal flaw in our relationship. Len needed to fulfill some of his fantasies and see what may be out there. It may not have been better sex than he was having with me, but he wouldn't know that. When he gawked at other women, and he did it often, he left me feeling inadequate. But I decided against going down that painful road in the midst of our weekend away.

We took the manual back to the Inn. While we were lying naked in bed and leafing through the pages, we found one that looked promising and tried it out. Len was certainly a new man in bed, experimenting, uninhibited.

It was pouring that night when we left the Inn for dinner. Since it was his birthday, I retrieved the car from the parking lot, held the umbrella for Len as I escorted him from the Inn to the car and then chauffeured him to the restaurant. He had no qualms about being catered to whether in bed or anywhere else.

"You make me feel like a king. And I love being king."

Len's birthday fell a month to the day after the first anniversary of Judy's death. I thought of what an enormous milestone that day had been for me. But Len had telescoped into several months what had taken me years.

We ate in a nearby Italian restaurant that looked very mundane, especially after the panoply of spectacular restaurants we were experiencing with Len's friends in New York. This was not Len's kind of place. But he drank four glasses of Pinot Noir at dinner and was in high spirits. By the time dessert came he was giddy.

He looked at me dreamily for a moment or two.

"What's the matter?" I asked.

"I love you," he said.

Stunned, I didn't say a word.

He continued, "I've been tempted to tell you so many times. I've loved you for a long time."

"I love you," I said.

"I've thought it a hundred times. I've whispered it to you when we made love," he responded.

I felt overwhelmed at this point, having witnessed a side of Len few people ever saw.

"Do you remember I said there would be some surprises in our relationship?" he asked.

"Yes, you told me that you're really six feet tall."

"I want to tell you about the biggest one tonight. I am really very rich."

He appeared also very drunk.

"I have about seventy-five million dollars in my accounts."

I didn't know what he wanted me to value more, that he loved me or that he was really wealthy? Or was I that awfully lucky woman who had found a rich man and he loved me? It was supposed to be, of course, the best of all possible worlds.

"I bet the people in here don't have a clue how rich I am," he said as we walked out of the restaurant.

I drove his car through the pouring rain down the dirt road back to the Inn. At one point I pulled over and looked at Len, with his seat pushed all the way down to relax his drunken body. Leaning over, I began to kiss and undress him and myself and climbed on top of him to make love.

On the following Monday morning, a massive arrangement of roses, peonies and calla lilies was delivered to my desk at work.

"I hope I've made you as happy as you've made me. Thanks for a wonderful weekend and the best birthday ever. Love, Len."

While my colleagues marveled at the flowers, I sat day-dreaming, enjoying my reflection in Len's eyes. The flattery from him was constant and filled with words like fun, smart, fabulous mother, sexy and sweet. It felt hard to resist that reflection, given that I had not seen, or at least had not been willing to acknowledge, such desire and flattery since Jake.

Next to my briefcase on the desk sat the latest edition of *New York* magazine. Turning to the back of the magazine, I began looking through the personal ads. Just as quickly, I closed the magazine and smiled at my flowers. Len had provided a way out of that singles world and I was hoping to never enter it again.

CHAPTER 13

October

On the list of people who were anxious to meet my new man, Jason and Elizabeth, two of my closest friends from Connecticut, ranked high.

Jason had interviewed me for my first job after passing the Bar, and within seconds of meeting him I knew I had landed in the right place. The first time I met him he radiated a warmth and kindness that struck a deep familiarity inside me. It took a few weeks to realize he reminded me of Jake.

After spending eight years as a mother, wife and caretaker, my legal skills were not rusty, they were untested. Yet it was Jason's gentle prodding that led me into that world that lawyers inhabit, and after a year under his wing, I was well on my way. His endless patience would leave me always feeling grateful to him.

His wife, Elizabeth, who maintained an Isabella Rossellini beauty, once worked as a prosecutor under Giuliani. She had later gone on to become an associate at one of the premier New York white shoe law firms, but would end up in-house just like the rest of us – shunning the big bucks to spend time with her two little girls.

We met at Smith's, an old, tiny, dark wood paneled restaurant overlooking the Connecticut River. The ceiling was low, the light fixtures hung even lower and the tables were dark wood with wooden spindle chairs.

"So Len, I hear you get to handle some interesting deals," Jason began.

"Yes," Len said.

"Must be quite a trip to be involved with deals that of that size," Jason tried again.

"Yes."

"I worked at St. Clair, James for a while and did some myself. The hours were exhausting. You must have a lot of stamina," Elizabeth offered.

"I do."

"I hear you have three great kids," Jason said.

"Yes, three great kids."

Silence for a moment as Jason, Elizabeth and I glanced at each other.

"I hear you live in New Jersey. I grew up there," Elizabeth said.

Len remained silent.

"Elizabeth, I'm going to the ladies room. Want to come?" I asked.

Once we were at a safe distance from the table, Elizabeth asked, "What's wrong?"

"I don't know. He certainly doesn't act like this with his friends," I said baffled and embarrassed by his behavior.

"Do you think we're not rich enough, not successful enough?"

What if she were right?

"He must be in a bad mood," I prayed.

So I tried again. Different friends, maybe a different outcome. The following week we arranged to meet up after work with my friends, Ann and Patrick, for dinner at Aquavit, the latest restaurant to be rewarded with three stars by the *New York Times*.

Delayed fifteen minutes en route, I found Len standing outside the restaurant on the sidewalk.

"You're late."

"I know. The traffic was awful."

"People don't keep me waiting, you know," he said.

"I'm not people, you know."

He stepped back and stiffly held the door open for me. We found Ann and Patrick standing in the alcove. The atrium of the restaurant shimmered with glass and a waterfall. The bar looked packed with twenty-something singles.

Ann, a charming conversationalist, was a tall, elegant lawyer who had worked for years at Pointer, one of the prestigious New York law firms Len used for his deals. Len had no choice but to approve of her. He later told me that one of his very prominent friends knew of her.

"Kate must be okay if she's friends with Ann," his friend had said.

Her husband Patrick was infamous for his big heart and extreme political views. We had been arguing for years, ever since he had tried to convince seven-year old Chloe to vote for Pat Buchanan.

"Ann, I hear you work with Steve. He's a great lawyer. I've done a lot of work with him, noteworthy deals. He's been invaluable. Tough guy," Len said.

"He is sharp. Have you worked with Don?" Ann asked.

"Don is the man you want at your side. He will never back down. Great team at your firm," Len replied.

After Len had consumed a few too many glasses of wine and had run out of war stories from work, he told Ann one more in his arsenal of tough guy tales.

"A guy hit my car about ten years ago, just a minor fender-bender. It might have been a big nothing, but I didn't like his attitude. So I pursued him, and I mean for years. In the end, I spent about fifty thousand in legal fees to screw this guy. I didn't care how long it took or how much it cost. For me, revenge is best served cold."

When we had ordered espresso, Len excused himself to go to the men's room. As soon as he appeared out of earshot I began, not able to withstand the urge any longer.

"So? What do you think, Ann? Do you like him?"

She sat quietly for a minute, and then glanced at Patrick who remained silent, nursing his drink.

"You're the best thing to happen to him in twenty-five years," she declared.

Me?

Len, who apparently had enough of the dinners with my friends, offered to take Chloe, Ben and me out for a meal at a sports bar near our home where we could watch the World Series. The Atlanta Braves were playing the Cleveland Indians and I frankly didn't care. But Ben appeared psyched while Chloe quickly disappeared into her room.

McNale's dark wood paneled walls were lined with three televisions and all three had the game already on. The place was packed, mostly with men, some with their young sons.

"The food here couldn't be worse than the concession stands at a stadium, could it?" Len said while surveying the place.

Ben looked around and appeared thrilled to be at a guy's place with a guy.

"I might leave you two alone," I whispered to Len.

He nodded and I headed out the door after explaining to Ben that I wanted to keep an eye on Chloe. He hardly seemed to notice my exit.

At home, Chloe came downstairs when she heard me open the door.

"Where's Ben?"

"With Len at McNale's."

"Hah. Good luck with that."

Two hours later they showed up, barely moving their Buffalo wings and chips laden bodies into the house. Ben headed up to his room. Len looked relaxed and one might almost think content.

"He's a great kid. We had a really good time."

Couldn't things always be like this with him? I hugged Len and kissed him gently on the lips. This meant more to me than any piece of jewelry he could possibly lavish on me.

CHAPTER 14

November

While Len headed to Dallas one weekend for a meeting, I drove Chloe, Ben and my mother south to D.C. for my cousin Alan's wedding. The entire family showed up – cousins, uncles and aunts – and we celebrated late into the evening. A ten-piece band completed the somewhat unsurprising atmosphere, a ballroom filled with two hundred guests. I missed having Len there that evening to introduce to my family but seeing my many cousins had definitely made the trip worthwhile. Chloe and Ben pooped out around midnight after dancing non-stop for hours.

It was long past midnight when the phone rang in the hotel room I shared with Chloe and Ben. We were sound asleep.

"Hi!"

I was thrilled to hear Len's voice. From what I could tell, he was in the midst of a very crowded room.

"How was the wedding?"

He sounded drunk. His voice giddy as he slurred his words.

"Typical. I would have loved to have you here, have you meet everyone. How're you feeling?" I asked.

"Great. We're having a great time. I'm with the other partners."

"You've had a few drinks, huh?"

"Yeah, quite a few. You wouldn't believe it. The office manager from Dallas is here. She's a blonde bombshell. She has the biggest tits you'll ever see, we all want to fuck her."

"Good night Len." I hung up.

"Kate, if you want to be with me and my friends you're going to need to be demure," Len had lectured me just the week before.

"I'll be demure, if you're dignified," I said.

Later that week one of his oldest friends told me of a dinner he had with Len in L.A. about five years earlier.

"The waitresses were gorgeous, with the largest fake boobs you've ever seen. Well, you should have seen Len. He was literally chewing on the table, reaching for these babes, he simply couldn't contain himself."

Len gritted his teeth and nearly fell off his chair as his friend continued to divulge the story. As Len teetered on the edge, I considered what a nice little kick to his chair might accomplish.

The weekend after his trip to Dallas, Len and his two closest friends went fishing in Florida. Len was a lousy golfer and refused to do anything in public he couldn't excel at so fishing was a possibility. Short of catching the monster fish that could become legendary in men's circles, it would be hard for anyone to judge him at his fishing skills. He had no patience for either golf or fishing, so I considered all of this an excuse to spend time with the guys.

Once Len had asked Ben to join him in a rare golf outing and had allowed Ben, only ten at the time, to drive the cart while Len and a friend watched from a distance.

"Ben drove the cart directly into me and flipped me over the front seat landing me on my back," Len explained when they got back.

Ben hadn't told me about this and I cringed, worried that Len had lost his temper. Although I worked hard not to laugh at the thought of Len knocked over by a ten year old.

"Ben just stood there waiting for me to scream so I said nothing. I knew he had no control of the cart."

"Thank you for not yelling at him," I said while breathing a huge sigh of relief.

I hugged Len and held onto him while I savored the moment. He had allowed what was probably a very embarrassing moment to pass without a word to Ben.

Len called me Friday night to say that the place where they were staying was a dump.

"I miss you terribly," he said.

Saturday afternoon he called again to say that it had rained that day and he had stayed in his room and worked. Finally, on Sunday they fished. He called again on Sunday night.

"I told Brad and Bill that we'll be married before I have a weekend like this again."

I said nothing.

"You ought to get to know Brad and Bill well. They're the trustees of my estate. If something happens to me, you'll have to deal with them."

He had told me just weeks before, "I just say things. You take them too seriously." I wondered how seriously I should take what he had just said to me.

■ ■ ■

My calendar was loaded with work meetings, Little League, soccer practice, Sunday School, car pools, teacher's conferences, trips to the orthodontist and everything else that suburban parents squeezed into their days. Chloe and Ben often went off for sleepovers with friends or had their friends camp out at our house. Meanwhile, I'd see Len one night on the weekend and once during the week while Myra, our wonderful au pair, stood watch over my children.

Managing the unpredictability of Len while working and juggling all the countless variables in Chloe and Ben's life was no small feat. But I felt lucky to have the chance.

"If Chloe and Ben made plans to sleep at their friends' houses tonight why don't we stay at mine?" Len asked the following Saturday night.

We ate dinner that evening at a quiet, small restaurant near Len's home. But it began to rain heavily as we headed to his car in the parking lot afterwards. The wind howled and the rain pummeled his car. Within twenty minutes we were safely ensconced in his warm, dry home.

"Go in the bedroom, get comfortable and I'll bring some wine," he said.

Turning on the lights as I headed upstairs, I heard the rain beating on the windows and wondered if any of the trees could be too close to the house and might do damage. In his bedroom, I undressed completely and slipped under the pale grey thick down comforter.

Len walked in with two large glasses of Pinot Noir and handed one to me.

"I can't think of a better way to spend an evening like this, " he said.

He put down the glass, sat down on the bed next to me and began to kiss my lips and fondle my breasts. He stood up, took off his clothes and stood up naked.

"Cheers," he said as he drank down the rest of his wine.

I sipped on my wine as Len got into the bed and began to rub his hand up and down my chest and belly. We were lost in each other on a stormy night and it felt heavenly.

When the phone rang I wasn't even sure what it was at first, I had become so immersed in the pleasures of his body. It was late and only trouble called at that time. Len picked it up immediately and I could hear a loud male voice.

"What?" Len said.

He sat up and a controlled, rigid Len emerged from the sensuous man of moments before.

"When?"

His face contorted.

"I'm on my way."

He jumped out of the bed, pulled on his clothes.

"Jennifer was in a car accident. That was Bernard. She's at the hospital. Stay here. I'll call you."

He ran out of the room, down the stairs and I heard the car drive away in the storm. No chance to even offer to go with him.

The nightmarish phone call Len received seemed all the more haunting on this stormy night. And I didn't even know the degree of injuries Jennifer sustained.

The rain continued to beat down and the wind rattled the windows. It felt creepy to be alone for the first time in Len's enormous house surrounded by the darkness and acres and acres separating me from the neighbors' homes. Worried about Len driving in the rain, distressed about Jennifer, scared to remain in his bedroom, I decided to turn on the lights in every room in that house and to make some tea.

Jennifer had just moved in with her boyfriend Bernard in Summit, New Jersey. While the hot water boiled, I tried to figure out the distance Len had to drive in this storm. But

Bernard had called from the hospital. I wondered which hospital.

With the tea cup in hand, I sat down on the black suede couch in the vast living room and began the wait for Len's phone call, for his return, for any news. Along one long wall, floor to ceiling windows faced the dark back yard and the windows seemed so vulnerable to the winds.

One a.m., the time passed so slowly and I felt so sleepy. But no word from Len.

"Hey, wake up," Len said as he sat down on the couch next to me.

Looking around, it was still dark and raining outside.

"How is she?"

"Bernard was driving, they went through a red light in the storm and someone hit them. She has a broken leg but that's it. He's going out of his mind with guilt," Len said.

"Are you okay?"

"I don't know how I got to the hospital. This was a night from hell. But she's going to be fine. Let's get some sleep. It's five in the morning."

We began to head for the bedroom.

"Why is every light on in this house?" Len asked.

"I was scared."

"Of what?"

I didn't bother answering. There were too many answers to choose from at this point.

When we got into bed, Len lay on his back and stared at the ceiling.

"You don't want to get a phone call like the one I did, ever."

Never having seen him unnerved, this rattled, made me wonder. Len always seemed to be the steel beam that held everything together. I put my head on his chest, my arm around him and held him tightly. His body felt rigid, regathering the strength that had escaped that night. I feel asleep thinking that Len might be a mere mortal after all.

WINTER 1995

CHAPTER 15

December

For several years I had been working at AvnnHealth, a company considered as secure as Fort Knox. People worked there for life. Company loyalty was fastened until a sudden decision was made by the CEO and Board to merge with a smaller, more aggressive company, whose management took over. Things began to unravel as colleagues began to leave in droves, and the general utility and vivacity of the office plummeted. The final straw for me, though, occurred when my boss Janet came into my office one afternoon.

"I need to talk to you," she said as she sat down.

"Uh oh."

"I'm leaving," she said with tears in her eyes.

"No!"

"I've taken a job and will be leaving in three weeks. I can't stay here anymore."

"How can I stay here without you?" I responded.

"You need to carefully think about your future too."

"But this is the only job as a lawyer I've ever had. And I'll never have a boss like you," I said.

"Don't call me your boss. I'm your friend. And it's not like when you first started. You're an experienced good lawyer now," she responded.

"I think I'm going to cry. I thought I was going to work for you forever. You are my friend and you've been nothing less than a saint helping me in my work."

She stood up, gazed at me and walked out of my office with tears flowing down her face.

Sleep became a rarity as endless nights came and went, filled with thoughts over whether I had the courage to leave Connecticut. At the Oasis, my friends looked somber.

"I don't know. My house is nearly paid for. Chloe and Ben are doing well in school," I said.

"You never wanted to live in Connecticut in the first place, did you?" Bonnie asked.

"I miss New York. We moved to Connecticut for Jake, for his work. When I think of the City, and I know this is going to sound strange, but it's as if I were a gyroscope and can only maintain my orientation when I'm in New York. The City feels like my center of gravity. And that means that the gyroscope will spin upright only when I call New York my home. I always felt a little off living anywhere else."

"We always knew that. We just didn't know why, " Zoe said.

The four of us began to laugh, which rarely happened during these lunches where we tried to transpose our legal skills to resolve conflicts onto the matter before us of Len.

"I used to occasionally tease Jake. I'd look at my watch and say, is it time, can we move back to New York today? He knew that the City was tugging at me. But Connecticut was perfect for when Chloe and Ben were little. They're just not young kids anymore."

"How's Len going to react if you move to New York?" Rachel asked.

"I bet he'll think you're making a move on him. It will be all about him. His friends, his family will think the same thing," Zoë declared.

"I don't care. Appearances are not going to factor into my decisions," I said.

"But is it about him?" Bonnie asked.

"He is kind of the elephant in the room, isn't he? Am I moving to New York to be near Len? Yes and no. He's a piece of my decision making but there's so much more."

Of course, I thought, I wanted to be closer to Len. But that wasn't the only reason to get back to New York. I'd lived there for almost half my life already and it was the home I kept in my heart. If Len happened to live and work in Providence, I would definitely not be heading there.

"I've spoken to several headhunters and they've been optimistic about finding the right position in New York. The job opportunities in the City are good while the few that might be here are not the right opportunities or salaries. Janet jumping ship did it for me and I have to move on," I said.

"What about Chloe and Ben? How will they react?" Bonnie asked.

"Not well at all. But actually Chloe's in a crowd of friends I don't like or trust. High school girls can be really nasty. As much as she would hate to change schools her senior year, she definitely needs to get her away from those girls. It would do her well in the long run."

"Chloe's a typical teenager now, spreading her wings. Your little trio won't be intact for long," Rachel said.

"But I want to make the right choice for my kids. I've always tried to be their mother and father and make the decisions of both parents. Chloe was so sweet and surprised me on Father's Day last year. She said I had been the best mother and father."

"A man would move in this situation in a heartbeat because of the changes at work," Bonnie said.

Rachel played with her bracelet as if they were rosary beads. Zoë could hardly sit still. Bonnie stared at me.

"So you're moving?" Bonnie finally asked.

"Yeah, I'm moving."

We sat there silently. My days at The Oasis were now numbered.

At dinner that night I broke the news to Chloe and Ben.

Chloe looked at me as if I had clearly lost my mind.

"What? We can't move. What about my friends?"

"We'd live in an apartment? I can't live in an apartment," Ben said.

"Chloe, you have one more year of high school."

"So wait one more year."

"No, people at work are leaving and I don't want to look for a job in Connecticut for one year," I replied.

"I feel like a caged animal when we stay in Grandma's apartment," Ben added.

"You'll get used to it, I promise. It's how I grew up."

"You can't be serious," Chloe demanded.

"Yeah, I am serious."

"Why are you doing this to me?" Chloe cried as she headed for her room and slammed the door.

I sat there trying to console myself with the thought that since the kids had lost their father, I had always put their needs first. Now I was going to choose based on their needs, but also my needs.

"I've made a big decision," I told Len over the phone.

"Really?"

"Now that Janet has left and my work is not the same, and Chloe has one more year till college, I want to move back to New York."

Len was silent.

"It's the right time. The kids have loved living here but New York will offer them new opportunities. And me too."

"You realize how expensive it is to live in New York?" he asked.

"Of course I do."

"And you're ready to ante up?" he asked.

"Yes. You don't sound very excited about me moving."

"I question whether it's the right thing and whether you've thought this out."

"Right now, I'm looking for the next good job and that's going to be in New York and not Connecticut. Remember, I'm supporting two children. I'm sure you can understand that my income and my career are crucial to me as a single parent. And hold onto your chair, but they're also important to me as a woman. I'm moving. I'm coming back to New York."

A week later Len, out of nowhere, changed direction.

"Would you and Chloe and Ben like to come with me to St. Bart's for two weeks over the holidays?" Len asked.

"We'll stay in separate rooms, right?"

"Of course. My kids can't come this year by the way. All three of them are traveling somewhere abroad for the holidays."

None of his children were available to spend the holidays with their dad? Of course, it was possible. Or maybe they just didn't want to spend their vacation with us. Len would never tell.

We were scheduled to leave on December 21st, the day after my birthday. One week before our departure, Len drove to Connecticut for our weekly Saturday night date. As we sat in the living room talking, Len pulled out a small box wrapped in green foil paper and handed it to me. I slowly opened up the package and found a radar detector.

"This is for you, hot rod. Happy Birthday!" he squealed.

"Thanks," I said.

And the night came to a close.

On the eve of my actual birthday, we drove to Len's house in anticipation for our flight to the Caribbean. Late that night, as the kids slept and Len and I sat in the kitchen, he handed me a large red Cartier box, the same kind my gold necklace had come in.

"This is your birthday present," he whispered.

Inside the box lay a dazzling platinum necklace with round brilliant diamonds that must have cost at least fifteen thousand dollars.

"I can't believe this! Thank you. This is just gorgeous."

He didn't respond and I assumed he felt hurt. My failure to appreciate his sense of humor with the radar detector wasn't sitting well with him.

Jake had only once splurged on jewelry for me. He paid twenty-five dollars for a pair of pearl earrings on my birthday our first year of marriage, a price dear to us at the time.

Along with the earrings, Jake had enclosed a card,

'To Kate, my life, my love.'

When he died those were the words that went on his gravestone:

Beloved Husband and Father
Our Life, Our Love

So what was I to make of this necklace that Len gave me, albeit with no card? Rich men were notorious for handing out fabulously expensive gifts to their girlfriends, gifts that attached no significance other than to serve as a reflection of the donor's wealth.

For the moment I chose to take the Cinderella route and just enjoy the moment. I never knew in my life when the clock might strike midnight.

Chloe looked beside herself the morning we were leaving for our trip.

"You realize this is going to destroy my social life. I'll be away from all of my friends over the holidays. For two whole weeks."

"It's going to be wonderful. Warm and sunny and you can swim. And you'll meet people there, people your age," I said.

We left that morning in a stretch limousine, the only vehicle that Len felt would adequately suit our loads of luggage. Len, who loved to reveal his hand slowly, spoke not a word to us until the limo arrived at Teterboro, rather than Newark Airport. Since we had never seen the place, Chloe, Ben and I looked around as if we had landed on another planet.

"What's going on?" Chloe asked Len.

"We're taking a private jet."

Ben quickly ran into the relatively small terminal.

The plane, chartered for a group of five of Len's friends and for us, sat waiting. The chaos of Newark Airport, replaced by a tall flight attendant who greeted us with an enormous smile as we entered the small plane, seemed silly. This was surely the way to travel.

The jet was pristine, uncluttered with noisy strangers and serene. How many thousands of dollars did Len pay to transport the four of us? It was worth every penny from the looks on the faces of my children. Maybe those guys on Wall Street knew where money did buy happiness.

To describe the island and all of its luxuries would be to close your eyes and taste the pure pleasure of a melting sweetness on your lips. From the moment we landed, I knew my feet had never touched a heaven like it before. Resting on countless acres of white sand and green gardens, the Hotel St. Barth-Isle de France looked commandingly beautiful.

We watched the sunset at dinner each night from the beachfront restaurant with large elegantly set tables and chairs stuffed with thick pillows. Spas and athletic facilities sat near luscious hills overlooking the sparkling of a clear and blue ocean. A huge pool and Jacuzzi nested within a short distance from the ocean. We were miles away from anything resembling home, and nothing had ever been more delightful.

Days of relaxation and enjoyment became routine, as Chloe and Ben quickly made groups of friends. They relaxed all day in the sun, and Chloe then left to party at night, at least until midnight.

On our second day Ben began hanging out with a boy his age he met on the beach.

"You know who that guy is?" Len said as we sat on our beach chairs and watched the boy's father walk over to chat with his son and Ben. The tall elegant man didn't look familiar to me, but that didn't surprise me at all.

"Not a clue."

"He's worth about ten billion."

"Ben doesn't care. Though the father might if he knew there are no billions in Ben's family bank accounts."

"He probably figures if you're here, you have similar fortunes," Len said.

"I do have a fortune, in ways that are not counted in dollar bills."

"Oh please. That doesn't pay the bill here."

At dinner Ben let us know that he'd been invited to spend the next day on the yacht of this family.

"I can go, right?" he asked.

"What's this boy like? Is he nice?" I said.

"He's fun. They invited me. I can go, right?"

"Was the father nice?"

Ben rolled his eyes and left the dinner table to join other boys his age who were playing ball on the beach.

"The father probably is thrilled to have his son around a boy like Ben," I said.

When Ben returned late in the afternoon the next day he seemed no different than the day before. Didn't ask if we'd be getting a yacht or why we didn't have one.

"How was it?" I said.

"Fun."

"That's it?"

Len seemed to enjoy watching Ben innocently making his way into this man's world, one that Len had never entered.

With Chloe and Ben entertained all day, I was able to go for long runs on the beach and plow through several books that I had been meaning to read for some time. After a few days the resort slowly began to feel like a home, and even more exciting, the four of us started to feel like some version of a family.

Len predictably did not leave unknown to me the identities of the other countless sun tanned, designer-clad bodies that filled the hotel. Some of the biggest players on Wall Street surrounded us at meals, at the pools, on the beach. If anything was made abundantly clear throughout our two-week stay, I was the poorest one in the place.

On New Year's Eve we watched fireworks explode at midnight and Len held me and said, "Let this be the year of Len and Kate."

After a leisurely late breakfast the next morning, we went to check out and the front desk clerk handed Len the bill for our two weeks. Len put on his reading glasses and carefully reviewed the charges. I stood idly next to him, not even glancing at the bill. As he read the last page he peered at me and put me on notice. He handed me the final page of the bill.

Total charges: $75,000.

Jake and I knew how to make that kind of money last for our rent, food and living expenses for years at a time. I wasn't quite sure what to do.

"Thank you," I said as I kissed Len on the lips.

After two weeks of heaven in the Caribbean, we went home and I knew I had to sell my house, find an apartment, quit my job, find a school for Chloe and Ben and then pack up fifteen years of memories in my house. My fantasy vacation was over.

WINTER
1988/1989

CHAPTER 16

December

It was time to leave for the hospital. Transplant time. The cancer center expected us to show up at four in the afternoon. The car was loaded with the kids and my mother.

Jake and I lingered in the house for a few minutes. As we were about to leave, he gave me a long, warm hug. His arms felt so strong around me. I closed my eyes and tried to forget what he looked like now.

Tears started to roll down my face and Jake quickly let go of me. We had been married long enough that we could communicate with a look, and in Jake's glance, I saw that he wanted no tears shed now, when there appeared hope for him now. The tears were willed away while I closed the door once again on my fears, and walked out to the car with my husband.

My mother and kids went to the hotel and Jake and I went to the transplant unit. In time this floor would be as familiar to me as the rooms of my house. Inside each room, behind the heavy wooden doors and tiny windows, was a bed, shelves stocked with medical equipment, a bathroom, a television, VCR, chair and a nightstand.

In front of the door to Jake's room, we kissed a sort of goodbye. For six weeks we would not sleep in the same bed, he would not see Chloe and Ben. Adults could visit Jake with scrubbed hands, sterilized gloves, mask and gown. He kissed me again and stepped into the room. A transplant was the cure so bring it on. He removed his clothes, put on hospital pajamas, and began serving his sentence on the cancer ward.

The transplant began with two days of chemotherapy. Then radiation treatments. The next day was called Day Zero. Jake received his cleansed bone marrow back and the nurses sang "Happy Birthday". Then began the countdown until his marrow was engrafted, his platelets and bloods stabilized and his discharge from the hospital.

The siege had begun. When I sat in Jake's room for long periods of time my hands grew hot in the gloves, it became hard to breathe behind the mask, and the room seemed smaller and more confining by the hour. Yet, I could leave at will.

One evening I began to reread articles we had taken out of the medical library on transplants. This time I read the actual words on the page rather than reading what I wanted to believe. Jake had only a fifty-fifty chance of being a transplant success. No matter how positive Martin was, the statistics just didn't back him up.

I pictured the faces of the patients on Jake's ward. Statistically, half of them would be dead in a year. Which ones? Certainly not Jake. Maybe this group would live and it would be people whose faces I would never see. Imagining myself a Nazi soldier standing at the head of a long line of people, I divided them into who should live and who should die. Jake would definitely live.

Jake sailed through transplant. He never got a fever. Yet another sign that Jake would clearly be one of those cured. Martin flew into the room one day and said just that.

"Jake, I'm not God, but you're cured."

When Martin left the room, Jake laughed. "I bet after one beer, he thinks he is God!"

Since Jake was doing so well, we decided to let Chloe take a peek at her father through the small window in the door to his room.

"Let's go visit your Dad today," my mother said to her.

"I'm scared," she said.

"That's why you should go. You'll see there's nothing to be scared about. And he misses you. Come on."

Whatever Chloe had pictured in her mind kept bothering her until the moment she stood on a chair, looked in the window to Jake's room and saw her daddy again. Jake smiled and threw kisses at her. She waved and threw her kisses back. Her imagination could stop now, there was her precious daddy and he looked well. She smiled and skipped down the hall on her way out.

On Day 26, Jake left the hospital. He got dressed, put on a mask to protect his very fragile immune system, and walked out. He was to stay for a short time at a condo near the hospital that belonged to friends of ours. Martin did not want Jake to leave the area just yet. And I was going to stay with him.

I sobbed all the way to the hospital. I cried for our kids and the revolving door life they were forced to lead; Daddy is sick, Daddy is cured, now he's not – Mommy's leaving again. And I wept out of relief – that the transplant had gone flawlessly, that it was over, that now Jake would be cured.

When Jake and I got into bed at the condo that night, it was snowing out and the room felt very cozy. A simple, sparsely decorated room, but not a hospital room. And so for us it could well have been a room at The Four Seasons Hotel. We cuddled under a warm comforter, and then I knew why we had endured the transplant. For the first time in months, we felt at peace.

Nervous about the cuddling, I wondered if one of my germs would attack Jake's compromised immune system. Then he reached for me. He had 70,000 platelets, over 500 polys – and Hickman lines coming out of his chest that were used to administer medications and withdraw bloods. The hospital instructions said 'No kissing or sexual intercourse until 50,000 platelets and over 500 polys'. They explained that polys were part of the white blood cells that fight infection. Very tenderly, very gently we made love. We both slept that night like babies, catching up on the closeness and sleep we had lost for months.

Four days later Martin let Jake go home to Connecticut. We surprised the kids who then made 'Welcome Home Daddy!' signs. Jake went into the den where he kept his medical books and journals. He was drinking in his surroundings and all the trappings of his career. All of it had been taken away, but now he could do what he loved to do most, practice medicine. He looked stronger just sitting there at his desk.

CHAPTER 17

January

The days flew by. Martin told Jake he could go back to work on February 1. One afternoon in mid-January I noticed that Jake seemed unusually sleepy, which surprised me because he had seemed almost back to his pre-transplant level of energy.

The next morning Jake was taking a shower and I was cleaning up the breakfast dishes when I heard the water in the shower in our bedroom go off only a few minutes after it went on.

Jake was downstairs in no time.

"I found a lump in my testicle."

I froze.

Jake paged Martin who responded immediately.

"Stop playing with yourself," he told Jake. "It's probably nothing."

But it wasn't nothing. That night in bed Jake found a lump on the side of his neck. I grasped the bed with both hands. We were falling back down the black hole of cancer and I didn't want us to go there. We called Martin again.

"This is nothing," he said. "It's much too soon after transplant for a recurrence. It just doesn't happen that way. The radiation likely caused the glands in your neck to block up. Calm down. Believe me, you're fine."

That night Jake got into bed and stared at the ceiling. I tried to reassure him that Martin had seen loads of transplant patients and if he didn't think it was a recurrence, then it wasn't.

As we went to sleep that night, I knew that the post transplant honeymoon we had been enjoying for the past few weeks was over.

The next morning the lump in Jake's neck was not only still there but bigger.

Jake called Martin.

"Jake, I told you, it's too early for you to recur. I'm an immunologist and I know that people's immune systems are responsive to their emotions. If you're going to panic like this all the time, you won't do well! You have to stop this Jake. You're asking for a recurrence!"

We were stunned.

"Martin's ego is on the line here –he said you were cured so many times I think he's denying the possibility that the great one could be wrong," I said.

"I've never in my life talked to a patient the way Martin talked to me. I wouldn't play with their emotions that way."

We both felt angry and helpless. Over the next few days Jake seemed to be tired all the time. Staring at his neck over dinner one night, I knew the lump was getting bigger. Jake took the kids upstairs for their bath and left me to clean up the kitchen. Instead I started to cry while running the water so they wouldn't hear my sobs. The cancer was back. I knew it, Jake must know it – and we couldn't say it to each other.

Two days later Jake noticed some spots on his leg that looked like herpes zoster, a form of chicken pox post-transplant patients often get. We headed back to the hospital and Jake was re-admitted after a month at home. A biopsy would be done and at least we would find out what was going on.

The results of the biopsy were due back Friday morning at nine a.m. On Thursday evening I left Jake's room around eight and went down the block to stay in The Morris Motel. I hated the place. The lobby was always deserted, and the hallways stretched as far as the eye could see with an alcove between each room door. To avoid walking down the long tunnel like floor, I asked for a room near the elevator.

The room was tiny and depressing with a faded brown plaid bedspread on a thin mattress that had seen better days, a brown dresser and brown carpeting that had worn out long ago. It had a connecting door, and the couple in the next room waged all-out warfare for hours. I began to make phone calls.

First Tim, a close friend of Jake's from medical school, one of his brightest classmates.

"Couldn't the lump in the neck be from the radiation?" I asked. "And the lump in the testicle just an inflammation?"

"It could be."

"So you think this isn't a recurrence?"

"Might not be."

"There are explanations that would cover these lumps other than cancer, right?"

"Right."

Next I tried Alan, a pediatrician who had worked with Jake for years. When he answered the phone I could hear his kids preparing for bed, family noises that made my throat ache.

"You think it's a recurrence?"

"I don't know, Kate."

"There could be reasons for the lumps other than cancer. Right?"

"Yes."

I hung up, wishing I hadn't been subjected to the sounds of his household, the kids laughing and yelling. Wishing I didn't feel so alone.

Finally, I called Jake's brother.

"This doesn't look good, Kate." Greg began to choke up, which threw me completely. He had always been so calm, so controlled.

"I can't bear it if Jake has recurred," I said. "What will we do?"

"I don't know."

We were both sobbing.

"He could die. Can you believe that? Jake saying good-bye to Chloe and Ben? To me? I want out of this nightmare!"

"I can't believe it."

"I wish the people in the next room would stop fighting already, they're giving me a headache."

"Why don't you call the desk and complain."

"Because the quiet might be worse than the fighting. At least I feel I'm not the only person on the planet. It's almost comforting to hear their voices, no matter what they're saying."

"I'm going to call Martin and see if he had any news, Kate."

"Call me right back."

Now I was in a state of panic. In the drawer of the nightstand there was a Bible. Not having looked at one for years, I didn't even know what to look for. There was Job –

hadn't he gone through this kind of thing? Reading some passages, I knew I wouldn't be hearing from Job's God that night and that there wouldn't be any miracles. We had prayed so much – and now this. What kind of God was this anyway?

But I prayed anyway. Down on the floor on my knees, I begged God for one last chance. Please save Jake. Help him. He's suffered so much already –

The phone rang.

"Martin says he can't tell us anything until he gets the results," Greg said.

"I'll have gone out of my mind by then."

We talked on and on for another half-hour; just hearing the sound of his voice soothed me.

"I'm getting tired," I said finally. "I may even be ready to get some rest. I'll call you in the morning – and thanks."

It was 10:30 p.m. One more call to the hospital to check on Jake.

"It's a good thing you called," the nurse at the desk said. "Jake is being worked on right now. His calcium is up to fifteen. That's very elevated."

Tumor cells could cause the bone to give off calcium. If the calcium got too high, there was the risk of kidney failure.

"They're putting in an additional line right now."

"Why didn't anyone call me?"

"Your husband said he didn't want to worry you."

Grabbing my overnight bag, I ran out of the motel and down the street to the hospital. The lights were horribly bright in Jake's room, his bed surrounded by interns and residents who had just succeeded in putting in a line near his groin. Jake was very groggy.

My heart broke at the sight of him. What more, God, what more? The cancer was back with a vengeance.

Sitting in the chair next to his bed until midnight, I was too overwhelmed with dread to stay in that room another minute. I called my mother, who was home with the kids. Her enormous strength had always been evident in her career but now it was my crutch. And her complete devotion to my children was the only reason I could handle my bifurcated life of Jake and my kids.

"I can't take this by myself any more!"

"Do you want me to come up? I'll come right now."

"What about the kids?"

"Aunt Nancy and Uncle Harold are here."

"All right come, I don't know how I'll make it through this one."

In the morning Jake lay on the hospital bed in a daze, terrified. I held Jake's hand and knew he had to hear the truth before Martin arrived, before the boom was lowered.

"Jake, I think Martin is going to tell us it's a recurrence."

Jake stared at me like a hurt, bewildered child.

"We'll get through this. You'll take that experimental drug that Martin's working on, and you'll be okay. We'll do everything there is in this world – you know we will. You're going to be okay."

Martin opened the door. "Jake, I just came from the pathology department, I looked at the slides myself. It's lymphoma. I cried on the way over here."

Jake took in a deep breath and held it. He was a doctor; he knew what this meant, far more than I did.

"Can he get that experimental drug?" I asked.

"We'll discuss it after we get him over this crisis. I'm sorry Jake. I love both of you and I didn't want to have to tell you this."

Jake could have said no at this point to further treatment

and acknowledged his fate and declined to fight.

Instead, he chose to continue on the path we had been taking. Life, if possible.

I left the room and found that I couldn't stop crying. All of last night's anxiety – all those phone calls, those pleas for reassurance – seemed ludicrous.

Over and over again, I walked up and down the halls.

Martin found me. "It's only a matter of months now," he said.

"NO!"

Jake would die of cancer, I knew that now. But not in months.

"You did something terrible Martin. When you yelled at Jake on the phone that this wasn't a recurrence, you hurt him. It wasn't necessary. The lumps in his neck and testicle were cancer, he had every right to be scared."

Martin was silent for the first time since I had met him.

"After all those promises of cure, Martin, how could you?"

"Kate, you have to be prepared for the worst now. A typical breast cancer doubles every six weeks. Jake's tumor is doubling every other day."

Now I had to tell my children that their daddy might not make it after all. We had always said that he was very sick but that the treatments and all the suffering had a purpose – that he would live. Now, the only hope I could give them – or myself – lay with an experimental drug.

We met at the same hotel we had used for so many weekends. The kids were their usual selves, running around the room, watching television, and playing Monopoly. They enjoyed the novelty of being in the hotel, the video arcade, the pool, and restaurants and gift shop. I loathed the place.

"I have to talk to you both tonight," I said. "I have something really important to tell you."

Chloe sat down on the bed and looked at me. Ben, always in constant motion, listened while he continued to play with his Lego bricks.

"Daddy's cancer is back. The medicines they gave him didn't work. Now the doctors are running out of medicines to give him. There's one more to try – we hope it will work, but it may not."

"What does that mean?" Chloe asked.

"It means Daddy could die."

Chloe's body jerked as she heard the words. She threw herself on the bed and cried while I held her. Ben didn't seem to take it in. Every few minutes he would cry briefly –as if imitating his sister – and then it would pass. Chloe was inconsolable.

Finally she got up, took a piece of hotel stationary and a pen and wrote in the lovely tentative handwriting of a seven-year-old.

Dear God,

Help daddy please?
I love him very much.
I don't want him to die.

Sincerely,

Chloe Newman

She went to the window of our room and pressed the paper to the pane with the writing face-out.

"What are you doing?" I asked.

"I want God to see this. He'll see it much better this way."

That night the three of us cuddled together in one of the double beds, and fell asleep glad to have each other but knowing that one very important piece of us was missing. I dreaded the future.

SPRING 1996

CHAPTER 18

April

From the moment Jake died, I became the widow with her nose pressed against the window of life. Watching my friends through that window, always hoping to get back inside, I ached with envy. And now, after what seemed like years wandering alone, I had arrived in the promised land. Being with Len was the answer to my isolation and deprivation.

More importantly, knowing that Len could and would take charge meant that I could and would relinquish some of the sole control I had maintained for my children and myself for all of those years. If anyone were listening for it, an enormous sigh of relief could be heard leaving my lips. No longer responsible for all that transpired in our lives, I cherished the feeling of having someone to watch over us at last.

Len arranged our travels, our weekends, and our social life. All I had to do was to mention that Billy Joel, Tina Turner or Bruce Springsteen would be in town, and tickets would appear. He was always arranging something, while I had lost that ability to feel so sure that the future was guaranteed. Jake's death had taught me to be more cautious, that planned events might not take place. Len was somehow unfettered with such inhibitions despite Judy's death.

But what mattered most to me was that Len was now arranging Ben's athletics. All of his life, Ben had been a terrific natural athlete and the fathers in our town had marveled at his abilities and determination. Ben's natural talents had carried him all these years as the other kids' fathers zealously worked on their sons' skills. Many a father had said to me that they would love to take Ben on a weekend and work with him.

"He's so good, maybe we could play a little ball," they'd say.

But they never called. So there had been no end to my attempt to be one of the guys, even serving as the first and sole female member of the Montwood Little League Board. When Ben was in elementary school, I managed his basketball team and coached his Little League team for a year. One father told me he objected to his son having a woman as the coach and I almost caved. But our team won because of Ben, and he even made me look good.

Even so, I was plagued with a vague notion that men knew something I didn't – that all of those years parked in front of their television sets watching sports gave them an advantage. I wondered what I could offer Ben as he grew older and the competition increased.

At one tennis match we attended, Ben had won the first set and the other boy had won the second set. There was a ten-minute break before the third set. The kid's father put his arm around the boy and began to coach him about mixing up his backhand with more slices and topspin. I had absolutely nothing to offer to Ben about tennis.

"Do you have to go to the bathroom? I said.

"No."

"Would you like some M&M's?" I showed him the ones left in my hand.

"No."

Ben went back out and lost the third set.

At tryouts for summer baseball leagues, there were always dozens of men and me watching the kids. And the fathers engaged in a lot of son promoting man talk with each other. Watching as they took their turns schmoozing with the coaches, pointing out their talented sons, I remained silent. Ben's abilities would have to speak for themselves.

One day Ben was pitching and I overheard the coaches discussing him.

"That lefty is really good. He's focused. What he has can't be taught."

I sat there wondering what Ben had and where he got it from.

As we were leaving I whispered to Ben what I had heard. He was beaming.

"You know you got your pitching genes from me?" I said.

"Yeah right!"

Well, Len took one look at Ben's abilities and was in charge immediately, the same way he had guided his own sons through their high school years in sports. And Ben loved that Len had played catcher in college baseball.

Len began to schedule Ben's pitching lessons and attend his games. At last a man who knew what he was doing could guide Ben in a man's world of sports. Len didn't know much about tennis but was able to advise Ben on the game certainly more than I could. I sat back and blessed my lucky stars. If Len offered nothing else to us, his stepping into this role with Ben was exactly what Ben and I had been praying for.

The natural result of this was a bond that grew between Len and Ben. Ben, surrounded in suburbia by involved fathers, seemed desperate for one of his own. And along came Len, ready to take him on.

Len was warming to the sweet, gentle nature Ben had developed over the years. Ben would snuggle up to him as they sat together on a couch watching whatever sport was on television and Len seemed to like the loving. They couldn't have been more different.

On the other hand, Len couldn't seem to muster much with Chloe because she kept her distance. Chloe, very adept at reading people within minutes of meeting them and a magnet for friends, was constantly surrounded by her coterie of teenagers. But she limited her interactions with Len and only occasionally allowed him to offer her advice about colleges. I chose to ignore what signals her radar might be picking up. And I dismissed her instincts, once again ascribing them to her age. No single woman would want to admit that her teenage daughter was better at judging men than she was.

■ ■ ■

Len and I sat at a table of eight in a gaggle of multimillionaires and billionaires. The frenetic energy of the celebration for the fiftieth birthday party of a twice divorced banker filled his penthouse apartment. The 360 degree view of the City from the floor to ceiling glass windows was simply spellbinding. A signed Picasso hung on the wall behind our table.

"Why is that guy at the next table staring at you?" Len asked while we poked at the pieces of rich chocolate ganache birthday cake in front of us.

"Lindsay? I went out to dinner with him on date a year or two before I met you."

Len leaned over towards me.

"Did you sleep with him? Why does he keep staring at you?"

"No, I didn't sleep with him. I didn't sleep around. You know that. I once had a guy spend $5000 on Yankee playoff tickets he got from a scalper thinking he'd get me into bed. He said he likes to spend that kind of money to take women to the South of France to seduce them. And here we were in the South Bronx."

"I gather he wasn't too happy if he didn't get you into bed."

"He was fuming when I got out of the cab at his building and walked away."

"What does Lindsay do?"

"I don't know. But he did inform me in the first fifteen minutes of our dinner that he's worth a few billion."

"I don't recognize him at all," Len said as he glanced once again at Lindsay.

"He's from Georgia. He actually told a story about when he was fifteen his father arranged a visit for him with a prostitute. Of course, he had to tell me that after they did it, she said how good he was."

"Damn, wish I had grown up in Georgia."

Two attractive New York socialites sat on either side of Lindsay. He looked quickly over at Len and me.

"Lindsay's tried to carry some of the charm of his family's old Southern ways to his current life. He has a housekeeper and said he rings for her with a bell."

"In New York City?"

"Can you imagine? I asked him where he found someone who would respond to his bell. He also told me that he has a masseuse come to his apartment once a week. I thought that sounded really cool until he said I'd have to earn a massage. As he tried to kiss me good night, I pushed him away and told him he'd have to earn it."

"I assume he's divorced."

"Of course. They all are, at least once. But when I explained I'm a widow, he blurted out that he wished his ex-wife were dead."

"That's classy. Did you actually kiss him?"

"Lindsay grabbed me when we left the restaurant and started kissing me very passionately. He pressed against me and I could feel his erection. So I pulled away and left him standing there on the sidewalk."

Len looked around the room for a minute or two.

"You have any more stories you haven't told me?"

"Just keep your eyes open for any other men staring at me."

The withering look on Len's face was probably the stuff of children's nightmares.

"That woman is wearing the wrong bra for her dress," he said a moment later.

A twentysomething woman in an off the shoulder Herve Leger bandage dress walked slowly by.

"You work quickly to even the score, don't you?" I said.

I turned to the man sitting on my left whose wife was busy chatting across the table.

"You look so serene in this room full of charged men," I said.

"I just left the world of investment banking after twenty years. There wasn't a single day in all those years I felt content."

This man definitely seemed different than the others. The pit bull ready to pounce energy must have dissipated when he made his exit from finance.

"What do you do now?"

"Not much. I made about twenty million a year so I have some leeway to figure it out. But I'm relieved to have left that world behind."

"Twenty million dollars a year? I would have left after one year."

He didn't laugh.

"There was never enough money. It's addictive. Until one day I turned fifty and realized it was getting late in the game to lead such a miserable life. My daughter paid a high price for my working so hard and never being home while my first wife, her mother, spent her time at our club and shopping."

"What's wrong with your daughter?"

"She's seventy pounds overweight and channels dead people at night."

He looked for my reaction. Stunned at his confession to a total stranger, I figured this man's head must be saturated with pain. Enough pain to have left twenty million a year behind. How often did that happen?

At that moment Len, now standing behind my chair, put his hand on my shoulder.

"I'm sorry to interrupt. We need to get going," he said.

I turned to the man on my left once again as I stood up. His face still portrayed the anticipation of something I might say to make him feel better about his daughter.

"I hope your new life works out just as you imagine and that your daughter finds her way. Life has many chapters and this could be a wonderful new one for both of you."

With a faint smile he stared off into the distance.

"What was that about?" Len asked as we left the party.

"Just another unhappy very wealthy man. Know anyone like that?"

CHAPTER 19

May

"C an I see you tonight after work? I'm just dying to make love with you. I was sitting in a meeting today, doing a two billion dollar deal and all I could think about was making love with you."

There was a pause as Len sighed.

"No one would believe what goes on with us. Do you think my kids would ever believe what kind of sex I'm having?" he giggled.

I pictured the oak paneled conference room, the enormous, obscenely expensive conference table surrounded by mostly male lawyers from Pointer, and St. Clair, James and their clients, like Len, who were paying these lawyers a thousand dollars an hour. They'd be doing the deal, the negotiations for a two billion dollar transaction sitting in the war room oozing machismo, the beat of war drums pounding in their chests, bluffing each other until the deal was done. Len had said that he was the master of walking away from the table, absolutely sure that the other side would yield because he was always the toughest one of all.

Len would be at the table in his white shirt, no jacket, his body to all outward appearances fully engaged in the war that was going on, but he was thinking of making love with me. I agreed to meet Len halfway between New York and Connecticut at nine that night since he thought he could escape for a few hours while the lawyers haggled over the contractual details.

Len's deal making testosterone levels must have been sky high that night. He was ravenous and I was thrilled to satisfy his hunger. After we made love Len held me in his arms.

"That was incredible. If I died tonight, I wouldn't care because I've had you." He kissed me tenderly and then continued.

"I was thinking that we should move Jake's body next to Judy's. That way when we die, we can be buried together. I'd hate for you to be in Connecticut."

I snuggled closer into his body.

"I feel like a king. You just ring my bell. I literally wouldn't care if I did die tonight."

I kissed his neck.

"I can't get enough of you. I love your joyfulness and playfulness. It brings out the best in me. You know, I feel like I know your body better than I know mine," he said.

A moment or two passed before reality set in.

"Have you thought about where you're going to live in New York?" he asked.

"Not yet. I have lots of options."

"I don't want you to make any decisions based on me."

I stared at him. One minute ago he had confessed to a willing foot in the grave having known the greatest heights of life because of our lovemaking. He was content to spending eternity with me, just not now.

"Does that mean you don't care where I live?" I asked.

"It means you make your own decisions. Don't factor me into them."

I pulled away from his body. How quickly he had transformed into a man with a steel heart. This part of Len scared me, and I dreaded any head on collision with him.

His sexual needs fulfilled, he was back at the table in the war room.

Several days later, it was late afternoon when the phone rang in my office.

"Kate, this is Linda from Dr. Mann's office. I have the results of your pap smear. You have Trichomoniasis."

"I have what??"

"Trichomoniasis. It is a sexually transmitted disease that a man passes onto a woman or a woman passes to a man," she said.

I stood up and began to pace around my desk.

"What?"

"Your pap smear shows that you have trichomoniasis. You'll need to take a medication and your partner will have to take the medication too to clear this up."

My heart was pounding as I called Len's office and asked to speak with him. He was in a meeting. I told his secretary it was urgent and that he needed to call me as soon as he was available. Then I sat frozen at my desk waiting for the phone to ring. It took only five minutes before Len called. I conveyed the news to him.

"I haven't been sleeping with anyone else," his voice was panicked.

"The nurse said that I got this from a man. You're the man."

"It must be the woman in Birmingham. I got it from her," he said.

"That was supposed to have been over a year ago. You told me you used condoms with her!"

Silence.

"We didn't. I was very inexperienced. I was too embarrassed to tell you," Len finally said.

"When you asked me several months ago what I had used for birth control in the past, you were adamant that I better have protected myself now that I was sleeping with you. And I asked if you used condoms with that woman. You said 'of course'."

The phone remained dead silent.

Len and I both took medicine to clear up our respective infections. He wanted to prove to me that the last time he had seen the woman from Birmingham was last fall. He wanted to show receipts from hotels. I wouldn't look at them.

"We didn't use condoms because I didn't even know we were having sex at times," he said.

He began to laugh, "I thought she raped me."

"You used that line on me. Remember The Madison?"

"My doctor says that the nurse was wrong about where you could have gotten this. People get it from dirty toilets, from past partners and it lingers," Len said.

"I'm not sure if you're just making that up about dirty toilets or your doctor is incompetent. But he's right about one thing. A man typically does not show symptoms, so it can linger in a man, a man like you."

Len had gone too far this time.

"Who cares where I might have gotten it at this point? You lied. The virus could have been HIV," I said.

MAY

For the first time since I'd know him, Len's face had a helpless look. This time, he had lost control of the narrative, a rare moment in this man's adult life.

CHAPTER 20

June

The master bathroom in Len's house was the size of most living rooms, and for Manhattanites, the size of their entire apartment. Set in the middle of the green marble floor was a two person Jacuzzi with gold plated faucets. Nineteenth Century antique English mahogany mirrors lined one wall over two hand painted porcelain sinks with fleur-de-lys design.

It was a lazy Saturday afternoon, Len had just finished running and we had several hours to spare before our dinner plans that night. When he went into the Spanish white tile shower, I joined him, a gesture he always appreciated since Judy had not showered with him in all of their years together.

We playfully washed each other's bodies and held each other tightly as the warm water covered us. I preferred the water much warmer and whenever Len closed his eyes to wash off, I reached over to the gold plated faucet and turned it to "H'. And Len immediately turned it right back to "C" as soon as I closed my eyes.

We dried each other off and slipped into bed, although it was against Len's productive nature to get into bed at five in the afternoon. But sex had taken a new priority on his agenda of what was important to accomplish.

Len looked tired from running and by lying on his back, waiting to be serviced, he made it clear he wanted to be catered to. I readily complied and we made love slowly in the late afternoon dusk. Afterward, we held each other for a long while before Len jumped up.

"I need another shower before I get dressed for dinner," he said as he headed into the bathroom.

When the water went off, I got up and opened the bathroom door to find Len standing naked in the front of the mirror by the sink. He was brushing his wet hair and in great spirits.

Len was about to lather his face to shave and was smiling to himself in the mirror, when he started wiggling his wide hips and belly – he was singing:

"Macho, macho, man…"

King Len, as I often called him, was certainly feeling like the Lord of the Manor tonight. He continued swaying his hips and singing over and over again those same words.

"Macho, macho, man…"

We were dining that night with some of Len's much younger colleagues and their wives. These women knew they would rarely see their husbands as the men amassed their fortunes.

King Len felt masterful when he was with these young colleagues and said so often. He thrived on their energy and enthusiasm but most of all on their complete admiration for all that Len had accomplished. He knew when he walked down the halls of Duke Heller, he was finally six feet tall in the hearts and minds of these young men.

"I didn't kill myself for twenty-five years just for the money, it was also ego," he told me many times.

It was the money and the ego because neither alone would have been enough for Len, a man in need of constant recognition. As long as an appreciative audience marveled at his triumphs, his enormous ego could relax.

"The best part of all is when I call one of these young guys into my office to work with me. They are terrified until they get to know me, of course, to know what a great guy I am."

"You should see when he walks down the halls at Duke Heller. People say 'there he is'," Len's administrative assistant told me one day when I called the office looking for Len.

Len knew he had truly arrived when he was able to donate large sums of money. He reveled in the booklets printed that listed his donation for all to see.

"When Judy died, I donated two million dollars in her memory," Len boasted.

"What a generous tribute. Who'd you give the money to?"

"To my business school, of course," he said.

"You're not serious."

"Why not? I was very happy there. And look what that school did for me."

"But this wasn't about you. It was about Judy, her cancer, her suffering. Why not help others who are now suffering?"

Len looked devastated. How could I not appreciate his largesse?

"I want to help others end up like me."

"You mean create more rich white men."

Len was furious. If I wasn't in awe of his generosity, what good was I?

"You know I do care about people. I helped my barber when he confessed to me he had money problems," he added.

"Wow."

The ultimate exertion of Len's power and ego was during a partners' meeting several years before when he wasn't getting his way.

"I stood up, picked up a Sixteenth Century Ming vase and threw it against the wall. I walked out of the room. Well, they did what I wanted after that."

Our social calendar was a non-stop affair. The following night we were having dinner at Len's country club. My middle class childhood had taken place in Manhattan and I had spent no time whatsoever in clubs. Not until several years after Jake died did I feel compelled to join The Golf Club of Montwood. Nearly all of Chloe and Ben's friends' families belonged to the one club in our area and all of their friends spent the weekends swimming together and hanging out there. It was not a fancy, expensive or large club and the members were all men – eight hundred of them.

On a crusade that my kids were to have normal fatherless lives, and determined that nothing would get in the way, including a male only club, I knew we were going to become members of the Golf Club of Montwood. My children had suffered enough and the fact that they were fatherless could never stand in the path of their swimming or hanging out with their friends.

I placed a call to the Club, asked for an application, and then asked three good friends, all three members and all three men, of course, to sponsor me.

Finally, I asked Janet, my former boss for legal advice.

After submitting my application, I let the Club know that if rejected, I'd pursue my legal options. I reminded them that the law delineates the circumstances when private clubs cannot discriminate on certain protected classifications, such as gender and race. They would have to let me in.

It wasn't long before I was invited to a member cocktail party to meet the guys. They talked about golf and I smiled nicely. There were now eight hundred male members and one female – me.

Len's club was filled with a different type of woman. When we arrived that night, sitting at the table were two investment bankers and their wives. Both women were bleached blondes, dressed in Escada suits, one bright orange and the other a blast of yellow, both cut very low to reveal large cleavage bursting out of push up bras. Large gold necklaces, enormous diamond earrings, heaps of makeup and perfect noses were the finishing touches to the twin fifty-year old Barbie dolls.

"Do I have to sit down?" I whispered to Len.

"You are being judgmental and narrow-minded," he said.

"I have nothing to say to them. They are artifacts waiting to be admired. And your friends are just going to talk business. This is going to be so boring."

"You need to know your role!" he scowled at me.

"Never," I scowled back

. . .

My house sold rather quickly. We didn't get much more than we had paid for it but I wanted out and took the offer. Getting a new job in New York also turned out to be relatively painless. A headhunter called with an opportunity similar to my current position. I submitted my resume, drove down for an interview and heard I'd been hired three weeks later.

And as the goodbye parties at work became more frequent, I looked forward to moving on. Once the General

Counsel left and with Janet long gone, I had to report to a very difficult woman from the new management. The decision to move felt right.

Now began the Herculean task of sorting through fifteen years of collected memories in my basement in preparation for the move. On the next weekend Len and I went down there to tackle the job.

The basement was enormous. Every inch of the concrete floor and walls was covered with the treasures of my life. It was a dismal place, with no windows, but for me it was a comforting reminder of where I'd traveled before.

I had saved absolutely everything that my children had acquired or created, including every one of their school papers beginning in nursery school – drawings, homework, precious penmanship papers from when they had first learned to write their names, their clothes from the day they were born, their tiny shoes from when they first began to walk. There were stacks of boxes of Jake's medical books, even his black medical bag from his residency. More boxes were filled with letters from my parents when I was at sleep away camp and acceptance letters to college. Rejection letters were nowhere to be found.

Slowly sifting through all of this, I felt a tremendous sense of continuity, understanding where I had come from and where I was now. My basement was me and all I had lived through.

Len kept urging me to discard; he obviously had no emotional attachments to all of this stuff. I tried to ignore him.

The first thing to go had not been from the basement, however, but from my bedroom closet. Two shopping bags were filled with two and three inch heel shoes to give to a charity for underprivileged women applying for office jobs. Jake was six-feet-five inches and those shoes were appreciated;

Len was five-feet-five inches and refused to let me wear them.

"You realize that my company would pay you to have someone else do this with you?" he said to me as we sat there sorting.

"Why?"

"Because my time is valuable. They wouldn't want me spending it like this."

"But you sit for hours in front of the TV watching football!"

"That's my relaxation so I can work better. Listen, I need to leave for a tennis lesson at home," Len said

"How am I going to do this by myself?" I asked him as he walked out.

On the Saturday evening before our move to New York, Jason and Elizabeth threw a farewell party for Chloe, Ben and me. Friends from work filled their home. Even Len reluctantly agreed to appear.

After an hour of eating from a buffet of Elizabeth's homemade cooking, we gathered in their large living room.

"Please sit next to me. This move is so unnerving," I said while settling down on their couch.

Len walked slowly to the back of the couch and stood off by himself. He had barely spoken to anyone the entire evening. Although my friends had arranged an evening to celebrate my family and me, Len was making sure to leave his sullen imprint on the party.

Neil, one of the senior lawyers at work, loved to dabble in poetry and we loved to indulge him. He sat facing the group.

"Ben, I've written something for you to read tonight," Neil announced.

Ben looked startled. But he stood up and, with his always game smile displaying shiny silver braces on his teeth, took the paper from Neil. Ben began to read.

Although I loved my life in Montwood
It's a pretty sleepy place
And I did my share of drifting
Into mental cyberspace.

I have learned the Tao of baseball
Touched the soul of water polo.
I'm at one with inner football
And the zen of flying solo.
Now Len's my Svengali,
On the arbitrage of sport
He's got me buying baseball futures
And selling Knick's seats short.

I've imagined playing hockey
With my mother's friends from work
They may skate like tax accountants
But the rules they play will get-ya
They hit the puck with gavels
Tied to ten foot wooden poles
They send the fights to arbitration
And negotiate the goals.

I have skied the Alps with Tomba
I've roped steers in Yellowknife.
I've jumped buses with Knievel
And I've nearly lost my life.
I have weathered icy blizzards
On a Himalayan ledge.
You can find my face in Webster's
Under 'Living on the Edge'.
But when I tell my story
Of each new hair-raising feat,
My family says that my sister

Will always have my record beat.

I have imagined disappointments
Like the game at Fenway Park
Where I'm the winning run on third
And I steal on a lark.
I beat the pitcher cleanly
And the crowd begins to shout,
But the plate ump isn't looking
And he claims that I am out.
It's reconsidered two years later,
And they reinstate the run,
'Cause I'm the Commissioner of Baseball
It's what my mother would have done.

And now my life is changing,
And I can't predict the way.
But regardless of the circumstance,
I'll always come to play.
I'll take on any challenge
For my life's been truly blessed.
I have learned from all the masters,
And I've played with all the best.

Almost everyone clapped and cheered loudly for Neil's rhymes and for Ben's poise while reading. I sat there feeling sad, second-guessing the decision to leave our small town and these dear friends. Len remained silent and grim faced. He looked uncomfortable and out of place. Moving to New York didn't seem like such a good idea after all.

On a beautiful day several weeks later, Chloe, Ben and I walked through our home one last time. For Chloe, the typical teenaged girl, this was a moment for melodrama. She was beside herself. Ben, keeping his feelings to himself that day, just walked out of the house. For me, the house was so imbued with Jake's bad luck, I was happy to bid it goodbye as if living somewhere else could reverse the curse.

"When I grow up, I'm going to buy this house back for myself," Chloe vowed. "And I'm going to live here with my husband and children."

Then with one final closing of our front door, we closed a chapter of our lives that ended with Jake's death.

We drove that afternoon to New York City in a subdued mood, silently hoping that this was the right decision. By selling an affordable house in Connecticut and renting in unaffordable Manhattan, I was no longer feeling as financially secure.

SUMMER 1996

CHAPTER 21

July

The wedding reception for the son of one of Len's colleagues was held under a tent in the backyard of the family estate in Alpine. It was a warm summer night and the guests mingled on the lawn behind the enormous dark brick house. There were no familiar faces around so I uncharacteristically stuck next to Len. He told me that Judy never left his side at social gatherings.

Just the week before, as we were walking to Times Square to hail a cab uptown after seeing the Broadway show "Rent", a homeless man standing next to me began to scream obscenities. I stopped midsentence, grabbed Len's arm and melted into his side. He held onto me and smiled.

"Miss independence, huh?" he said.

The more the man yelled, the tighter I clung to Len. As I buried my face into his shoulder, Len gripped me around the waist. He loved it when I needed him and worked hard to cultivate my dependence on him. He often asked me when I would quit working altogether.

And now, because I knew no one at this wedding, I shadowed Len around the tent. Finally, the waiters ushered the wedding guests to their tables.

The man sitting next to me belted down a gin and tonic. He asked the waiter for another one.

"Good evening," he said.

"Hi. I'm Kate."

"Donald."

"Do you live in Alpine? It's really beautiful here."

"Alpine? Alpine is fine."

The waiter arrived with his gin and tonic and Donald took a long swig of it.

"The shops in nearby towns are full of rich kids demanding to have everything bought for them. Brats. Women in their forties have been dumped by their husbands who want a younger woman. They're miserable," he said.

At this point, nothing one of these uber wealthy men said to me would be shocking.

"I'm sorry you feel that way," I said.

"No apologies needed. I'm in the midst of a very ugly, very expensive divorce and just venting."

"Do you have any children?" I asked.

He paused to take another long drink.

"My daughter is forty and just separated from her husband. Her ex-husband is a wonderful guy but they never should have been together in the first place. She's a bitch. All women are bitches."

At that moment the eighteen-piece band began to play and I threw a look at Len. A desperate look of get me out of here. I also loved dancing and had managed over time to get Len to dance most times I asked. He had a funny little move where he bounced up and down and looked silly, so unlike the dignified image he so carefully constructed.

The band began to play "Twist and Shout" and Len, having had several glasses of wine during the cocktail hour, began to twist with me. He was doing the whole thing – up and down and round again. Laughing at his lack of inhibitions, his apparent joy in twisting, I hugged him when the music stopped.

"I don't recognize him," one of his friends said to me as we were making our way to retake our seats, "I have never seen Len like that." The continuous comments from his friends about the sea change in Len were encouraging to me. Len was finally enjoying himself.

We sat down at the table. Thankfully Donald wasn't there. But I couldn't help but overhear Len's conversation with his friend on his right.

"Len, you look so happy," his longtime friend said to him.

Len paused.

"It's so difficult still," Len replied somberly.

He couldn't possibly confess to his friend what he had revealed to me recently.

"I'm so happy with you, Kate. Does that mean it was good that Judy died?" he asked.

"Life does go on," I had answered.

My experience after Jake's death was that the world did not stop while one grieved. You had to choose one day to catch up with the world and yet I had grieved and grieved for years. Memories of the depths of those years were as good as reason as any to stay with Len, turning a blind eye to all he stood for.

"I loved Judy when we got married and she was perfect for me when we were twenty. But we grew apart and by the time she died, she was not the woman I would have chosen to be with. But you're not the woman I could have handled at twenty. I needed Judy at twenty. Now I need you.

"When we were in college, Judy wrote a four-page love letter to me. I rewrote the letter in my handwriting and sent it back to her. She called me, all excited thanking me profusely for the letter, not realizing what I'd done. She was the right woman for when I was twenty."

At dinner the next night in a secluded New Jersey steak house with Len's friend Thomas and his wife Linda, we discussed the recent revelation amongst Len's colleagues regarding the fiftyish chairman of a huge multi-billion company. He had resigned his position, left his wife and four kids and run off with a thirty-year old secretary.

"I can understand his desire to feel young again," Thomas said.

Linda, sitting next to him, appeared easily into her fifties.

"Len, how would you feel if Jennifer came home with a fifty-two- year old man?" I asked.

Len cringed.

"I get why the older men do it, but why would a woman in her thirties get into bed with a man in his fifties?" Thomas asked.

Was he kidding? Women in their thirties only got into bed with rich men in their fifties.

"Well, I've never dated a woman younger than forty. I'd be too embarrassed for Jennifer's sake," Len declared.

"If much older men did not lavish much younger women with jewelry, trips, clothes and a lifestyle, we could actually discern if the woman really cared about the guy. Maybe there really is love between the two of them. But I bet a man in his sixties is so grateful to have his arm candy that he'd never put it to the test," I said.

"Well, I have friends who are in the sixties and they won't date women any older than forty-five. My friend Bob is sixty-eight and dating a woman in her forties and said he's getting the sex he wants. He thinks women in their fifties lose interest in sex," Thomas said.

I looked at fiftyish year old Linda who remained silent.

"I'm in my forties and I wouldn't go near a sixty-eight year old man. And I know two women in their thirties who told me they never had much interest in sex. It's ridiculous to write off women by their age. Don't you think it's surprising and unpredictable who turns out to be a great lover and who does not?" I said wondering how Len would react.

"So Len's been that surprising and unpredictable great lover?" Thomas laughed.

Len put his arm around my shoulder and squeezed it tightly so everyone could see.

"I am under no pressure to say he definitely has been."

"Why wouldn't you want a trophy wife?" I asked Len as we drove to his house.

"Because I am the trophy."

I laughed. Trophy women were beautiful. But Len had meant it.

We were driving along dark unlit roads on a moonless night with thick woods on either side of the road. Len turned on the windshield wipers as light rain drizzled on the car. I missed the bright lights of the City.

Len was speeding along the curving country roads.

"You know Raskolnikov in *Crime and Punishment*?" he said.

I didn't answer. The last time I had thought about Raskolnikov was my freshman year of college in a Russian lit course.

"He is the one in a million man who tried to get away with murder. I am that one in a million man," Len said.

"You're kidding?"

"Not at all," he replied.

"Raskolnikov was an arrogant man who thought that the moral restraints of ordinary men didn't apply to him. He thought he was superman," I said warily.

"Yes, do you remember when he says 'I wanted to turn myself into a Napoleon, and for that purpose, I even committed murder'?" Len asked.

That night as the rain began to pound on the car and we drove the dark, back roads, I got the chills. The connection between Len's arrogance, his love of money and power, his disdain for my common friends and his identification with Raskolnikov was alarming. And then my skin crawled with the thought that I had chosen to give my heart, for only the second time in my life, to this particular man.

CHAPTER 22

August/September

Our move to Manhattan forced Chloe to evaluate her schooling options, and after rejecting out of hand the idea of carving her niche among high school seniors in New York City, she decided to spend the year abroad in Spain. She hadn't been exactly pleased with my decision to uproot the family, but also realized that months of fighting with me would have no impact at all on my decision.

As the summer passed by quickly both Chloe and I soon began to comprehend the reality of her upcoming departure. I watched helplessly as her eyes grew wider with fear as each day passed, as the letter from the family she would be staying with in Barcelona arrived, as she desperately tried to form sentences in Spanish with a woman who lived in our building who knew no English.

"I'm not going to be with my friends this year," she said one morning.

"But you'll make new friends. Why don't you find out the name of someone going on your program who might live nearby? You could make a friend before you go," I said.

Chloe called her program immediately and found that Dave, who was also going to Barcelona, lived an hour away. She phoned him and they agreed to meet that weekend. At least there was one potential friend in sight.

"I'm scared. I hate making changes! What if I have no friends?" she asked as she lay shivering in my bed.

She asked the same questions over and over, her mind distant in a far off unfamiliar world.

"You hated when first grade finished. You cried and told me you didn't want to go to second grade. And after second grade, you said you were too sad and didn't want to go to third grade. You've been uncomfortable with transitions ever since then. And I understand, but they always seem to work out great for you" I reminded her.

"I'm so worried about Chloe," I confided in Len one night.

He said nothing.

"I hope she makes friends. I hope she's not too home-sick," I continued.

"Jennifer wouldn't behave like Chloe is behaving."

"Why do you always have to compare them? Jennifer is an adult now and Chloe is a teenager," I asked.

"Because Jennifer never behaved like Chloe."

"How would you know? You were never home."

The surprise bon voyage party I arranged for Chloe was held in the back of a small unpretentious SoHo restaurant. Thirty of our friends and family sat in Café Rouge waiting for her to appear. Len volunteered to pick her up and deliver her to what was billed as a farewell dinner with my mother and a few relatives.

As Chloe walked into the restaurant, she squinted and tried to focus her near sighted eyes on the people in front of her. Her glasses were back at home as usual. She was practically in our laps before she covered her mouth and let out a scream of surprise finally making out the faces of her friends who had come in from Connecticut for the evening.

We sat Chloe down in the middle of our group and Lyla, one of my friends, began.

"Chloe, everyone here knows that you are a little bit scared about your new adventure, a bit intimidated to go off to a foreign country without knowing anyone, without knowing the language even well enough to get fed!"

Chloe was busy nodding her head.

"Well, because your mother is such a thoughtful, compassionate person, she has at great expense flown over from Spain your new family!"

"She what!" Chloe looked panicked that I might have done just that.

"And here Chloe is Maria, your new Spanish mother."

At that moment I emerged dressed in a rented toreador's costume: red short tight pants, a red jacket with gold and black braiding and epaulets and a black velvet hat. Chloe burst out laughing and buried her face in her hands.

"And now, Chloe, here is Eva, your new Spanish aunt."

With that, my sister-in-law pranced out dressed as a flamenco dancer with her body squeezed into an off the shoulder flimsy black blouse and a flaring red skirt. She flitted around Chloe.

"Finally Chloe, we all know how much you're going to miss your grandmother. So here is Alba, your new Spanish grandmother."

My mother, eighty years old, dressed in a furry bull's costume, charged out at Chloe. Only her face and thick glasses peered out of the dark grey headpiece topped with horns.

Everyone roared with laughter, and most had tears rolling down their faces. The smile that appeared on Chloe's face was the first in quite a while.

. . .

Nothing could measure the day that I had to drive Chloe to Logan for her flight to Barcelona. Tears kept falling like rain from her delirious eyes and her breathing was so deep and heavy that I was forced to pull the car over to calm her. Despite the fact that she was going with a group organized by one of the premier private schools in the country, it was a surreal experience preparing to put my teenaged daughter on a plane to Spain for a year, and one a mother can never quite prepare herself for. I wondered if she would actually board the plane.

Yet as we arrived at the meeting room and she began to greet the other sixty teenagers who would accompany her on the trip, I watched as the calm and color returned to my daughter's face. After a meeting of the parents and the kids held by the director, it was finally time for the kids to depart.

We stood, facing each other in front of the bus that would take her to the plane, and she smiled and hugged me goodbye. Optimism had filled her worn down body with a slight sense of relief, and for this I was glad. Yet, as she boarded the bus, I began to lose it. Watching the bus pull away seemed like an eternity, with me frozen in an instant of separation and loss, an emotion that had become too familiar.

As I walked the corridors of the airport slowly back to my car, I suddenly remembered that Len had promised to meet me at Logan for the drive home. He couldn't understand why the group flight wasn't leaving out of JFK for which I had no response. It was the last thing on my mind.

I turned a corner of the long hallway and a glance revealed his sympathetic and familiar face. He had flown to Boston that afternoon to drive me back in my car to New York. His support was welcomed with open arms, as I never could predict when I might expect it. It was these acts of kindness that were so random that I never knew what would elicit them, and certainly not how to reinforce them.

SPRING 1989

CHAPTER 23

March

The doctors treated Jake with more heavy-duty drugs to get him out of crisis. Now his blood counts were going to fall and this was the beginning of an unpredictable siege.

That day my in-laws and my mother left the hospital to take the kids back home. Watching them drive away in our station wagon was devastating. I saw their two little heads in the back seat as the car pulled away and wanted to scream. Jake and I were no longer in the picture in that wagon.

I went up to Jake's room. It was just Jake and me now.

Now the race was on. As Martin explained it, a lot depended on which came back first, the tumor or the counts. If the tumor did, they would treat it and that would knock his counts down all the more.

In the meantime Jake and I settled into our home away from home, a small hospital room. At first there was only a chair in his room to sleep on every night. I was told to speak to the nursing supervisor in charge of cots.

"This hospital has a policy," she said. "No cots for visitors unless the patient is DNR – Do Not Resuscitate."

"I know what DNR means. I also know this is a cancer hospital. My husband is dying of cancer and I'm staying with him. If you want me to sleep on a chair every night, I will."

"It's difficult for the staff to have family staying in the room, Mrs. Newman."

"The nurses have told me many times how helpful it is to have me there."

"I'm sorry. This is hospital policy."

"The nights are long and hellish for my husband. I'm going to be in that room with him."

She glared at me.

When it became clear I would be there for the duration, night after night, a cot finally appeared in Jake's room. It is not as if we ever had a night's sleep anyway, the nurses checked on Jake constantly.

But Jake and I talked. We were together. And somehow that enabled us to give each other the strength to go on.

It's amazing how you can live anywhere if you have to. For five weeks Jake and I lived in this world of bright lights, shiny linoleum floors and nonstop activity.

We were used to living in a house on a dead end street. When snow blanketed the many trees surrounding our house and closed off our road, we felt like we lived alone in our world. Now we were in Grand Central Station with a steady stream of nurses, doctors, interns, residents, lab technicians, janitors, and other patients coming in and out of our room. There was no sense of privacy, of home.

Jake and I established a routine that helped us survive the exhausting weight of another day spent in that institution. There was a rhythm to the day that enabled us to keep our sanity. It felt like we were living on death row, and in some sense we were, and I admired Jake's courage for enduring his sentence, having committed no offense. He, in my eyes the kindest of all people, didn't deserve to be on death row.

Each morning Jake took a warm bath. The two of us would sit in that tiny bathroom for the longest time, not caring how much time passed, and talk while he soaked. I looked at Jake's body in the tub and wondered how it had all gone so wrong. After the bath we would walk the halls, read, watch television, or talk to other patients and their families. Martin would dash in and out so quickly that you only could tell him the headline: Jake's counts were the same.

The interns and residents made their rounds, also running in and out of Jake's room as rapidly as possible. They were kind to him but he was very much a contemporary of theirs and he was dying of cancer. The reflection in the mirror made them run.

Every day it was the sorry task of Jake's nurse to walk in the room and tell us that his counts, taken that morning, were not back yet. No counts, no experimental treatment. No counts, no going home. No counts, no cure.

We began to wonder whether his counts would ever come back. We watched patients get discharged, we watched new ones get admitted, always curious to see who else was entering our world.

The weight of time ticking by was enormous. We wanted nothing more but time, time to be together, at home, with our children. Not time spent like this. And so we would daydream and nap and watch some more daytime television, anything that was on, and wait for results.

The evenings were quieter. You knew you weren't going home for another night; there was a sense of lock-up time for the night on death row. Everyone had a television on, for hours. Whatever people may say or write about television, it is essential to survival in a hospital.

Around eleven o'clock each evening I would climb into my cot. We went to sleep every night with the hope that tomorrow would be different, and every morning we woke up to the same day.

Martin was not promising an early end to our siege. Our house and everything in it, everything we had acquired over the years, was left behind.

We were back in the state when we were first married. No money, no children. Chloe and Ben were in Connecticut with my mother and my in-laws. It was just Jake and me in this room.

It was unimaginable that we had worked so hard to purchase a couch in our newlywed years. We had been in such a hurry all the time. There had been so many things to worry about back then - careers, money, houses, furniture, vacations. The days had flown by while we did all the things young couples do. That is, young couples who know they'll live forever. Now the days were endless, even as they drew to an end, and we were no longer doing what a still young couple should be doing. We were facing the end of life and all those things we had worried about, no longer mattered. Now it was just us, a bed and cot, a bathroom, a television, and the angel of death hovering over us waiting for the grab.

Hardest of all, of course, was not having Chloe and Ben with us. We saw them only on weekends when my in-laws and my mother drove them up after school on Fridays. We couldn't wait to see them running out of the elevator, down the hall and into Jake's room. We couldn't hold them tight enough or stare at their faces long enough.

Chloe and Ben felt very at home in the hospital. Maybe because Mommy and Daddy were living there, they never seemed to focus on just how awful a place it was. If Jake wasn't in his bed, they'd press the buttons that made his bed move up and down and then put on rubber gloves and face masks and pretend they were doctors. When they got restless, they rode the elevators, played games they had brought in the waiting room and ate snacks.

Jake loved seeing the kids but he could only take their exuberance for so long when he wasn't feeling well. It hurt us to know that their lives were going on without us.

But nighttime was a problem at home for the kids. No more Daddy in Chloe's room and Mommy reading to Ben while he fell asleep. If they were upset, we would often get a call around eleven.

"Mommy, when are you coming home? I need you. I can't go to sleep without you," Ben sobbed.

"We'll be home as soon as we can. We love you very much."

"I need you Mommy."

"But Daddy needs me too right now."

"I need you more."

"Oh, Ben, I miss you so much. If I tell you a story, will you try to go to sleep?"

Ben always agreed.

Chloe would take Ben's hand and say, "Don't worry, Mommy and Daddy will come home one day and we'll be a family again." She would rub his hand and softly sing, "Don't worry Ben" and finally he would fall asleep.

Then in the middle of the night, Ben yelling for her would awaken my mother.

"Please sit in here until I fall back asleep. I'm scared."

My seventy-three year old mother would wrap herself in

a blanket and sit on a chair until he was asleep. She got little rest those days. Jake's cancer was exacting an enormous toll on all of us.

The rest of February passed in a numbing haze. Jake's best hand had already been played. We groped for a reason to slog through each day, and that reason was to make it to Martin's experimental drug.

Then one day both of the nurses who cared for Jake walked into the room beaming.

"They're back. Your counts are back!"

Jake had a smile on his face for the first time in weeks.

"We're out of here, Jake!" I was joyous.

CHAPTER 24

Early April

From the protocol Martin gave us, we learned that the purpose of giving Jake this experimental drug, the potentially toxin ricin, was to determine the maximum dose a patient could tolerate. Jake would be a guinea pig. Everyone made that very clear. Only one human being had ever received any benefit from the drug Jake was about to receive. What did we focus on? We focused on that one man. We narrowed our world down to one man, a one in a billion chance.

The tests revealed that cancer was rampant in Jake's entire body. We were both wrung out at this point, at the end of our wits. He looked awful – thin, pale, bald, sitting hunched over in the wheelchair. He could no longer walk even a few yards without feeling dizzy or having pain. This thirty-eight-year-old had two children, a wife and a career he loved. It was all slipping away. Where the hell had he gotten this cancer? Was it the water? The food? Something in the air? I looked at Jake slumped in his wheelchair and clenched my fists for a long, long time. Then I held the rage in for another day.

The news from Martin was good, Jake would qualify for ricin. On our way once again.

The week Jake received the experimental drug was a welcome and wonderful hiatus in a miserable string of months. We both were convinced that this would do the trick. Each day was the same. The drug flowed in, and I held my breath knowing how toxic ricin could be. As the week progressed Jake managed walking a few steps. For the first time in months, flashes of his personality, the personality that had been buried under all the apprehension and sickness, appeared.

We left the hospital at week's end ready to get the next dose the following month. All Jake had to do was not recur in the three weeks at home.

Once home, we tried to act as if our lives were about something other than cancer. But there was no getting away from it. I was walking along the front walk when Ben yelled to me "Don't step on the cracks, Mom!"

As I turned around, he yelled, "Watch it!" I was about to step on one of the cracks.

Ben began to sing-song "Step on a crack, you'll break your mother's back." But his version was "Step on a crack, you'll get cancer."

My three-year-old son knew one thing that was worse than breaking your mother's back.

A few days later Jake was so constipated that he asked me to call the doctor. Martin recommended various laxatives, none of which worked.

"I need you to disimpact me. I can't take this," he begged.

"Tell me what to do."

"Put on rubber gloves. I'll lie down on my side and you'll put your finger in my rectum and remove as much stool as you can," he explained.

Slowly I removed the very hard stool from him. It took a long time and was not a pleasant experience for either of us. Afterwards, he lay down on our bed, exhausted, and I lay down next to him and thought about, of all things, our wedding day. Jake had worn a black tuxedo and looked stunning; I held his hand at the altar so tight it must have hurt.

"How much more?" I whispered to the Rabbi, halfway through.

"Ten minutes."

"Can you cut it in half? I'm too nervous."

The ceremony over, I relaxed and thought how lucky I was. All of my girlfriends were there, from nursery school through college, none of them married, all commenting on how lucky I was to have Jake. I was twenty-two, Jake was twenty-six. We had a lifetime of good things ahead of us.

Now I lay next to an exhausted husband whose body was riddled with cancer and I thought of our vows.

"For better or for worse, in sickness and in health," I had promised him.

WINTER
1996/1997

CHAPTER 25

December

We were sitting at a table of ten at yet another gala at The Waldorf. Or was it The Plaza? No, it was The Pierre since I recognized the headwaiter. The parties and dinners were becoming indistinguishable from one another. Crowded rooms, women in beautiful gowns and meaningless conversation. Dinner after dinner, party after party.

I now had a closet full of dresses from Bergdorf's and my party jewelry, thanks to Len, consisting of a gold bracelet with sapphires, two pairs of gold earrings – one with pearls and one with diamonds – and of course my birthday necklace. Before we left for the party that night Len showed me a large gold necklace with diamonds he had bought for Jennifer for her birthday.

"It's beautiful."

"You've had your share of jewelry this year," he said.

Len would always point out to me who the major players were at any event, how much they were worth, what interaction, if any, he had with them. For me, the most astounding aspect of every one of these events was how many very rich, very successful people there were in Manhattan.

Four hundred people packed the Grand Ballroom of The Pierre for this party. The party was over the top with two bands, glass centerpieces filled with gardenias, orchids and tulips that reached for the ceiling and endless courses of food covering the tables. One of Len's investment banker friends, a sixty-year old divorcee was dancing with two beautiful twenty-something women. He was at least thirty pounds overweight and had lost his hair, but these two blondes were grinding their bodies against his.

Several of Len's partners were sitting at our table. I didn't know where Len might be at the moment and his partners had consumed way too much champagne as they celebrated a deal they had just finalized.

"Kate, how are things with Len? You've been together…how long now?" George asked.

"Two years. We've made it two years."

"Then you are quite the hero," George said as he downed another glass of champagne. The other partners burst out laughing.

"Funny you say that. I was quite apprehensive about dating him, out of fear that…you know, as an investment banker he would be somewhat of a bastard," I replied.

"Well you got the biggest bastard of all!" George laughingly volunteered to the table.

Feeling adrift, wondering where I belonged in this crowd, I realized that I wasn't sure where Len was. Edging my way through the hordes, I found him standing at the edge of the very crowded dance floor.

Len was standing with his arms folded, staring at a woman. She looked very thin, very bleached blonde, and covered in makeup and jewelry. Most of the women had on long black dresses and she was no different.

I walked over to Len and nudged his arm.

"What are you doing?"

"Isn't she pretty?" he responded.

"Why are you staring?"

"I think she's pretty."

He continued to stand with his arms folded staring at the woman. Could I have done the same? Mock him, find some man to gawk at? No, it wasn't me.

"When I'm negotiating a deal, I always look for the weaknesses of my opponents and then play on them continuously," he said.

"Well, you're playing on mine. Perfectly. Why? Am I just another one of those acquisitions that you end up gutting?"

The next day Zoë and I were walking the streets of the West Village on one of her frequent visits to New York.

"Maybe you should consult that psychic about Len," Zoë said as she pointed to a sign outside a brownstone.

'Readings by Maria. Third Floor.'

"I would but she'd have to promise not to tell me anything bad was going to happen," I said.

"You could tell her that. But they usually tend to give the good news and the bad news."

"I never told you what the psychic said about Jake?"

"I need to sit down to hear this," Zoë said as we entered a small tea shop and ordered.

"Jake and I went to a party about a year before he got sick. One of my friends, a television news producer, held the party and she went all out. The food, the drinks...she had a DJ and even had a palm reader," I said.

Zoë was sipping her tea and paying close attention. She'd obviously never heard this before.

"We were there about two hours, drank two glasses of wine, Jake was busy talking to some friends...so I walked over to the palm reader. She asked me to hold out my left hand, paused and spoke slowly as she appeared to be reading the lines on my hand. I wasn't really into palm reading or psychics at the time, it was just something to do at a party," I explained.

"I think I did it once. They tell you about your love line, your life line," Zoë said.

"Right. But after a few minutes of saying stuff like that, she said 'Your husband will get ill in a year'. I froze. Did she know about Jake's first cancer? I couldn't believe those words had come out of her mouth."

"Did you tell Jake?" Zoë asked.

"No, of course not. He was so happy and content at the time. Chloe and Ben were precious. Things were so good. And then I completely forgot about what she said until Jake became ill. It was not like it hung over me, or I was waiting for something to happen. But when Jake got sick and I remembered her words, I had this eerie feeling. It's hard to ignore when something like that happens."

"I think we better not pay a visit to Readings by Maria. I dread to think what she might say about Len," Zoë said as we walked out into the street.

■ ■ ■

Len and I were getting ready to go to a birthday party for one of his close friends the next night when I put on a white silk sleeveless blouse and an off white skirt with sandals.

"If you wear that, you're not going!" Len looked at me with disgust.

"What's wrong now?"

"You need a whole new wardrobe. That's what's wrong. I'll buy it for you. The blouse is too see-through. I hate it when women wear blouses like that."

"Really, then why're you always gawking at them?"

"I don't gawk. And your skirt is way too short. You're a woman in her forties trying to look like a twenty year old."

"My friends tell me I have nice legs and I'm not hiding them till I have to," I said.

"You should look dignified."

"You mean matronly. You gawk at other women but you don't want me to be looked at."

I had seen pictures of Judy. She was at least twenty-five pounds overweight and her skirts covered her knees and her blouses were buttoned at the collar.

"I feel like you're chipping away at me, piece by piece. You're constantly criticizing me," I said.

Len didn't respond. I could see in his eyes he was calculating the risks of what he was about to say.

"That's just what Judy said to me, " he finally said.

"What?"

"Judy said the same thing to me."

A victory at last. Was there an official scorekeeper taking notes?

"I'm going to the party and I'm wearing this outfit," I said.

"Why do you have to show other men what is mine?"

"My friends tell me that their husbands love when they wear sexy clothes and they can show them off. Their husbands make them feel attractive. They don't criticize each and every part of them."

"You're a reasonably attractive woman. The only motive any man would have to be interested in you is because of your personality."

I sat down on the bed.

"I don't know if I can endure this kind of loving. You're wearing me down."

He sat on the bed next to me.

"But we are so compatible. You're the smartest person I've ever met," he responded.

"I'm not the smartest person you've ever met. I just know what you're up to."

"The only time I ever relax and enjoy my life is when I'm with you," he tried again. "I've never let anyone into my life the way I've let you in. I've never been so intimate with anyone. I hope I've made you feel half as good as you make me feel."

"But what about Raskolnikov? How do I trust that man?"

It had taken me a few years after Jake's death, to realize that I wanted to recreate the love affair that I had with Jake and to marry again. And now after two years of dating, Len and I were besieged by people asking when we were going to marry.

"I want a strong independent woman in my life, not a 'yes' woman again," Len said one evening after a dinner with friends of his.

"I thought you told me you needed to be in control at least eighty percent of the time."

"When did I say that?"

"Several months after we met. I didn't think there was a man alive who thought that was a viable option with a woman these days, not with the women I know," I said.

"I think I should be able to call the shots on how you dress, where we travel, who we spend time with, and if your comments at dinners with my friends are appropriate."

"My old fashioned mother thinks I should just humor you. And then do what I want. Does that work?" I asked.

"Don't humor me."

Len's scolding eyes frightened me.

"It used to be very comforting to surrender some of my control to you. But the price is getting very high. Your endless criticism of me makes me wonder if I can do anything right anymore. And you say that you want a strong woman in your life now but I think a strong woman just reminds you of your mother," I said.

He looked away for a moment.

"I'm so fucked up. My family was so screwed up, I'm so sorry."

We drove to Connecticut the following weekend to have dinner at Rachel's house. On the way home, I asked Len if he could ever love me the way Rachel's husband loved her.

"No. I could never love like that."

"But that's what I want. Your ambivalence reminds me of my mother."

"But Edward looks like a deer stuck in the headlights," Len insisted.

"When I think of a deer stuck in the headlights of a car, I see fear, imminent danger. Is that what love means to you?"

"People love in different ways. I can't love a woman that much," Len admitted.

"But that's what I need."

"You feel things more intensely than I do. That is one of your most alluring qualities. But I'm not you," Len said.

"Well, I don't want to put you in a place you don't want to be."

"You often see the world in black and white. And sorry to mix metaphors, but sometimes I have to watch and wait for the weather to change."

Len the weatherman. It was a gloomy night as we drove

along I-95 with few cars on the road.

This conversation was only adding to the bleak view outside.

"And when my friends ask when we're getting married I tell them I'm waiting for my feminist girlfriend to ask me," he chuckled.

"Is that what you're waiting for?"

"No, this will be done my way when I'm good and ready. I'm not going to tell you when that will be."

"Don't you think I should have some say in this matter?" I asked.

"No."

Len, the weatherman, did change his forecast when he invited Chloe, Ben and I to St. Bart's again for two weeks for Christmas vacation.

"I want us to stay together in the same room this time," he said as he made the reservations. "I want your kids to see that I have good intentions."

"Are you joking? You know what staying in the same room means to my kids? It means we're 'doing it' I can hear them now, 'Mom, that's so gross'."

"But it does mean that we're out in the open to your friends. And I appreciate that. What about your kids?" I added.

"Jennifer is going to Hawaii with Bernard, Peter is going skiing in Switzerland with friends, and Dale is studying. I'll miss them but they're adults now."

Len bought a ticket for Chloe to fly from Barcelona to St. Bart's and she, and Ben were staying in another room. Len then arranged for their room to be as far as possible from ours. We had possibly become a family in some sense, although his children were absent from the picture. And now we appeared to be going along for this version of a family ride.

CHAPTER 26

February

I have to go on a business trip to Frankfurt over Valentine's Day. Will you go with me?" Len asked one night as we lay in bed.

"I've never been to Frankfurt. It's not the city you think of first for Valentine's Day but of course I'll come."

"Well, the plane stops in Paris on the way to Frankfurt. So you'll get at least an hour layover there. Should be enough time for a café au lait and a croissant."

In preparation for the trip, I bought *Fodor's Germany* and read up on Frankfurt.

"I've booked a room for us at the Steingenberger Frankfurter Hof, the best hotel in the city, of course," Len said.

"Of course."

On the day of our departure, Len instructed me to meet him at the Delta International Terminal at JFK at five. The cab dropped me off at the domestic terminal and by the time I made it over to the correct terminal, we nearly missed the flight. It was a good omen for the trip though that we boarded the plane without a single remonstration from Len. But mechanical problems with the landing gear on the 747 delayed our takeoff for four hours.

Landing in the City of Lights the next morning, the plane for Frankfurt had long departed.

"Let's have lunch in Paris," Len said.

"I haven't been to Paris since high school. I'd love to. "

We hopped into a cab and Len, always the dealmaker, tendered the terms.

"Here's the deal. If you let me have my way eighty percent of the time over the weekend, we can stay in Paris until Monday when my meeting begins in Frankfurt."

"Will a kiss seal the deal?"

"I'd like that," Len said as he put his arms around me and began to kiss me passionately.

Len told the driver to take us to the Hotel Ritz, and I settled back to gaze out the windows at Paris, at last. I had yearned for years to return for a romantic weekend, and it seemed the moment had arrived.

As we checked in, it became apparent that Len already had a reservation for the weekend.

"What's going on? I thought the plane delay was the reason we're in Paris."

"This was my plan all along. Our delayed plane just helped me along," he said.

We went upstairs to our elegant and enormous Versailles-like room.

"This is like a dream," I said while gazing at the Louis XVI décor, the fireplace, the fifteen-foot high ceilings, the lavish beddings and the view of the Place Vendome.

We walked the streets in the 7th and 8th arrondissements for hours that day gorging on sinful pistachio, almond and chocolate macarons, and eclairs stuffed with a creamy coffee custard and a luscious chocolate icing. To warm up after hours in the freezing cold, we drank the richest hot chocolate that Paris had to offer. I spent my first night in Paris afraid to close my eyes, fearing to wake up in New York the next morning with the trip having only been a sweet dream. Len knew that another beau had offered me a weekend in Paris, and I had refused, hoping to go with Mr. Right.

In the morning we woke early since Len was on a mission for bargains on Art Deco antiques at the Parisian flea market at Clignancourt. The air felt freezing that morning and we wandered for hours up and down the stalls until my feet and hands went numb. Len was calling the shots for the weekend and he relented at last to take a break for some baguettes and café americains in a small café. But time in his mind did not stand still and we quickly moved on in search once more. Len finally purchased a green enamel liquor box for $3000 and seemed very pleased with his find.

After defrosting in a hot bath perfumed with lavender salts at our hotel, we headed to Le Caprice, a small French restaurant in Montmartre that was hosting a Valentine's Day dinner. They garishly decorated the tables, the walls, even the menus, and provided female patrons with cupid picture frames and tiny teddy bears carrying hearts. We were eating in a Hallmark card store.

When the waiter translated the menu, Len and I laughed as we heard the choices: wild boar, venison, or rabbit.

"Guess I should have called ahead," Len joked.

"Any fish or pasta?" I asked the waiter.

"Non."

The waiter was all attitude, acting as if I had mistaken the place for McDonald's.

Len managed a few words with the maitre d', and the kitchen reluctantly agreed to rummage around and create something for me.

"They're going to make something that wasn't shot today," he assured me.

The tables in the restaurant fit very close together. Valentine's Day might be a shared experience that night.

"The French really know how to celebrate Valentine's Day," I said quietly.

Suddenly Len reached into his pocket, took out a huge diamond ring, placed it on the table in front of me and asked me to marry him.

He appeared nervous as hell. I glanced at him and then at the ring. The diamond looked enormous, four or five carats, in a very beautiful Tiffany setting. The ring felt a little tight as I tried to place it on my finger. Not terribly graceful, but I managed to get it on. Len didn't slip it on my finger and he didn't get down on his knees, although it would be hard to imagine him on his knees for anybody. I don't even remember if I ever answered his question.

The awkwardness of the proposal made the ritual feel so contrived. And that was it. The moment I had waited years for passed and it felt no more touching, no more thrilling than if we had spent the evening watching reruns of "Friends" on TV. The couple at the next table witnessed the whole thing and smiled at us. Guess it looked authentic to them.

We returned to the hotel and I called Chloe in Barcelona.

"Guess what? Remember Len and I planned to go to Frankfurt? Well, we ended up in Paris, and tonight at dinner he asked me to marry him."

"What about Daddy? What happens to him?" she said.

"Daddy? This has nothing to do with Daddy," I replied concerned about what Chloe might be thinking.

Chloe's unexpected reaction made the evening even more anti-climatic and sad. She harbored thoughts about her Daddy that she hadn't shared.

I called Ben. My mother was staying with him for the weekend.

"Ben, Len asked me to marry him!"

"That's great Mom. Hey, guess what?" he yelled to my mother.

"Len asked Mom to marry him!"

My mother was on the phone in no time.

"I'm so happy for you. So happy. Can I tell everyone?" she asked.

"Of course you can."

We could barely make love that night, an awkward tension evident in our bodies felt like a sign that getting engaged may have been wrong. My second night in Paris I went to sleep dazzled by the rock on my finger but scared that our anti-climatic engagement might be more cubic zirconia than Tiffany diamond.

The next morning, after a delicious breakfast of Eggs Benedict at the Ritz, we set out for the Biennial Antiques Fair at the Grand Palais. The furniture would be beautiful and very expensive. Len was itching to buy something.

Time stood still that morning in Paris as he raced around the Fair, trying to figure out what to buy. We were surrounded by gorgeous objects, plotting how to spend more money than some people earn in a year. Len had already indulged me in a minor take of this extravagance in New York when he picked out an antique Regency style dresser for his bedroom that cost $12,000. This must be a Raskolnikov moment for Len.

After two hours of careful searching, he decided on an elegant mid-Nineteenth Century hand carved Italian rococo table for $20,000. The decision was based on a simple calculation of what Len could shell out, and that most of the other pieces were way beyond his means. Len was simply out of his league when desks were $500,000 and armoires a million.

We returned to New York and the following weekend my friend Ann threw a small engagement dinner for us. Everyone gathered in the private room of La Cote Basque and Thomas stood to make the first toast.

"Len, you've finally met your match!"

My brother held up a glass.

"Len, you must be nuts!" my brother cheered.

I watched Ben and he appeared thrilled with the evening. Len's kids, even Jennifer, congratulated us with hugs. We laughed and drank and for the first time, it felt like we were celebrating the moment. Our engagement had become so much more for others than what Len and I experienced that night in Paris.

"Sarah, Len and I are engaged." I relayed the news on the phone.

"Congratulations! Are you good with this?"

"What do you think?"

"Did Jake ever give you 'permission' as it is called?"

"No, he was so sad at the time. I think he just assumed I'd move on. We never discussed it. It would have been too painful," I said.

"Sorry for the therapists hat being on, but have you thought that's why you are ambivalent about all this engagement stuff?"

"I've had worse thoughts than that."

"Uh oh. Tell me," Sarah demanded.

"What if Len is my way of sabotaging any possibility of

moving on past Jake? What if he's just so wrong for me and then Jake stays in my life?"

"Oh baby. So Jake still occupies your heart? That's a real problem if that's true."

■ ■ ■

Once a year several of the managing partners of Duke Heller, all close business associates of Len's, held an intimate dinner. This year they decided on Le Bernardin, often cited as the best restaurant in the City. Terribly expensive, elegant with an incomparable menu, it made perfect sense that the dinner should be held there.

"This is my fiancé, Kate," Len said to one partner as we walked in.

His words stunned me for some reason. The first time hearing them since our engagement.

Len walked away to chat with another couple.

"I don't know how to say this other than you've done a great job on Len. He seems so relaxed and happy," the partner said.

Who was this generous-hearted man?

"That's so kind of you to say."

"No. You've made life easier for all of us."

I started to laugh since it was all about him.

"My pleasure."

At dinner the men drank to their successful year while the women leaned back into their chairs. My two lives. As if I needed a passport to cross over the deep divide into the world of these women. Len was watching me, possibly to see how I'd behave. Straddling the chasm, I reached for my glass of wine. I'd need all the help I could get.

We sat in our cocoon of astonishing food, glistening jewelry, designer clothing, pleasantries, and an overwhelming air of confidence that filled the room. Why would one ever want to leave this bubble?

As the evening wore on however the endless pleasantries grew tiresome. The talk about money and deals by the men went on and on. The women didn't discuss their work, if they did work, and I certainly didn't get asked about mine. No talk about the latest play or movie, or even our children.

Like high school girls readying for the prom, we rambled on about where we had bought our dresses, had our hair and makeup done, and where to buy the best shoes. My friends and I could indulge in that girl talk for quite some time, but they would not have recognized me after two hours of it.

As we ordered dessert, I faded. I knew the bubble had burst.

■ ■ ■

"We should live together and see how it works," Len said after we made love the following Saturday night.

"You mean get an apartment together, not live in my apartment?"

"Yes, I'll have Susan Carpenter, my real estate agent, start looking. If I see something I really like, I can buy it and keep the house in New Jersey."

My apartment, a small, nine hundred square foot, two bedroom apartment, was not a place Len would be settling for. The next week we began looking at apartments that cost millions on the Upper East Side. It was an out of body experience as we walked around these apartments with Susan. None of them appeared quite right for Len.

Each time we entered another apartment we walked around silently witnessing a stranger's bedroom, closets, bathrooms. Some of the apartments looked pristine, while some owners must have rushed out in anticipation of our visit leaving a pile of dirty dishes in the sink. Behind the facade of elegant buildings at the right address were apartments with an enormous price tag and an attempt to make a home in a city of millions of people. Len and I just couldn't see any of them as our home, not yet.

When Susan finally showed us a very large, four bedroom, Len actually confessed to me he didn't have the money to pay that much. It was just what we had been looking for with an understated elegance on 79th Street close to Fifth Avenue.

"I'm growing impatient with this. We need a place and this is going to take a long time," he said to Susan.

"Why don't you rent in the meantime and we can keep looking for something to buy?" Susan replied.

So we decided to rent for the time being a twenty four hundred square foot, three bedroom on the twenty-second floor of a thirty-story building. An ordinary apartment with white walls, white tile bathrooms and a small kitchen, offered a view off the terrace that was breathtaking. The rent listed at $10,500 a month.

"You should pay forty percent of the rent," Len said.

"Let's think about what tiny percent of your income I earn and compare your assets and mine," I responded.

"I didn't ask for fifty percent. We need to be equally responsible for this. This is only till we're married."

"Fine. If that's what you want. That's fine," I said.

"The lease must be in your name. There are tax implications for me in New York if it's in my name. I'll give you my share every month. And they're going to want a large security deposit since the lease will be in your name," he said.

Our first night in the apartment we lied in bed and looked out at the gorgeous view and the lights of the City.

"I can't believe we're living here. It's beautiful," I said.

Len took me in his arms.

"And I get to walk the streets of the City with this ring on my finger. People just stare at it, it's so big," I added.

"Are you still unhappy that I never got on my knees to ask you to marry me?" Len asked.

"Maybe."

And with that, Len got out of bed, walked over to my side and got down on his knees.

"Will you marry me?" he asked.

"Yes."

We made love that night slowly and passionately. It was unlike anything that I had experienced with Len. Our bodies could not get enough of each other, could not pleasure each other enough. When we were done, we lie there knowing that no matter what else happened, we had shared a moment of bliss together that seemed to make our troubled ride worthwhile.

SPRING 1989

CHAPTER 27

Late April

It was time to see if Jake would qualify for the next dose of the drug. When we arrived on our usual floor everything was the same – so familiar, our second home. Our friends had beach houses. We had the cancer hospital. There was even a cot set up in the room.

Jake's calcium was very high, an indication that the tumor raged in his body.

"At this point some families would elect to go home and let the patient die," Martin told me in the waiting room.

"We are not some families. Treat Jake with whatever you have."

"You might be deluding yourselves," Martin said.

"I don't care. Right or wrong, we want a miracle. We will fight as long as there is life left in Jake's body."

Now I knew on some level that Jake would die, although I refused to truly acknowledge the reality. At the bookstore near the hospital, I bought Elizabeth Kubler-Ross's book *On*

Death and Dying and hid the book from Jake until the weekend when the kids came to visit. After they went to sleep I read until the early hours of the morning.

I learned that Jake was disengaging from his friends, his children and that it's easier for someone who is dying to say goodbye if they slowly withdraw from their former life. All Jake seemed to want now was me - he was removed from everything else in his life. He disengaged from all that had given him so much pleasure, so that he could die.

I wept for hours that night. When Chloe and Ben woke in the morning, I went into the shower and cried some more. We were now veterans of the cancer wars, which we had lost, hadn't we? What was Jake thinking? Was he agonizing over everything he would miss as Chloe and Ben grew up? Was he worrying that we might lose our house if we ran out of money? Was he wondering if I would lose my mind when he died? I was.

The next evening it was time for the kids to leave the hospital.

"I don't want you to go there tonight," Jake said.

I stood next to his bed and just looked at him for a long time.

"Why?"

"I need you here. I don't want to be alone."

Only a very few times during this whole nightmare had I been impatient with Jake. He had been so victimized and what was being taken away from him justified whatever he did.

"I need this time to be with the kids so I can make it through another week," I said.

"What about me?"

"All right. I won't go." And I stomped out of the room.

Ben started crying when I told him I wouldn't be spending the night at the hotel. My mother took them in a taxi. I needed to be with them so badly, and once again what I or the kids or Jake wanted or needed just didn't matter any more.

I went upstairs to Jake's room.

"If I were the one who was sick you would have just kept on working and never have been able to do anything for me." I regretted the words the minute I said them, but they were out.

"I would have done whatever I could," Jake replied.

We were silent for a few minutes, and in the silence I realized I wasn't angry at Jake but at cancer.

"You can go if you want," he said. "If you need to be with them, go."

"No, it's too late." I thought of Ben crying.

"I just don't feel like you're with me here. I need you."

"I'm here."

That night I went to sleep furious at being torn between my children and my dying husband and woke up repeatedly despairing.

The next day we celebrated what we knew would be Jake's last birthday. Was there a right way to celebrate a dying man's birthday? The nurses brought in a cake, Martin made an entrance, and we all sang the song. We didn't give him a present since he wanted nothing and needed nothing, at least nothing that we could buy.

Jake's condition continued to deteriorate. He was retaining fluid in his lungs, in his belly, and in his legs. In the hallway Martin drew me aside.

"I need to talk with you. Why don't we sit down in the waiting room?"

"I want more treatments for Jake, no matter what."

"Just come in the waiting room."

I arched my back and marched down the hall. I would fight for Jake even if everyone else had surrendered.

Martin closed the door.

"Jake is very ill now, Kate. He has pneumonia, and there's fluid near his heart. If something happens, I need to know if you want him resuscitated."

I glared at Martin.

"I have discussed this with Jake's brother and we both feel that he should not be resuscitated," Martin said. "There's no need to prolong his life."

My mind reeled. I thought of my friends back home. What were they mulling over in their minds this Sunday afternoon: should they have dinner in or out tonight, should they put the blue wallpaper in the kitchen? Why was I deciding whether or not to put a DNR request on Jake?

"I will have to see if and when the situation arises. I simply can't tell you now."

"Then we should talk to Jake."

"NO!"

"Jake should have the right to make a decision as important as this one."

We walked down the hall to Jake's room.

Jake looked horrified when Martin explained why he was there. For so long we had been in the same boat, sailing on the good ship Denial.

"I'll have to let you know, Martin, I can't give you an answer now."

Martin left. Jake turned his head to me.

"I want you to decide if the situation arises. Tell him that."

"I already did."

Later that night Jake appeared to have reached a new low point. It was dark in the room; he slumped low in the bed and could no longer move without help. We had always maintained an unspoken pact – there would be no talk of an end, of failure.

As I sat on his bed and brushed a few tears from his eyes, I held back my tears for Jake's sake until I couldn't control myself anymore. I sat there and cried my eyes out.

"Please get well. Please, baby, please."

"I can't believe I won't see Ben get on the kindergarten bus for the first time. I won't see him play Little League. I won't see Chloe get married. I have such awful thoughts. I think about the kids at the funeral. About them having to make it without a father."

"What about me? Won't you miss anything about me?"

Jake's eyes embraced me.

"I won't grow old with you," he said.

We had felt like children wandering through the halls of life together. But it was not meant to be. Jake's journey would end at thirty-nine. He would not get his wish to grow old with me, and I would have to grow old alone.

When I woke up the next morning my entire body was covered with hives. The stress was breaking me down. And then Jake said the words I never wanted to hear.

"I want to go home. I don't want any more treatments."

He was right. But I was stunned. It had finally happened. The two world-class cancer fighters were going to give up. Cancer had won.

All of the nurses and Martin came to say goodbye. They were really saying goodbye this time. We would not be coming back this time; there would be no more admissions, no more long sieges in the hospital, no more battles over cots. We were done, and done for. Martin gave me a big hug and we went on our way, an ambulance ride to the hospital back in Connecticut.

Had we known the true nature of Jake's tumor from the beginning, would we have made other decisions, explored other options? Maybe just have gone to Hawaii and enjoyed his last months on earth in peace. But we were so vulnerable, so gullible, so desperate.

They had made promises to us of a cure based on the premise that chemotherapy was a science, not an art. Yet one oncologist now told me that chemotherapy was a witch's brew and sometimes the doctors get lucky and sometimes they don't.

Our arrival in the hospital where Jake had worked was a relief. People flowed into the room, all the familiar faces. But Jake had a new edge, something he had been unwilling to show Martin. He begged Henry to get the fluid out of his swollen belly to relieve the discomfort.

"Get me out of this. I've had it."

A cot was set up in the room after a simple request. Jake was on high doses of morphine, but nothing seemed to take the edge off. He woke me every hour, very alert and nervous, obviously very aware that death was imminent. As for me, I felt physically and emotionally finished. There was nothing left.

Whenever Jake woke me that night I pleaded for a few more minutes rest. Finally, I took my pillow and climbed into bed with him. There was very little room for me. Jake's body was swollen, intravenous lines trailed across the bed, an oxygen tube rested on his chest. And yet for a brief time, it was wonderful to be laying in Jake's arms again. I snuggled against him, against his right side, where I had always fit next to his body, closed my eyes and listened to his heart beating. But there would come a time soon when, if I put my head on his chest, there would be silence.

Jake, who seemed to draw enormous comfort from my body next to his, seemed to relax for the while as we both dozed off until the doctors arrived with the sunrise. I left our bed, our moments of intimacy ended by the start of another day in the hospital.

"Sit next to me," Jake said, "I want to be alone with you."

Jake remained alert. He did not go into a coma. I sat next to him, holding the oxygen to his mouth. He closed his eyes, opened them to look at me. Then he took a deep breath and this time his eyes rolled up. He was dead. It had happened, and I was not prepared. All those talks with Martin, all that crying, all that preparation and I was shocked. I ran from the room to get help and fortunately, Jake's doctors were on their way in.

"What's going on?" I screamed.

They raced into the room and began to resuscitate Jake. Only yesterday I had agreed to a DNR order. But that was just in theory. I wanted Jake and was not ready to let go, even now.

I stood in the hallway and wept. The nurses tried to comfort me. Some of Jake's friends, physicians, gathered in the hallway. Then I ran to the phone and called my mother. She and my in-laws left immediately for the hospital. The doctors managed to stabilize Jake.

Again, Jake was alert, aware. He was telling the nurse how much oxygen to give him. When I pumped on the oxygen bag for a few minutes he whispered, "Get someone who knows what they're doing".

Then he laughed. He was cracking jokes at his own resuscitation. He had crossed to the other side and come back and he was at peace now.

My mother and in-laws came into the room and held his hand.

"I love you," he said.

"I love you, Jake."

The doctor asked me to leave the room.

"I won't resuscitate him again."

"I know."

He hugged me and went back into the room.

"I'm going out kicking and screaming," Jake said.

Jake would never "go gently into the night".

"I'm so tired," Jake kept saying.

"Then close your eyes for a few seconds," the nurse said as she pumped the oxygen bag.

"No. If I do, they won't open."

He was right. It happened. Jake took a final breath, died, and this time he stayed dead. There was no resuscitation. He was gone. The body was there but there was no Jake inside it. I had never understood death before and now I felt it and I knew it.

"I have to get out of here," I said. "Fast."

I couldn't look at Jake like that any longer. I felt guilty leaving his body, but I had been there when he needed me.

His mother and father, my mother and then I kissed him goodbye.

"I love you, baby."

We left the hospital crushed. The bright lights of the day outside hurt my eyes. All the people around us seemed to be rushing. We walked as if in a fog, four dazed people getting into our car – no, it was my car now. My father in-law drove. He pounded on the roof of the car every so often, but no one said a word. We drove to my daughter's school.

My father-in-law went inside to get Chloe while I waited in the schoolyard. Chloe walked out smiling, happy to get out of school early for the day. Her smile faded when she saw me.

I picked her up and held her close.

"Daddy died."

As I said the words, I felt the sweetness of the word 'Daddy'. Chloe looked at me, not quite comprehending yet what I had said. She held me tightly as I carried her to the car. No one said a word as we drove home. Ben was playing outside on the neighbor's lawn when we drove up. As I opened the door, he happily jumped in on my lap, then looked around.

"Where's Daddy?"

No one answered him. We all got out of the car.

"Where's Daddy?"

"Daddy died," Chloe said.

The tears started to fall down my face. My three year old son stood in the doorway to the garage and tried to comfort me.

"It's okay. It's okay. We'll be okay, " he said.

In my bedroom, I sat down on some pillows that were on the floor by the bed. I didn't know what to do with myself so I called Martin, but the operator said he was out of the building.

My mother came upstairs.

"Would you like some lunch? The kids are eating," she asked me.

The kids were eating, but I wasn't with them, cuddling them, helping them through these first awful moments. Having lived for so long without me, they naturally went to their grandparents. I wasn't ready for them – at any moment I thought I would die from the pain.

When the kids went to bed that night, I went to sleep downstairs on the living room couch. I couldn't sleep in my bed without Jake.

During the next day there was an avalanche of flowers, visitors, phone calls. Jake's obituary was in the newspaper. In black and white they had summarized and finalized Jake. It didn't seem possible, I wanted them to print a correction. There had been a mistake.

Ben was obviously confused by everything going on. That night as I put him to bed, he held me very tightly.

"Did I die too?" he asked. "Will I be sick like Daddy?"

"I don't want to go to the funeral," Chloe told me the next day.

"Me either!" Ben mimicked.

"You don't have to. Don't worry about it. I'll have someone stay with you and you'll be fine," I told them.

Chloe woke up the day of the funeral with spots on her face and back. Chicken pox. For fifteen months we had lived in fear whenever one of the kids was exposed to chickenpox at school. Now that the chicken pox couldn't hurt her daddy anymore, Chloe seemed to have finally succumbed.

Jake's brother announced it was time to go and held me tightly as we walked into the funeral home and saw the coffin for the first time. I froze. He whispered into my ear.

"That's not Jake, that's not Jake."

"How long will this take?" I asked the Rabbi. I didn't think I would last long.

"I'm not sure."

"We have to cut it short."

I was back at our wedding, Jake at my side, squeezing my hand.

The Rabbi began and the hundreds of people who had come to say goodbye quieted down. The Rabbi put my anger into words.

"Death, whenever it comes, leaves a trail of tears, of pain, of suffering. But the tragedy is searing beyond compare when someone so young, so good, so sweet, kind and saintly dies…"

The eulogy was given by a doctor with whom had Jake worked for years. He was shaking as he stood up and I wondered if he would make it.

"Jake taught me a great deal about being a doctor. Jake was called on to perform intrusive procedures on the most fragile of all patients, children. He did this in a gentle, extremely capable manner. His consummate skill and concern for families created a quiet revolution at the hospital where parents had never before been allowed to stay with their children. Many a parent made a point of telling me how Jake made a potentially traumatic test tolerable and the kids certainly remembered him not with fear but with fondness.

"Jake taught me the most at this bedside. He bore this excruciating illness with dignity and resoluteness. He never stopped fighting. I wanted him to go outside and scream at the heavens in unbridled anger at the injustice of it all. I will always miss Jake, but I will be a better physician, a better husband and father and a better person for having known him."

He continued to speak and well before the time he finished, I had faded. More of Jake's colleagues spoke, but I couldn't listen anymore.

That morning we buried Jake in a peaceful, small cemetery in our town. I kissed the coffin goodbye and left. It was over. Jake's pain ended, the full depth of mine was just beginning. I had done everything with Jake up until now but die with him. I felt very intimate with death now, it didn't scare me any more.

SPRING 1997

CHAPTER 28

March

Two weeks after Len and I became engaged we arranged to have dinner at one of our favorite romantic restaurants in New York. But it had moved. Sonia Rose was an intimate, charming French restaurant that had relocated into a larger but soulless space. We walked to our table disappointed that one of our favorite restaurants for romance had been lost.

I finished my second glass of Pinot Noir and was feeling the effects when Len started.

"We need to do a pre-nuptial. My friends have advised me that since we're living together we could have palimony issues."

"Fine. I've told you all along that I would do a pre-nuptial," I said. It wasn't lost on me that Len had all the money in the relationship and that his kids deserved to inherit his estate.

"I've been reading some of the provisions that should go in."

I had drunk enough wine to not really care what Len was saying, yet.

"One provision is that if I die and you want to get remarried, you should move out of wherever you're living. I assume I will have paid for it."

The effects of the wine immediately wore off. Was Len attempting to control me from the grave?

"Don't worry," he said, "You'll get money to buy another place and when you die the money will go back into my estate for my kids."

"What if I want to remarry at sixty after living in my home for fifteen years? I will have to move from my home?"

"Yes," Len said.

"I am a widow. What if Jake had told me to move out of my home?

"You are aware of what I went through during Jake's illness. The doctor at the cancer center told me that in his fifteen years there he had never seen anyone care for a dying person the way I cared for Jake. And you've seen how I have behaved as a widow. It took me years to get over Jake. What do you care where I'm living? You'd be dead."

"This is what I want. I don't see what's wrong with it. You get a certain amount of money to buy a place, maybe not as nice."

"Don't most men think about what they can do to make their widow's life easier, not more difficult?" I asked.

"I saw other provisions that were much worse. Just be glad I don't want those."

"Maybe if you were more flexible, then I could be more trusting," I responded.

We left the restaurant and drove back to New Jersey to Len's house for the night. As we crossed the George Washington Bridge over the Hudson, I looked back at the glittering lights of the City wondering what price I would pay for more time spent in Len's world.

As we walked into his home, Len headed towards his den.

"I have work to do," he said.

"But it's Saturday night."

"You've had your two hours."

The same two hours he allocated to Judy on Saturday nights. Not much had changed, I gathered.

The phone rang that night at 9:30.

Len was sprawled out on his brown leather chair, reading SEC filings and drafts of contracts, watching television and often dozing off. Some time around midnight he would make his way down the hall to the bedroom.

I rarely answered the phone in Len's house, even after all this time, so I let it ring three times before assuming he had dozed off. It was my dear friend Rachel.

"Hey dudette. How are you?" she said.

In case the phone had awakened him, I carried the portable into the bathroom upstairs. I definitely didn't want Len to hear this conversation.

"I'm okay."

"I just got home from dinner and couldn't stop thinking about you and Len. I hope this isn't a bad time. Now tell the truth, how are you?" Rachel said.

"You really want to hear this? Len and I are in a tug of war interspersed with daily sex, extravagant presents, great trips and a few laughs."

"Can't either of you slack off the rope a little?"

"I think we've both tried. But we're both too scared of the advantage the other one will gain."

"You don't trust each other?" Rachel said.

"I think we love each other – for whatever that's worth. But trust, absolutely not."

"This won't work without trust. I do understand you think he's rescued you from some of your responsibilities so you've forgiven him many times."

I tried to explain to Rachel how much I wanted the relationship. Len was always taunting me that I'd been a widow for years, that I'd dated scores of men and would never do any better than him. He had said a hundred times that I didn't appreciate what I had with him. But I knew what it felt like with Jake.

"I'm not sure I like Len's insides – his soul, as corny as that sounds. Guess you could say I'd be settling after Jake."

"You love everything about him but who he is," Rachel said.

"Len's the consummate concierge – get me tickets to anything, arrange whatever I want. But tune in to my feelings? Have my back no matter what happens? Hah."

"Then why won't you get out? Are you crazy? His universe is one of domination. That's his work," Rachel, who never gave relationship advice, was doing just that.

I thought about Len's world, filled with relationships, with marriages like this. It was obvious that a deal had been struck. They didn't care about being soul mates or best friends. The relationship was a deal and the perks made it worthwhile for each partner. The woman was younger and beautiful and the man was very wealthy and often got that way by being a bastard.

I put my ear to the door just to make sure Len wasn't somewhere nearby.

"Are you ready to move on then, to date other men? You know it's not Len or nothing," Rachel asked.

"The thought of dating again is unbearable. You have to wonder how I'd go from someone like Jake to a Len."

My mind wandered to all the times in the past year Len had asked me why would I want to be with him – he was older and I was too good for him. He had told me that he was never at peace except when he was with me. And that the only people that matter to him were his kids, his best friend Bill, and me. He made this so difficult because he wasn't all bad.

"He actually told me he loves me more than he ever loved Judy."

"I'm not surprised about that. I would love you more than Judy," Rachel giggled.

I thought I heard a sound outside the bathroom.

"One second," I said very quietly.

Silence.

"I need to whisper in case Len is around. This is like high school. Talking to your friends on the phone so your parents can't hear."

"That kind of says it all, doesn't it?"

And then I remembered the strangest thing. A friend of Bill's wife Heather called me about a surprise birthday party for Heather. I'd met this woman at various dinners and she seemed to relish gossip more than anyone I knew.

She must have heard from Heather about any troubles Len and I might be having because she confided in me that Bill and Heather didn't really like Len all that much, and that their friendship was all about business relationships and keeping them in place. I was stunned. Was there anything real in his world?

"Kate, you're losing your confidence, your sense of joy. You were always the one who lit up a room. Would anyone want this man without his money?" Rachel asked.

"But that's who he is."

"Is that who you are?" she said.

"He says that I make him very happy but he doesn't think he can make me happy."

"He's right, Kate, because you probably want to be with a different kind of man."

"I can't start dating again. I never talk about this but the truth is, I have always lived with someone. My parents, then college roommates, Jake, my kids. I'm genuinely scared to live alone and I'm worried that if it doesn't work out with Len and Ben leaves for college, it will be the first time I'll have to be alone."

Rachel was quiet for a moment. "You cannot change him and you cannot twist yourself into a pretzel to be someone he can control."

"I have to try, Rachel. No man is perfect. You know that expression – a tickle and a slap? It pretty much sums up my time with Len. Wonder how many women in Manhattan are in the same boat."

■ ■ ■

I rarely remembered my dreams but that night Jake appeared in one and I longed for him when I awoke. Looking over at Len, I missed being in Jake's comforting and forgiving arms. And that's what I had dreamed about, Jake holding me in his arms, because of Viola.

When I was six weeks old, my mother went back to work and she hired Viola to be the housekeeper and nanny. Viola landed as the conduit between my mother's focus on her work and my needs.

She might have reached five feet tall and pictures show her just as round. She lived with us in our two-bedroom apartment for twelve years, sleeping on the pull out couch in the living room. Only when she met Jackson and moved to Pittsburgh to marry him, did she finally leave.

Viola had her own agenda of things she wanted to teach

me, like the importance of being a lady. From an early age she made me practice sitting with my legs together. I couldn't imagine at the time why that mattered. She held my hand when we walked somewhere, pushed me on the swings in the playground, asked me how school had gone that day, and hugged me if I cried.

For the ten hours each day that my mother worked, Viola reached out to me when it felt like I was on my own in the universe. I loved Viola and when she left us, the pain eased only because all of my attention at twelve shifted to boys.

Jake and I went to visit her once in Pittsburgh and she came with Jackson to my wedding. I called her every week. And then one night, a year after our wedding, Jake was on an overnight hour shift during his residency. Alone in our apartment, I dialed Viola's number. A woman picked up but the voice didn't sound familiar.

"Is Viola there?" I asked.

"She died today."

"She what?"

"She had a heart attack and died."

Whether it was the loss of Viola in my life or the shock of her sudden death, I became hysterical. Normally, I wouldn't think of bothering Jake at the hospital and never had, but nothing felt normal. He must have heard the havoc in my voice.

"I'm coming home. On my way," Jake said.

"How can you come home? Who's going to cover for you?"

"I'll find someone. Just hang in there, baby."

Jake walked into our apartment within an hour. His friend Kevin immediately agreed to cover for him overnight. It was the first time Jake had done this, left his responsibilities at the hospital behind. He held me tightly while I cried.

Being in his arms got me through the night. I had lost Viola, but I had Jake.

But I didn't have Jake except in my dreams. Len, lying next to me, slowly opened his eyes and I braced myself for the day.

Driving back into the City from Len's house the next day, as if an IV were pumping into my veins, life reappeared in the throngs of people walking the streets on the early spring afternoon. A car accident had completely stopped traffic on the Henry Hudson. Forced to make my way down Broadway and the side streets of the Upper West Side, the windows of the car open to the warm air, the sounds of the City revived me.

Sitting on the steps of the brownstones near Columbia University, hanging out on sidewalk cafes, playing ball, the energy of my fellow New Yorkers felt invigorating. The Upper West Side, an area allegedly filled with writers and artists, was well known to be less pretentious than the Upper East Side where Len and I lived.

Whether just a City girl or reeling from the tension with Len, I felt so grateful fleeing the isolation of that mansion. I wanted out of his big empty home. If only I could stop and tell each one of the folks sitting on the steps of their brownstones that you may not have Len's money or his big beautiful mansion but it was okay. Believe me, it was okay.

CHAPTER 29

April

At dinner that night at Sonia Rose, Len led me down a slippery slope from which the climb back seemed daunting. The terms of the pre-nuptial were too much for me. Time to confront him with the Sisyphean nature of our relationship.

"It makes me sad that I love you and yet you repeatedly hurt me. Please name one time when I've hurt you," I said at breakfast that weekend.

Len just sat there.

"This isn't love like I had with Jake and it isn't the love I wanted. You know what it will take to make this relationship work and you aren't willing or maybe not able to do it."

"Kate, I'm just plain weary at this point. I argue with people all day long and I don't want to argue with you all night long. I need peace in my home. That's what Judy gave me. Peace."

"Hah."

She had given him a Prozac induced peace.

"Ok, I understand your weariness. You are who you are

and I can't change you. You have to tell me if you're willing to do this with me because I can't survive in the type of relationship you had in your marriage," I responded.

Len said nothing.

"I want someone who's a best friend and a lover. We've had fun – dinners, trips – it's all very nice but it doesn't provide the glue. I feel like I live in fear of you. I just can't relax around you."

"I realize I am a deviation from perfection," Len said.

"A deviation from perfection is one thing. Not being nice is something else."

Len gave me a steely look. I sat there wondering how many people had confronted him over the years. Certainly not Judy.

"You can be kind but then ...you lose your way. I love you and want this to work. Please think about what you want," I said hoping to melt the steel.

"You have faults too. You know so little about so many things. Finance, opera, ... I could go on, " Len said.

"While you were sitting in your corner office on Wall Street, I was raising two children by myself and earning a living as a lawyer. I might have been a bit too busy to be worried about Adam Smith and Wagner," I glared at him.

Twice a week at lunchtime I escaped to Carnegie Hall to attend a ballet class for amateurs, of course. Just walking into that storied building made me feel graceful. More important-ly, ballet entailed focusing on the shaking in my hamstrings rather than from Len's comments. And straining to remain on my toes, the pain began in my calves and seared my glutes rather than my heart.

"Push your chest forward, your butt back and squeeze your abs in. That will give you the strength to lift up and stay up," Nicolas, the French instructor, said as he pushed us to repeatedly relevé.

Forcing myself to hold my abs as tightly as possible, my neophyte version of the strong, long, lean ballerina appeared in the countless floor to ceiling mirrors that lined the walls of the large room. The classical music, the grace, the challenge allowed me to pretend for two hours a week that I was someone other than the woman entangled in a mess with Len and bogged down in a stressful legal job. Grateful that I could lose myself in the beauty of ballet, I worked hard to impress Nicolas.

Little girls may dream of being a ballerina because of the pretty costumes, the beautiful movements. And though I wasn't wearing anything other than leggings and a tight gym top, occasionally a movement worked and Nicolas would reward me with one word, "excellent".

But today, he pushed us harder than usual to hold in our abs, to reach the needed core strength. Nicolas, often very strict with us, seemed more intent than ever on achieving his goals for the class. He obviously led by example. Just one look at the way he moved his very muscular, lean and elegant body about the room and through the moves he wanted us to repeat inspired me.

"When Juliet dies in the ballet *Romeo and Juliet*, you see as they carry her dead body that her abs are perfectly tight and her feet are perfectly pointed. Perfectly tight, perfectly pointed. It is essential, even in death. The appearance of perfect control," he said.

Len. He returned to my consciousness as the consummate ballet dancer on Wall Street. Always in perfect control. And now desiring that perfect control even in the pre-nup, even in death.

. . .

We both hired lawyers to handle the pre-nuptial. The document consisted of twenty pages of provisions that reduced our relationship to legalese with timeframes for death and divorce. If we were together less than three years, between three and six years, six and ten years, at least fifteen years, Len would only pay the following sums.

Len appeared to approach this as if he were negotiating another one of his deals that he had to win. I would acquiesce and he'd be in charge. A most unlikely scenario. Or else he knew I'd never agree to the deal and two weeks after asking me to marry him in an elaborate trip to Paris, he'd presented me with his escape route. A no win situation for me in either case.

"My lawyer says I'm being cheap and unfair," he relayed to me.

"And what did you say?"

"I said that nobody was going to tell me what do with my fucking money.

"Listen," he continued. "I want you to sign this document no matter what it says. This is not a negotiation. You have to trust me."

"Why would I just trust you?"

And he didn't trust me. One provision in the pre-nuptial amused my friends to no end.

11. Kate and Len each acknowledge that privacy is important to each of them. In order to keep all information that Kate has learned or may learn about Len, or Len has learned or may learn about Kate, from becoming public, each agrees that any and all information that he or she acquires from any source concerning the other, the personal and business affairs of the other (the 'Information') shall be held in confidence. Kate and Len each agrees that she or he will not violate the confiden-

tiality of their relationship and attempt to benefit from said relationship by engaging in any of the following; (a) writing, authoring, co-authoring, publishing or revealing Information for the writing of any books or articles or the selling of the rights to any books or articles to publishers or other involving the other; (b) conducting any interviews, press conferences or giving any press releases about the other or the relationship between the other; (c) selling any movie, television, theatre, documentary, or any other rights concerning the relationship.

"Who does he think he is? Warren Beatty? His ego has no bounds, does it? And what if you wanted to write a flattering book, hard as that is to imagine anyone doing," Sarah said when I read it to her over the phone. And then she began to sing Carly Simon's song "You're So Vain" but she had changed "song" to "book" as she sang.

We couldn't stop laughing.

"I'm never going to meet this guy, am I?" Sarah asked.

"I doubt it. You definitely wouldn't approve of Len."

"But you obviously don't want to hear what I might say. I understand."

"Sarah, what you don't appreciate is how carefully constructed Len's life is, and that I am certainly not going to be allowed to deconstruct it. Len told me that he wasn't worried that I would write about him since he had the goods on me. What does that mean?" I asked.

"Don't sign the pre-nuptial, but I think writing a book about him is dangerous. Remember Raskolnikov? But I wonder if Len is as confused as you are, Kate," Sarah said.

"Len confused? About me? About what?"

"Because people underestimate you and you like that. You want them to underestimate you, don't you?" she asked.

"You are so much stronger than people think you are," Sarah continued, "you can be the consummate tease because of your infectious joy. You can be strong and smart. He's probably wondering what hit him. And so he's in deal mode. He needs to win this one. And something tells me you're not going to roll over and play dead. You will not be another victim of his. It's his loss," Sarah said as she hung up the phone.

.   .   .

Len and I tried many things to salvage the relationship. We tried a couples therapist who met with me alone after several sessions together with Len.

"Kate, Len can give you diamonds and Paris and St. Bart's but he won't be there for you when you need him most. He doesn't understand the vulnerability that you feel from losing Jake," she said.

"But he lost his spouse."

"Len saw Judy's death as an opportunity, and seemed able to make the transition instantaneously between partners. You need to think about whether this is what you really want. Len seems to have a limited ability to be intimate, to love, to empathize. You two have a bad connection in that area. What you need most he is least able to give," she cautioned.

"Therapy is bullshit and I'm not going to change for anyone. I'm not broke and there's nothing to fix," he said when I repeated her comments to him.

I looked at his stern, cold eyes, took off the diamond ring and put it on his bedside table.

"I don't want this anymore."

Stunned, Len gave me a withering look.

.   .   .

As the plane continued its steep climb into the sky, the tears streamed down my face. We left Chloe behind in Barcelona and were heading back to New York after a ten-day visit to see her and the Spanish family hosting her for the year. Chloe landed in a honey pot with the sweetest family and we received the warmest of welcomes from them. To see Chloe that happy, and her school experience so enriched because of a year abroad, allowed me to feel vindicated after our move from Connecticut.

But despite the hospitality of the family and Chloe's successful year, Len and I spent the ten days in our continued state of misery. Now, even our lavish trips, staying in the best hotels and flying first class, provided no relief.

The jet flew out over the Mediterranean and then made a wide turn west to take us home. Chloe wouldn't return for another two months, just in time for graduation from high school. As we passed over Barcelona, I looked down at the city knowing that somewhere far below was my daughter. I missed her enormously already.

Len, busy reading his papers for work paid no attention to my tears. When a certain calm returned, I turned to him.

"Why wouldn't you comfort me when I'm missing my daughter?"

He looked up over his bifocals and with icy eyes glared at me. "What are you upset about now?"

"Leaving Chloe behind in Spain. She won't return for another two months."

"I wouldn't feel sad if we were leaving Jennifer."

"But this isn't about you. I feel sad. I'd even comfort a stranger if he sat next to me on a plane."

"Chloe is fine. What's the big deal about leaving her?" he said.

Len went back to reading his papers.

Len and I sat far apart in the back seat as the car service drove us home from JFK. He looked straight ahead, his mind churning apparently, as always.

"I forgot to tell you Dale called. He met a girl in medical school and he thinks this is the one," Len said.

I wondered if she knew she'd be swallowed up in Len's world.

"Dale says she's very close to her family, especially her mother. I worry that I'll lose him. Girls do tend to stick to their moms."

The car moved slowly in the traffic as I thought of Ben and whether he would drift away if he met the one.

"Her father's a high school math teacher and her mother's an administrative assistant. So they're probably pretty middle class. I'll just give her expensive jewelry, buy them a house, a car. Bring her on our vacations. Whatever it takes."

I looked at Len. Was he laughing? His comments all a joke?

"You're buying her affections? It will say a lot about her if that works," I said.

"Worked with you."

"The past tense is appropriate."

Len turned his head for a moment. Provoking a man with a killer instinct had to be risky.

"I wonder what I'll do when Ben meets someone. I don't have the means to bribe his future wife. We'll actually have to rely on her loving Chloe and me enough to want to be with us."

"Good luck with that.

We rode the rest of the way in the Lincoln Town Car in silence.

"So this is what it's like to be more alone in a relationship than to be alone with oneself," I explained to Sarah on the phone the next day.

"How is it living together?"

"Len has not stopped complaining since we moved into our apartment. He hates having to ride the crowded elevator and exercising in the small gym in the building with other people. At night, he says the sounds of the City, which are music to my ears, drive him crazy."

"He's not a City boy."

"But he has barely moved any of his belongings into the apartment. That's the most telling sign of all. If only Len could get a heart transplant, from someone nice."

"Hah! But do you have the courage to leave him?" she asked.

"No, I don't. If I were alone again, I would always be plagued by whether I had made the right decision."

"You're fighting against a man with more structural defects than just his heart. This one has a steely spine and what appears to be an empty soul. You're going to drive him away eventually. He'll break up with you," she cautioned.

"I know that. Len needs peace in his home life so he can take on the world. There will never be peace at home with me there. It's so funny. I walked the streets of New York with this knock 'em dead diamond ring looking like the luckiest woman in the City. If people only knew."

. . .

Len left work at four to watch Ben pitch in his first game for Barnes Academy. The game was scheduled to be played on a field adjacent to the Hudson on West 98th street. The cars flew by on the West Side Highway during the rush hour exodus out of Manhattan.

As Ben took the mound and began his warm-ups, I started pacing by the benches.

"Kate, stop it. He can see you," Len said.

"I can't. I'm nervous."

Len walked away from me, pacing on his own, anxiously watching Ben. He looked almost as jumpy as I was. Ben pitched, I paced and Len mumbled to himself, as was his habit, about the coach, the other team, the other players. In the end, Ben had a good outing striking out six and walking two.

Afterwards, as Ben parted from the team, Len put his arm around Ben's shoulder.

"That was a good start. You held your own," he said.

Ben smiled at him apparently enjoying the comfort of Len's arm.

I drove through Central Park with Len in the front seat and Ben in the back. All of the windows were open, allowing the cool April breeze to relax three weary people after a tense game. I loudly honked at a woman on a bicycle as she rode directly in front of our car and then continued through the Park. The car was stopped at a red light where Central Park and Fifth Avenue intersect when the woman on the bicycle pulled up next to Len's window, threw a handful of dirt in his face and took off.

Len slowly erupted, his body contorting first at the waist, the anger rising through his shoulders until his head was held rigid. His fury looked volcanic. I grabbed his jacket as he started to bolt out the door of the car after the woman.

"No! Don't Len, please!" I yelled.

He ran up Fifth Avenue after her as fast as he could.

"He'll kill her. We'll have to get him out of jail." I yelled to Ben.

Since traffic flowed down Fifth Avenue, I couldn't follow Len. I crossed to Madison and started to drive uptown. Ben and I searched everywhere for Len. After only one block, we saw him walking desperately trying to catch his breath. He got in the car.

"I think I injured my leg running," he said.

"What did you do to her?" I asked not really wanting to know the answer.

"She didn't think I could outrun her bicycle, but I did of course. I caught up to her halfway up the block. She stopped, got off her bicycle and froze. The people on the street naturally thought I was attacking her so they stopped too."

"So what'd you do to her?"

"I yelled at her. That's it," Len said.

"You mean you just told her not to do it again?"

"I wanted to scare the hell out of her. She was shaking in her boots."

She was not the only one. Ben sat frozen and wide-eyed in the back seat trying to comprehend what had just happened. He had never seen anything like this.

Ben looked very relieved to say goodbye to us and head to his best friend's apartment on the next block for a weekly sleepover.

Len and I rode the crowded elevator in our building in silence. Another couple exited at the same time and walked to the door adjacent to ours. We had never bumped into them before, a typical experience of apartment life in the City.

As we reached the alcove where our doors abutted, Len showed no apparent interest in speaking with them. He seemed to prefer never to venture outside his insular world of bankers where their net worth and connections to deals were well known to him.

"Hi, I'm Kate," I said.

"Russell. And this is Gabrielle. Would you like to come in for a drink?"

Len gave me a 'not in a million years' look.

"That would be lovely."

They had to have a decent bank account to be living in the building so I figured Len would survive.

"Please sit down," Russell said as he ushered us into their very contemporary one bedroom apartment.

Len and I sat on the sprawling cream leather sofa. Gabrielle curled her long thin legs up on a large matching leather chair while her thick blonde hair cascaded down her shoulders. Her skin tight black leather pants looked like they might rupture from the exertion. The cat jumped up on Gabrielle's lap and nestled in.

"Wine?" Russell asked as he brought over a bottle of Grand Cru Burgundy.

Len smiled at the expensive bottle and relaxed a bit as he obviously approved of the choice. Quite a starting offer from Russell.

"Have you lived here long?" I asked.

"Gabrielle and I moved in together about a year ago."

Len and Russell began a modest exchange of information about their work.

"I started the company thirty years ago and it's my baby," Russell said.

I looked at Gabrielle, who must have been an infant at that time. She sat very quietly as she and the cat engaged in synchronized gazing at Russell. He seemed to glow in their attention.

Maybe that's what Len needed. A much younger woman who would look up to him, listen to his every word, follow all of his advice. But one reason older men chased women like Gabrielle, to validate their sexual identity, could not possibly be an issue for Len.

I walked over to their large living room window to compare their view to ours.

"What does Kate do?" Russell asked Len.

As I turned around Len responded, "She's a healthcare lawyer."

Was that even a tiny hint of pride in Len's face? But Russell gave Len a "bet you got your hands full look".

"Gabrielle, what do you do?" I asked.

"I work at the Georgette Klinger spa," she said.

"Len gave me a facial there as a present. I loved it."

"I tweeze eyebrows."

Something told me that Russell didn't care much what Gabrielle did for a living. This was about how she made him feel in the eyes of others at an age he might fear becoming invisible to women.

Len stood up.

"I have work to do tonight. Thank you for the wine," he said as he ushered me to the door.

"It was lovely to meet you both," I added.

Russell appeared disappointed at our quick exit.

"Let's do this again," I offered knowing well that Len would be fuming at my words.

When we entered our apartment, Len looked at me sternly.

"What's the matter now?"

"You should learn how to act like Gabrielle," he said.

"A lap cat who's in it for the money? My advice to Gabrielle is that if she's going to do it for the money, go big. In New York, there are much bigger fish than Russell."

We woke up Saturday morning to heavy rain and wind. I was cuddled under the down comforter as Len returned from the bathroom and sat on the edge of the bed next to me.

"I need to tell you something. You know the company that I invested so much of my money in. It may be in trouble. I may not have nearly what I thought I had," he said looking me squarely in the eyes.

My mind was racing. Maybe he couldn't afford the apartment on 79th Street because of this? Had the heavens sent me a test: could I love Len without his money? Or maybe the company wasn't in trouble?

CHAPTER 30

May

Len moved out in early May after a horrible fight. Jason and Elizabeth came to spend the night with us in the apartment and Len simply wouldn't talk with them. My friends had been my lifeline for years and he was obviously attempting to cut them off.

"How could you do this?" I screamed.

The more upset I got, the more Len steeled himself.

"I learned to control my rage growing up. If I ever let go, I'll probably kill someone," he had told me once.

I believed him. His anger avoidance seemed a good hedge against acting out on his destructive instincts.

After he left, Ben cried for hours. He may have heard the fighting but that probably was not what hurt the most. He probably liked having a man in certain parts of his life to take control as much as I had at one point.

"I feel like Daddy died all over again," he sobbed.

Len moved back in within the week. I emailed my former boss and good friend Janet hoping for some of her priceless wisdom.

"Should I give Len a second chance?"

I awaited her response which I knew would consist of one part Oliver Wendell Holmes and one part Thelma and Louise.

"Let me start with a reasoned approach. As a general rule, I think people are entitled to second chances," she wrote back. "I've been given more than a few myself – and I suspect so have you. I'm grateful, and I'll bet you are too. That said, not everyone is worthy of a second chance in every situation. I guess the determinative factor for me is the likelihood of success (however defined) the second time around. Some things can't be changed or improved e.g. no matter how many chances I'd be a lousy singer, painter, dancer. For some people a loving faithful nature, is the same, I think. Who can say on what side of that line anyone fails? Past behavior is an imperfect predictor, but the greater number of mistakes, the less likelihood of staying the course, I'd say. How many screw-ups are we talking about? And how much is it worth to you? I'd be more willing to give a great love another go, and less willing to reconnect with someone about whom I had misgivings even without the screw ups.

Despite the fact you need to make your own decisions, if you really want to know what I think about Len, I'd say run for the hills and hide! Change your phone number, take a very long vacation and don't tell him where you're going. Consider moving. You get the idea. But you decide what you want, but don't take revenge and don't take him back to avoid being alone. Lots of love, Janet."

Janet's advice was to run for the hills. Since that night at Passover when she first met Len, Janet had not rendered her verdict on him. Until now. As I read the counsel from a precious friend, I realized I wasn't listening anymore. I was in too deep with Len.

FALL 1997

CHAPTER 31

September

At the end of the summer Chloe left for Brown, the same college where Jake and I had gone twenty-five years earlier. My heart was pounding as I delivered our child to the campus where I first noticed her father walking by. Len and I kept the peace for one day so I could send Chloe feeling secure and prepared for her acclimation, although only a minor adjustment after her year in Spain.

Len's hostile behavior over the past few months had me thinking about his greatest passion, his deals. I tried to learn about Len's work sitting in the den with him, when he allowed me to, listening to several conference calls with his colleagues. That same deal making mentality had obviously seeped into Len's idea of a relationship with any woman post Judy.

Using my very limited understanding, I attempted to apply the structure of his work to our relationship since he certainly, as it was second nature by now, had done the same. I knew he'd be laughing in my face if I conveyed this information to him. But who cared at this point? Len's modus operandi was getting into focus and it scared the hell out of me.

Bypassing any of the knowledge gained in business school, it still appeared to me that Len wanted to maximize his returns while maintaining, what he would consider, a controlling interest. The acquisition itself, otherwise known for the moment as myself, did not necessarily have to be a benefactor of the transaction except as Len thought appropriate. A Wall Street deal transposed by Len onto of all things – me. And when Len's greed was not satisfied because I was not one to be acquired or controlled, would he think it time to move on to the next acquisition?

A few nights after we dropped Chloe at college, Len sat in the corner of the couch in the living room of our apartment whispering into his phone. In our bedroom, I could hear him man giggle every so often, a flirtatious giggle.

Finally, I stood at the door to the bedroom and attempted to listen. The words were impossible to distinguish but the tone and the man giggles were not. I walked into the living room and stood squarely in front of him. He would not look at me and continued listening to the voice on the phone.

What was I supposed to do? Stand there watching him? Pull the phone out of his hand? The thought of another confrontation with Len seemed purposeless. I wondered if I just didn't care anymore or if I was just too exhausted from banging my head against his steel frame.

Or maybe Len had done something that would finally encapsulate his character, relieving me from the desire to consume his bitter pill any more. He had obviously begun to see another woman. Yet it was only then, listening to him on the phone, that I became convinced of her existence. I went to sleep that night wondering about a possible escape route.

But on the very next day I learned that I was pregnant.

"I don't want to be tied down in any way. I don't want any more kids, mine are grown and I'm done. You have to get an abortion," Len said.

"Do you remember when Bill said that we should have kids when we get married?"

"I don't care what Bill said. I don't want more kids."

"If you don't want any more kids, ever, then you should get a vasectomy."

"No way. It's safer for you to have an abortion."

I couldn't even respond.

"There are no complications with an abortion but there are with a vasectomy. And those are the kind of complications I can't even think about."

"You mean there are no complications with abortions that will affect your body."

We had used condoms as usual but one condom had obviously failed me at the worst possible time. Len felt so alien at this point and now something of his was growing inside me. There was a sense of urgency about this and I knew that Len's behavior had determined my choice. I would not carry Len's child.

"I'm pregnant," I told Zoë that night on the phone.

"Oh no! What are you going to do?" She almost yelled.

"I'm going to have an abortion. Len told me I have to get an abortion."

"It's your body and you don't have to get an abortion, you know that?"

"I know that. I'm going to have an abortion for my reasons, not for his. I would have done anything to have more children with Jake. We even talked about it. But not with

Len," I responded.

"I don't think you need to pay the consequence for a failed condom the rest of your lives."

"Look, I am not an eighteen year old impregnated by her teenage boyfriend. I know what it means to bring up a child and by myself. If I had the baby, I would be tied to Len forever."

"But there are women who would keep the child, just to keep Len in the picture financially," Zoë said.

"I have no interest in leveraging Len. You know that."

"I do know that, Kate. I'm so sorry about this."

Other than Zoë, I did not discuss this decision with anyone. There could not be a more personal action that I would have to live with the rest of my life. And a chorus of pro-abortion or pro-life voices in my head would not change my mind.

■ ■ ■

At first Len wasn't sure that he would even come with me.

"Nine out of ten men I know who are working on a deal like this wouldn't bother coming with you."

We took a car service to the doctor's office on West Broadway. I sat very still thinking about what I was about to do. Len babbled on about work.

"So the lawyer I worked with last night told me he thought I'm the best negotiator he has ever encountered," he said.

I remained silent.

"I guess you don't want to hear about this right now."

He couldn't possibly be trying to provoke a fight, even at this moment, could he? The benign bargain I had struck with myself to stay with Len as a safety net after Jake's death was turning malignant.

As the nurse put the needle in my vein and the anesthesia began to take effect, I suddenly panicked and thought of capitulating to Len. Terrified of being alone, my final thought as I passed out was surrender.

When we finally left the doctor's office, Len warned me that he'd be working on his deal throughout the night. I quickly called my mother to come spend the evening at my apartment. The sadness of the day felt overwhelming.

Long after Ben had gone to sleep, my mother and I sat on my bed while I recounted to her all that had recently transpired with Len.

"If you'd like, I'll spend the night here, in your bed. You need the company," she said.

For the first time in my life, my mother crawled into my bed. I desperately needed the comfort of her warmth and love and she was there.

CHAPTER 32

October

One week later, on a beautiful brisk October morning, I went out for my first post-abortion run around the Central Park reservoir. Still emotionally distraught and hormonally unbalanced from the abortion, running felt a welcome relief. Len hated this path, too many people who didn't have the sense to get out of his way. Neither the beauty of the skyline nor the tranquility of Central Park in the midst of the frantic City stirred him.

When I came back upstairs, Len sat reading memos from his staff.

I showered and dressed.

"It feels so good to run again."

He looked up at me with a patronizing smile and returned to reading his papers. I pecked him on the cheek goodbye and left for work.

At noon I had an appointment with my gynecologist, a woman I had known since college and who had performed the abortion. She examined me quickly.

"Everything looks fine. Are you feeling okay?" she asked.

"Yes."

"And that man who came with you? Things okay with him?"

"Not really," I said.

"I'm not surprised. I only spoke to him for a few minutes, and I really shouldn't say this but I've known you forever. I didn't like him at all."

At three o'clock that afternoon the phone rang in my office.

"I've packed my stuff and moved out," Len said.

I sat at my desk for a moment and dreaded the thought of being alone.

"Please don't. I'm sorry about arguing over the prenuptial, for not trusting you," I said.

As the words left my mouth, I felt horrified that I'd said them. I knew Len could not change. Compromise was part of the art of relationships. And I had compromised with Len, having bargained away so much of myself. But we had crossed the line, hadn't we? The line when too many concessions of what felt important to me, to my character, to my happiness, left me a skeleton of my former self.

"I had already called my lawyer to put you in my will. I knew you weren't after my money, you just wanted security for your kids, didn't you? You should have trusted me on the prenup," he said.

My lawyer had told me that the prenup clearly stated that it took precedence over his will and that Len had left me in a worse position under the prenup than if I were in his will. The lawyer explained that the protections a wife received in a will under the law were waived under this prenup. Len was underestimating me but I kept thinking what being alone would be like.

"Look, I'm sorry. I shouldn't have fought with you so much," I tried.

He said nothing.

"And...I really thought you were attractive," I offered.

Could I possibly be saying this? No one would believe it. These strange words were leaving my mouth but there had to be a limit to my desperation to stay with this man. I should have just felt relieved but I didn't. Since I couldn't be the one to walk out, he finally had and I should have happily skipped out through the exit door. But I couldn't, yet.

Nothing but silence from Len.

"Can we try just one more time? I won't say anything bad," I said.

I was scared enough to keep us going, even though I had known for months that life appeared more pleasant in a Gulag, and that I didn't want to end up like Judy, on medication. Len had taken control and I had lost it.

But could he really walk out a week after the abortion? Could there be a more cowardly way to end our relationship? And then I found my strength.

"Men like you think they come out on top because of a willingness and ability to win at any cost, and you do win – for the moment. But that meanness, that anger defines you. The money, the connections to powerful people won't compensate for the person inside. I know you won't hear or understand what I'm saying. You learned from a master, your mother, and chose to treat people as she taught you. You had the opportunity once to live as a good man."

Len remained silent.

"I wanted you to save me after Jake. And I am grateful to you because you did save me. You showed me your world of Wall Street, of privilege, and what's in your heart. There are good people with enormous amounts of money who do wonderful things with that money. But not on your block. How someone earns that money defines who they are. So thank you. You saved me, alright. From spending any more time on the outside wishing I could enter a world that isn't worth the price of admission."

There was silence for a moment.

"Goodbye Kate." He hung up.

I had embraced Raskolnikov. No reason to be shocked now to find what he was capable of.

Three weeks later Len left me a voice mail.

"Please let me know when you'd like to pick up your things at my house."

Zoë came to visit for a few days and sat near the phone when I called Len back. I pushed the button for speakerphone so she could witness the conversation.

"Hi, this is Len, please leave me a message and I will call you back. Thank you."

"Zoë, I know the passcode to his voicemail." Zoë looked at me. I pushed it.

"You have one new message," the voicemail reported.

"Hi, I got the flowers. They are just so beautiful. Thank you so much. I love you. Can't wait to see you this weekend," a female voice cooed into the phone.

. . .

It came as no surprise, however, that my friends let out a universal yell of joy and relief. As I told each one, their replies were uniform. "Finally." "Good riddance." "I'm thrilled."

I wasn't so sure, often finding myself feeling lonely and sad without Len or maybe the life with Len. Not quite as confident as my friends that he had done me an enormous favor.

And then Zoë summed it up with a quote from Oscar Wilde.

"Kate, think about this and which one is you and which one is Len. *Some people cause happiness wherever they go. Some people cause happiness whenever they go.*' Let him go…" she said.

■ ■ ■

One night that fall driving home very late from a birthday party for a colleague in Westchester, Zoë called me. It was long past midnight and she sounded in an unusually thoughtful mood.

"I went for a long ride today. The leaves were gorgeous. Did you notice?" She didn't wait for my response. "Last year, I bet you didn't even notice there were leaves, let alone the color of the leaves. Life must have been like watching a black and white television the last year or two you spent with Len. Is it back to living color?"

"You know what I realize now? I don't care about country clubs, jewelry, designer gowns. I want to travel to Antarctica, Bhutan and Africa, not St. Bart's. I can leave Len's world behind," I said.

"And be grateful you didn't marry him because that soon would have been your world. It's not you, honey. Figure out what Kate wants and find a man who enjoys what you like. Don't just fit into his life because he has money."

"Sometimes I think there is more method to my madness than I get credit for. I might have bumbled my way through the relationship and stayed too long, but I didn't marry him. And I walk away with an even better sense of what I want and don't want. I didn't need him to rescue me after Jake's death after all."

"That's the Garth Brooks 'Thank God for Unanswered Prayers' theory. You rescued yourself," Zoë laughed.

SPRING/
SUMMER 1998

CHAPTER 33

April

On a lovely warm spring evening, I had just walked in the apartment when the phone rang.

"Kate. This is Heather, Bill's wife," she said hesitating.

Bill had been one of Len's closest friends at one point. Surprise didn't begin to capture the strange feelings her voice evoked in me.

"I've waited a long time. But I miss you and wanted to talk. How are you?" Heather continued.

"I'm good. Really good. How long has it been? Six months?"

"What I was hoping...that you might meet me for lunch one day this week and we'd catch up." she said.

Bergdorf's small restaurant on the lower level was filled with Ladies Who Lunch and we met there at one that Friday. Perfectly coifed, Prada and Chanel-clad women eating salads chatted away.

Heather stood waiting, dressed in her typically understated cashmere sweater and black pants. A tall blonde who allowed herself to age gracefully, she had an elegance that appeared more and more rare amongst the nouveau riche women inhabiting the Upper East Side of New York.

She wore simple earrings and no other jewelry. Her straight shoulder length hair and little makeup looked out of place in Bergdorf's. Then again, I didn't look like I belonged there anymore either.

When she saw me she looked pained, which left me wondering just how good an idea this lunch might be. We ordered our Cobb salads and iced teas.

"Guess we should talk about Len and get it over with. Do you know the latest on what's going on with him?" Heather said as she carefully placed the cloth napkin on her lap.

"How could I? And I'm sure you can understand I prefer not to. Although he has called my home a couple of times and hung up. Once, he called in the middle of the night, waking me up of course, and I kept saying 'Hello? Hello? Hello? Who is this?' He finally hung up."

"He got married again, to a woman who just turned thirty. He must have called right before it," Heather said.

"So I was replaced as easily as Judy?"

"He took her to Europe to propose, although not Paris. Sound familiar?" Heather replied.

"A few nights before we broke up Len said that if we didn't make it as a couple, he wouldn't date for a long time. He needed a time out to think about how he deals with relationships. Looks like he had already picked out his second wife. But at the end I knew something was going on."

"How'd you know?"

"Over the summer, we had stopped seeing some of his friends, long-planned trips were cancelled, and I would find Len giggling at messages left on his voice mail. I asked him what the story was, who was leaving the messages. And he yelled at me, saying that I didn't trust him."

"Well, get this – she's pregnant. He bragged about how pleased he was that he could get a woman pregnant at his age. I don't know why, it's not unusual."

Heather frowned as she sipped on her iced tea.

"You didn't know that I was pregnant a week before Len moved out?"

"With Len's baby? You had an abortion? I'm starting to feel sick," she said as she pushed her plate aside.

"Why are you here? Why did you want to tell me these things?"

"I felt so badly about what happened and it looks like I didn't even know the worst of it. Now I feel really awful," she said.

Heather appeared on the verge of tears as she leaned over the table and reached for my arm.

"Do you think she knew about you? I bet he didn't tell her he was living with someone and the someone he was living with was pregnant."

"I don't care what she knew," I said.

Heather stared at me apparently in shock at all she had heard.

"I've moved on. I don't need to hear about Len. He's still threatening me that he wants money for the security deposit. I used it to stay in the apartment while Ben finishes the school year. You can't imagine how ugly this has become. He has sent some of the nastiest letters, even by his standards," I said.

"Obviously, it's not about the money since he doesn't need it. He's doing very, very well."

"I reminded him in my letter that he often told me that when he was wrong he needed a graceful exit from an argument. To save face for him, I gave back all of the jewelry."

I didn't tell Heather but my friends had flipped when I told them about returning the jewelry. Every one of them argued they would have kept all of it and relished wearing it, to boot. They assured me that time would erase the memory that Len had purchased the pieces. And that the jewelry, at the time Len gave it to me, honored real feelings.

Despite my friends' efforts, I felt good about returning every piece of it. The jewelry meant nothing to me and I never wanted it anyway. I certainly wanted no ties to Len. And I wasn't so sure about those real feelings as Len's motivation when he gave me the pieces. He probably just wanted the woman on his arm flashing expensive jewelry.

"He still says he's going to sue me," I said.

"How did you respond?"

"I spoke to a good friend of mine who's a divorce attorney who's used to men who are bullies. She advised me to write a simple note back saying go ahead and sue and ignore his threats. I haven't heard from him since. He knows a lawsuit would be public and expose all the details of who he truly is."

Heather looked around the restaurant as if searching for the nearest emergency exit door. Oh, how she must have regretted arranging this lunch.

"I've heard enough about Len for a lifetime. Tell me about Bill and your kids."

Heather and I chatted for another ten minutes about our families. She always struck me as a kindhearted woman untouched by her enormous wealth and it should not have been a surprise when she reached out to me. But as we parted, exchanging hugs, I felt sure Heather and I would never cross paths again.

■　■　■

It was finally time to rebuild the woman Len had torn apart and try to believe in love again. For some women at this juncture, giving up on men and on love is the only possible course, even by default. For me, the end of Len was different than losing Jake. It was not a great loss but a betrayal. Maybe Len had done more damage to my head than Jake's death had done to my heart. But I had forever learned from Jake to never give up, and I needed the sweet memories of him to believe in love again.

Jake was born in early April in a once in a lifetime blizzard. Twenty-two inches in one day. On his birthday each year of our marriage, I took note of the invariably spring like weather and teased him that snow on his birthday was simply impossible.

Now sitting in my office, looking out over the Hudson River, I remembered it was Jake's birthday. The past week had been unusually warm, in the seventies, and the prospects of a boiling summer in New York City loomed ahead. But that day started out cold and overcast. And while I sat there, thinking about how much I needed to remember the love of a good and kind man, it began to snow. Within several minutes, the Hudson was blanketed with white flakes. Jake had sent a sign to me and the tears rolled down my face.

A colleague came running into my office.

"Can you believe it's snowing?"

Nothing was impossible – not even snow from heaven that day.

That last summer with Len, I had soaked in the luxury of his enormous marble Jacuzzi, close to being another victim of his personalized version of corporate raids. Now that I was out of the elaborate maze he had constructed for me, I could again notice that the leaves were gorgeous.

All my adult life, people had told me how much they savored my joie de vivre. Len had almost sucked the joy out of me, leaving me no buffer against his unstoppable power.

And then on a crisp morning when Chloe was home from college for the weekend, I woke up and realized that in all of the time since I had lost Jake, I had never felt so good, so thoroughly pleased with my children and with myself. If I hadn't been so desperate, I would have been done with Len years earlier. But he had smelled the desperation and the advantage was his.

Chloe and Ben sat at dinner that night laughing over our family joke of how Ben was born with both Chloe's and his fair share of the athletic genes. Watching them I sat quietly, completely satisfied with the moment. Ben was now six foot four, almost as tall as his father and just as handsome with his father's heart of gold. Chloe was now the daughter I had always wished for – strong, beautiful, hardworking but always ready to play. I had brought these two up single-handed.

Gazing at the heavens from our twenty-second floor window, way above the twinkling lights of the City, I whispered a message back to Jake.

"I did well with your kids. You'd be so proud of them. And you'd be so proud of the woman I've become. You can rest in peace now. We'll be just fine, Jake. I have survived the toughest one of all."

■ ■ ■

Traffic in the Bronx crawled as Ben and I headed to his game on a Saturday afternoon. Ben looked stone-faced listening to music, getting psyched to pitch, while I prayed the pitching gods would smile on him. At the ballpark the mothers always huddled together in the bleachers, holding our collective breath until one of our sons walked off the mound after his last throw, either a hero or a bum.

The car windows opened to the spring air while Nirvana blasted on a tape. As we stopped at a light, a fire engine red Camaro pulled up next to my driver's side window. The two guys inside bopped their heads in time to the sounds coming from our car.

"Hey mama, love your music," one called out.

My music? I sort of smiled back at him trying to disguise the fortysomething woman chauffeuring her son around.

"Cool, very cool," he said and they drove off.

"Guess your mama is cool," I said bopping my head.

Ben cringed with teenage disbelief covering his face.

"You want to be cool?" he said.

I stopped bopping.

"You know my friend Tyler. His older brother just climbed Kilimanjaro. That's cool. You've always had a lot of courage so why don't you climb?"

And then Ben turned away to listen to "Smells Like Teen Spirit".

Kilimanjaro? A native New Yorker who had never slept in a tent, let alone climbed a mountain. Was that a curve ball Ben threw me? But something about his comment left me wondering. There remained a void after Jake's death that supposedly could only be filled by a man.

Standing on the top of the world's highest freestanding mountain might be that moment that could make the past vanish in thin air. Literally. Hiking in Provence would not do the trick. It had to be this kind of challenge.

Yet what Ben didn't know, just two days before a friend introduced me to Ted, an acquaintance of hers, at a party.

"Ted's a criminal defense attorney who handles high

profile cases that make headlines. He has his own firm. And if that's not enough, he climbed Kilimanjaro two years ago," she said that evening as he stood erect by her side.

With a pin stripe suit, Ferragamo tie and thick grey hair, he looked every bit the part of a senior partner on "LA Law". The climber in him appeared evident in his tall, strong body.

"He's divorced and very successful," she whispered in my ear as she turned and left us standing alone.

"You have soulful eyes. Lots of deep emotion there," Ted said.

Not sure about the proper response to that, I just kept my soulful eyes looking into his.

"I assume you came alone," Ted said while he appeared to laser into my eyes as if he could take control of me if he did it long enough. Did this work when he cross-examined witnesses?

"I feel like I'm on the witness stand. You must be quite intimidating."

"Of course I am. I've got some very important clients counting on that. Let's have dinner. Give me your number?" Ted said as he took out his business card and handed it to me.

"If you'll tell me about Kilimanjaro."

After Ben's comment, the thought of climbing Kilimanjaro consumed me. Since the end of my relationship with Len, I had vowed to never let anyone treat me like that, ever. And despite the deep wound of Jake's death, somehow I wanted to open my heart and love completely again.

I wondered if I could risk loving like that once more knowing one day I'd have to feel the inevitable pain of saying goodbye. But I didn't want to go through the next thirty years feeling nothing. Maybe by climbing Kili, building a core strong enough to climb that mountain, I could yet again engage in life and start over. Get a sense of our place in this world. And then by finding love and going with it. Uphill. One step at a time.

Ted and I met for dinner a week later at The Four Seasons, a meal that lasted for two hours while Ted unexpectedly poured out the story of his tumultuous life. Surrounded by the elegant décor and the power brokers of New York, Ted began when his alcoholic father physically and verbally abused him as a child.

Then he narrated the saga of his two failed marriages. As Ted retraced the wounds of his life, my mind reeled with the thought that Ted might just be another version of Len. The grown man never able to overcome and always compensating for a very damaged childhood.

The two hours passed before I interjected myself into his world, having literally not uttered a word for the entire time.

"Tell me about Kilimanjaro. I'm seriously considering the climb," I finally said.

"I did it for charity with some other lawyers. We organized an eight person group to raise money for Alzheimer's research."

As he stood up, Ted threw me a supercilious look.

"I doubt you'd make it up Kilimanjaro. You don't look terribly athletic or strong," he said.

The memory of Len's criticisms began ringing in my ears.

"Not quite the support I was hoping for."

"Why don't you come back to my apartment?" he asked as we walked out of the restaurant.

I turned my head to look at him with not a trace of warmth on my face. He glared back at me.

"You know when I was in Vietnam, we had a saying about the enemy. 'If you grab them by the balls, their hearts and minds will follow.' Women should know that applies to men," he said.

"Thank you for dinner."

I quickly threw myself into a cab.

CHAPTER 34

May/June

All that time craving the security of Len and now I was making plans to climb Kilimanjaro. Alone. Scheduled to leave for Tanzania on Friday July 3rd, it became obvious I was on my own in this adventure. Chloe and Ben loved the idea for me but expressed no interest in coming along. Everyone in my life questioned why climb any mountain, let alone Kilimanjaro. Some even let out snippets of "It's just plain nuts".

"Do you know what you're getting yourself into?" one friend asked.

"No, but that's never stopped me."

. . .

The route required a seven day climb up and two day descent, all told about sixty miles. The focus turned to my body and how to turn it into mountain climbing material in the next eight weeks.

On the summit of Kilimanjaro, which is 19,340 feet, the amount of oxygen in the air is only half that at sea level. This causes altitude sickness in some people, but it's not predictable who will succumb. Climbing Kili didn't require technical skills or special equipment like ropes, so it really was all about getting in the best possible shape.

"Do I need to train on some mountain in Colorado or California?" I asked the trainer from the trekking company over the phone.

It didn't make sense that people would prepare by climbing mountains in Colorado and I'd be walking the flat sidewalks of New York with designer clad women in sultry stilettos passing by.

"The workout regimen I'm planning will push you in the same way as climbing a mountain. The fact that you live at sea level is no problem," he said.

Central Park quickly transformed into a training ground for several hours a day several days each week, squeezed in between my obligations to my work and caring for Ben. It felt idyllic at first, surrounded by joggers, children playing and endless trees smack in the center of Manhattan.

But by the second week, after walking the six mile route with twenty-five pound weights in my backpack twice around the Park for the third day in a row, I wondered if it would be a waste of taxpayer dollars by dialing 911 to have a couple of muscular guys carry me back to my apartment on a stretcher.

The phone rang at eleven at night and I must have answered it, but exhaustion clouded any conversation that took place.

"Why don't you come over to my place and I'll show you what I kept from Kilimanjaro. Might be some things you could use. Saturday. At four," Ted said.

In a half conscious state, I agreed to the visit. Although, in the morning I wondered if the call even occurred and then tried to rationalize spending any more time with this man as a means to learn more about Kilimanjaro. Ted, the victim of his father, earned enormous compassion. But Ted, the man who appeared as crude and tough as his abusive, alcoholic father he had told so many stories about at our dinner, engendered none.

His apartment on the Upper East Side, the seduction den of a successful bachelor, seemed ready for a magazine spread. A masculine aesthetic pervaded the dark wood bookshelves lining one wall, the abstract art hung over the huge brown leather couch, and the large Tibetan beige silk rug trimmed with brown leather.

Ted had gathered some of the equipment from his climb. On the ottoman were some well-used hiking poles, binoculars, insulated gloves, and two thermal shirts.

"You can borrow these. They've already made it to the top and might bring you good luck."

Ted handed me a bronze leather album. The photos inside chronicled the story of his trek along with several of Ted standing next to a tall, pretty woman, neither of them looking particularly happy. I thumbed through the various pictures.

On the last page a certificate with Ted's name, the date and the words 'Gilman's Point' was supposed to be the climax of the story. The signatures of Chief Park Warden of Kilimanjaro National Park and the Director General of Tanzania National Parks lined the bottom.

"Pretty impressive, don't you think?" Ted said.

"Gilman's Point isn't the summit," I blurted out.

His face contorted, probably like one of his clients on the stand caught in a lie by the prosecuting attorney. All those books I'd been reading told me that Ted needed to climb another two hours to get to Uhuru, the summit. In Ben's world of Monday Night Football, Ted had made it maybe to the fifteen yard line. Not a touchdown.

"They mixed up the certificates when we got down," Ted said.

But there was a picture of him with his group standing next to a Gilman's Point sign. The summit picture is taken next to the Uhuru Peak sign.

Ted sat there silently. Embarrassed for him, second guessing if I should have blurted out the truth, I couldn't look him in the eye. The tale he spun of making it to the summit hovered over us. He may have been accustomed to dealing with folks on the witness stand when they were lying, but I sat there speechless.

"You're going to have to work a whole lot harder training if you think you're getting to the top," he said.

There was a harsh look on his face that he must have inherited from his father. At that moment, I knew that Ted would be my foil. The high profile attorney who lied about attaining the summit and tried to diminish me because he couldn't make it. Another version of Len had truly come back to haunt me. Only this time things were going to work out differently, very differently.

"Thank you Ted. I'm getting to the top," I said as I stood up to leave his apartment and him behind.

∎ ∎ ∎

With exactly one more month of training left, I was wiped and needed a day of rest. Feeling strong, trim, and firm, I had on heels rather than the boots I hiked in every day to break them in. For one day at least, New York could be savored and not simply endured on its endless sidewalks and pseudo trails.

But as I crossed 8th Ave at 58th street, the heel of my shoe hit one of the countless New York City potholes and my foot turned under. It hurt like hell.

Not with Kili a month away. Limping along the street, the pain grew worse. I turned and headed back to my apartment. It couldn't be broken, it just couldn't be.

Three hours later, Dr. Craig, the orthopedist examined the X-ray.

"You fractured your fifth metatarsal. I'm going to give you a boot and you need to take a month off from your current training. You can schedule your climb for September."

I felt so rattled it didn't even occur to me that the climb might be rescheduled. After Jake died, my bottom line was that if it's fixable, then there's nothing to get upset about. A broken foot is fixable. I just never thought the day would come when I get the results of an X-ray showing a broken foot, not cancer, and I would flip out.

The training plan metamorphosed into swimming a mile three times a week and riding a stationary bike for an hour three times a week, while nursing my broken foot gave me the time to read more books. But now I wanted to know what compelled climbers to endure freezing temperatures, extreme physical exertion and sometimes risk their lives. Just the opposite of the life craved in the lush world of the Upper East Side.

Extreme climbers confessed to two attractions, reveling in nature and savoring the risks. But those didn't resonate with me at all. Smitten with the idea that there were mountains that could teach me lessons, I felt compelled to climb. The hard labor of training felt just like the prelude to giving birth, but I had no clue this time what might be born out of all of this.

SUMMER 1998

CHAPTER 35

July /August

A long summer of working out lay ahead once the heat settled into New York. While many of New York's residents escaped to the beaches, certainly the Hamptons, training continued day after day. Some days the exercise seemed so hard and I felt so exhausted that even my bed felt like a mountain to climb in and out of.

But the thought of tapping into something in life greater than what we experienced everyday waited for me on Kilimanjaro. I kept going for two months and finally crossed a threshold where my body seemed to transform into a simple exercise machine.

■ ■ ■

As I was stretched out on the couch engrossed in another book about the Seven Summits, the phone rang. To hear Heather's voice again shocked me.

"Did you see the Obituaries in the *Times* today?" she asked.

"No, but I'm getting the paper right now."

I grabbed the newspaper on the glass coffee table in front of me and started flipping the pages.

"Look at Section D, page 7," Heather said.

The page displayed a picture of Len from ten years ago. Len dead?

The Managing Directors of Duke Heller are deeply saddened by the passing of Leonard Miller, a member of the firm for over twenty-five years. Mr. Miller joined Duke Heller as a general partner and went on to lead the real estate investment banking services division as a Senior Director. Mr. Miller was the epitome of the Wall Street investment banker for all who knew and worked with him. He was a mentor, advisor, strategist and inspiration to all. We extend our deepest and heartfelt sympathy to his beloved wife, Peggy, and three children, Jennifer, Dale and Peter.

Heather broke the silence.

"Len was hit by a taxi. It happened about one in the morning. Five days ago."

"One in the morning? Was he working late? Coming out of his office? I thought you said his wife is pregnant."

"He was leaving an apartment building near the corner of 65th and 2nd. A cab was trying to beat a yellow light, hit him and dragged him halfway down the block trapped under a tire. There was one witness who heard a screech and called for help. They rushed him to New York-Presbyterian where he died."

Heather's words seemed surreal. I almost felt sorry for Len for a moment.

"What was he doing in that building at that time of the night?"

"Turns out, Len was visiting a woman who has an apartment there."

"Someone he works with? Maybe he was picking up documents."

"She's a saleswoman in the lingerie department at Saks."

"You're not serious."

"I wish."

Len's picture evoked nothing other than enormous sadness for his family. All I could think about was that fate, or karma, or just bad luck had caught up with the powerful Wall Street man who had run over so many on his path of greed to secure and enjoy his many millions. He was run over by a cab driver hustling for a few extra bucks.

"I feel terribly for his kids, his pregnant wife. Can you imagine?" I said.

"What a mess he left."

"I'm so sorry Heather."

Len was dead. I was about to climb Africa's tallest mountain. Go figure.

FALL 1998

CHAPTER 36

September

When the day finally arrived for me to leave, Ben hugged me goodbye while the taxi driver waited impatiently after putting my duffle bag in the trunk. He kept twisting his head back to watch us and then turned on the meter to let me know I could linger as long as I'd like but it would cost me.

"Be good. Have fun. Don't do anything stupid and I'll try to do the same," I said.

His face betrayed an understandable mix of worry and excitement. Chloe, already back at Brown, was so lost in her world that her parting words on the phone had been brief.

"Good luck Mom."

The trekking company carried satellite phones on Kili so I knew if they needed to reach me or I needed to contact my children, it could happen. I wouldn't have gone otherwise.

The taxi began to pull away from them and then my tears came. It felt so strange to be on my own. Was this the most boneheaded thing I'd ever planned? Leaving my children behind didn't seem an auspicious beginning to an adventure like this.

The day before many friends called to wish me well. Janet, my constant source of wisdom, offered advice, "pay attention to your intention". I didn't pay much attention to her words until they resurfaced on the way to the airport.

So I rode in the taxi struggling to make clear my intention and it appeared to be very simple: getting to the summit of the mountain and back. I had never backed down from any challenge before, so climbing to the summit of Kilimanjaro was next. All the rest of what might happen would be revealed on the journey, whether my intention or not.

■ ■ ■

On the plane from Amsterdam to Kilimanjaro my terror surfaced. A dark moonless sky covered Africa so we saw nothing of the continent below. About thirty of the men and women on the plane wore hats and t-shirts from various trekking companies. And of all of the climbers I could see, it appeared I might be the only one traveling alone. Alone. I tried to settle into my small coach seat on the long ride, comforted by the knowledge I'd be heading home in two weeks no matter what happened.

Or at least I assumed I'd be going home. Around ten people die each year attempting to scale the mountain. They die from pulmonary edema, cerebral edema, heart attacks, acute mountain sickness, falls and the rare avalanche. Those ten are among the 40,000 people who attempt to climb Kili each year. A thousand people are evacuated from the mountain. Roughly 15,000 climbers actually make it to Uhuru, the summit.

When we finally landed at the tiny Kilimanjaro airport packed with climbers, the group of two women and five men who would be trekking with me introduced themselves as we gathered our luggage. They appeared in the age range from thirty to sixty. As we stood there, the power in the terminal went off. The unexpected and unpredictable, something we craved on this journey, had just begun.

Just as we arrived at the small rustic lodge where we'd stay before our climb began, another group of climbers checked in ahead of us. Standing at the end of the line, a man caught my eye. A tall handsome guy wearing a black t-shirt and khaki shorts, he had an athletic, muscular build with well-defined arms and legs. If getting up this mountain required a body like his, then the joke had to be on me.

We had a long, leisurely dinner that evening as we chatted and tried to gauge the chemistry of our group. By the end of the meal, the moment came when we looked around at one another seated at the large wooden table. For the next week our lives would be intertwined in potentially dangerous and difficult conditions. Each one of us appeared pleased, apparently relieved, that the group at first glance might be a very lucky role of the dice.

■ ■ ■

The next day we remained in neutral. A day to acclimate. As we took our time eating lunch on the porch of a small wooden structure built for viewing the scenery and giraffes, elephants and zebras wandering in the distance, climbers from the other group sat down at our table, including the athletic looking man from the lodge. He introduced himself as Drew. Across from Drew sat a husky, serious looking guy who kept eyeing him.

"Can't wait to get this show on the road. Enough of this hanging around. I came to climb," Husky said.

He directed his comments at Drew. Only a certain type of man could utter those words and the streets of New York had its fair share of them. A man who let competition and impatience drive his every move.

Drew lifted his head, as he had been concentrating on the food, and just looked at Husky. Drew's body shouted to anyone listening that he'd known his fair share of battles in sports. But he didn't respond.

Husky left the table, frustrated with Drew's restraint.

Finally, the next morning it was game on. The journey began in the forest zone where the lush, dense rainforest sounded filled with birds and the occasional colobus monkey. We hiked for four hours including some big uphill climbs and reached 9,500 feet.

But the real test began after our dinner. Turning on my headlamp and heading for the tent, dread of the cold, the dark and being alone hit me. My training should have included sleeping at night in a quiet tent without city sirens and horns and lights from blocks of office buildings coming through my open blinds.

No sleep would mean exhaustion and lessen any chances of success. Since enduring the nighttime was a pivotal part of the package of climbing the mountain, soothing myself "one night at a time, I can do this" ran over and over again in my head. Conquering the mountain included the darkness.

Our tents were set up just a few feet apart and it wasn't long before the sound of snoring in the next tent became nature's version of background music. Although not a city sound, it helped. I crawled into my sleeping bag, turned on the flashlight and fell asleep exhausted.

. . .

Samuel, the Tanzanian head guide, and I trekked in the middle of the line our group formed along the trail on the second day of our ascent. He told us our objective of reaching 12,200 feet in about five or six hours.

The scenery had changed. No longer encased in the forest, our view looked wide open now on large heathers and unusual looking shrubs. Small boulders filled the trail and my eyes focused down on them.

"There's Kibo, the top!" Samuel said.

I looked up at the summit of the iconic mountain for the first time. And at that moment my foot tripped on a rock and I fell flat on my face. Lying there for a second, panic set in. Not in Africa, I couldn't have broken something, again. All that training. I had to climb Kili. Please.

I waited for the pain to surface. But nothing happened. Nothing hurting meant nothing could be broken.

Standing up, I started giggling and Samuel seemed to relax.

"I need to keep my eye on you," he said.

. . .

Drew and Husky were sitting on some large rocks, far apart from each other, the next afternoon when we arrived at our campsite

"What'd you take the long way? We've been here for hours," Husky said.

They weren't in our group, and Samuel wasn't responsible for their health and safety but that didn't stop him. He knew the risks of going up the mountain too fast.

"Does your guide know what you guys are doing?"

"I'm not in your group pussyfooting my way to the top," Husky said.

He waited for Samuel to take the bait and when he didn't, Husky stormed off to his tent.

I sat down on the rock next to Drew.

"It's such a beautiful mountain. Why would you climb it with him?" I asked.

"I love competition."

"But why are you here?"

"To beat him to the top." Drew said.

Drew spoke in a gentle voice as if his strong physique and dark handsome features drew enough attention.

"Seriously."

"I've dreamed of doing this for so many years. After hiking out west over and over again, it was finally time. What about you?"

"I've dreamed about it for four months. This dormant volcano is supposed to surface something dormant in me." I said.

"You seem to really enjoy this physical challenge.

"But my idea of a physical challenge and yours aren't even in the same league."

"They are now. Same mountain, same goal."

As the climbers gathered for dinner, we noticed there were two less in another group.

"Remember there was a guy shouting at his wife the other day? He kept yelling at her that she was holding him back. Well, he was vomiting, had diarrhea. He couldn't do it anymore and went back down. He seemed very disappointed," Samuel announced to our group at dinner.

We all snuck in the tiniest smiles at one another. Not one of us would miss him for a minute.

"And his wife?" I asked.

"She went down too," Samuel said.

"You're kidding, right?" Drew asked.

"No, she escorted him down."

"She should have made the summit just because he couldn't," I said.

. . .

Frost covered everything inside the tent the next morning. Shivering in my sleeping bag and with no other source of warmth, I piled on some layers of clothing and hurried to get out.

From six in the morning when the sun rose till sunset at six at night, the temperature on the mountain felt comfortable. But the minute the sun went down, the brutally cold air settled in and we could not escape it anywhere. Each day became more clearly defined as heavenly between sunrise and sunset and hellish from sunset to sunrise.

I woke up every morning freezing. But once I fled my tent, saw my fellow climbers and the sun, it all made sense. Our view of the mountain was spellbinding and it looked far more enormous in person. At the first sighting of Kili each day, it seemed daunting to imagine how we'd get to the top.

The morning also revealed how dirty my body became with my long hair tangled and filthy, my lips chapped so badly they hurt and my fingernails black with dirt. We couldn't shower but simply washed off the parts of our body that we managed with a wet cloth.

I missed Chloe and Ben terribly and longed for contact with them. They hadn't called the satellite phone so it seemed reasonable to assume they were doing okay.

"Today we reach 15,000 feet and that's when the altitude might really affect you. I need to know how all of you are feeling," Samuel said while we ate our breakfast.

He tested our pulse and oxygen levels and we waited for disastrous results that didn't appear. No excuses. Keep climbing. And we did, all day.

But Drew, whom I hadn't seen since the evening before, looked different late that afternoon as we headed into our campsite.

"I've got a bad headache," he said.

"That's probably altitude sickness. Maybe you need to let this go with Husky?"

Drew's muscular body, now hidden under many layers of clothing, could surely handle this. But the interjection of Husky meant that ego, bravado and testosterone could be driving them higher and faster up this mountain than what their bodies needed to acclimate. Was there no stopping a man in this mindset?

The women in our group appeared at ease with each other. The lack of contention amongst us didn't mean for a minute that we weren't all working as hard as we could to get to the top. But from the moment Husky encountered Drew, it became a race to the summit for those two. I wondered if Husky wasn't just plain jealous of Drew's physique. Husky kept baiting the jock in Drew and Drew kept biting.

My tent felt no warmer that night than the outside frigid air and as I pushed myself into my sleeping bag with two layers of long thermal underwear, a down jacket, wool hat, gloves, and two pair of socks, I thought about Drew and Husky. Just as Husky became Drew's foil to persevere up the mountain, Ted served as mine. And not just for himself, but as a surrogate for Len. But lucky me, I didn't have to see my foil every day egging me on.

■ ■ ■

The Barranco Wall at 14,000 feet stood before us the next day. We'd be climbing up the steep 800 foot wall of rocks, equivalent to an eighty story building.

"Manhattan girl climbing the Barranco Wall?" Noah said.

Noah, a mediator and family law attorney from California, had lost his first wife to cancer six years before. We became friends the moment we met.

"This Manhattan girl is up for anything at this point."

Matukuta, one of the guides, positioned himself so he could instruct each of us as we scaled the Wall.

One by one, our group headed up the wall. We occasionally looked up at how high the Barranco Wall reached and then at the long way down at where a misstep might land us. There was no way to go but up that wall. Finally, I began to climb.

"Ok, put your left foot on that rock," Matukuta called.

I put my foot on the rock.

"Put your *other* left foot on that rock."

"Whoops."

I looked down at the jagged rocks far below and immediately did as he said. But this Manhattan girl started laughing at the wonder of finding herself scrambling up the Barranco Wall. It just didn't get any more surreal or better than this.

■ ■ ■

The air in the dining tent the night we camped at 16,000 feet felt icy cold on our faces and we ate in down jackets and hats. Noah sat across the table. After finishing their dinner, all the others left to get some sleep. The next day we would head for the summit and Noah had waited years to do just that.

He and his second wife, Amelia, attempted Kili three years before. Noah came back by himself for another try.

"I couldn't possibly imagine doing this again, ever," I said.

"I've never taken a trip like this by myself and it's very empowering. I really want to be close to the spiritual ethers, so to speak, on the summit, make peace with some inner demons. A spiritual cleansing."

"Wow, and I did this just to stop dating the wrong men."

Noah finally let out a laugh.

"I couldn't figure you out right away. There was a sense of nervousness about you that first night and I wondered if your mood was more bravado than jocularity," Noah said.

"It was definitely both. Some people back home didn't think I could do this."

I thought of Ted and also of Len, the men who underestimated me in life.

"So you're like on a crusade. I do think your good cheer has been contagious, taking something arduous and making it fun. One more day and hopefully you'll be able to say Kate did Kili," he said as he stood up.

■ ■ ■

On summit day, six hours of steep climbing separated us from the top. For the first time on our trek, it felt like the mountain was going to deal its toughest hand. Few of us chatted while the group moved very deliberately up the steep path of rocks. The hours passed slowly. Drew and Husky had to be hours ahead of us and already heading down.

We entered the fourth zone, the arctic zone. Huge and gorgeous glaciers as tall as eighty feet high framed our view as we climbed to the top of this dormant volcano that Hemingway immortalized. The air felt biting cold on our bare faces.

Gazing down, we saw a vista of clouds way below covering our view of Africa all around. A stillness surrounded us as we approached the summit. And then we saw the iconic large brown rugged wooden sign, covered with stickers from previous climbers, at the top.

CONGRATULATIONS.
You are now at Uhuru Peak, Tanzania.
Africa's Highest Point. World's Highest
Free-Standing Mountain.

Our group hugged one another repeatedly and took endless pictures in front of the sign as proof that we had propelled ourselves up this giant mountain to the top. Typically, climbers spent ten to fifteen minutes at Uhuru since the altitude above 18,000 feet is considered extreme. We lingered, reluctant to leave, and already thirty minutes passed.

"How are you feeling?" Samuel asked.

"Great. I can't believe it," I said.

"Prove it. Do a push up."

I got down on the ground and did a push up on the summit of Kilimanjaro. Showing off on top. Elation filled the freezing air.

"You're really strutting your stuff," Noah laughed.

"You bet."

Samuel ushered us away from Uhuru.

"We still have a five or six hour descent ahead today to get back to 12,500 feet. Let's get going."

We ascended the mountain slowly approaching from the west, gaining altitude in careful increments. But now, we could go straight down as fast as our knees would carry us on the steep trail. Several times we saw stretchers lined up along the side of the trail.

Another guide going by stopped Samuel momentarily and they spoke briefly in Swahili. The changed look on Samuel's typically placid face betrayed the news.

"Someone died up there earlier today," Samuel relayed to us.

No one moved a muscle.

"Who was it?" Noah said.

"I'll tell you when we get down to camp later. "

After an endless five hours of the difficult trek down the mountain negotiating the scree, we arrived at our campsite completely depleted. Samuel pulled us aside.

"Remember I told you someone died up on the summit today?"

We all held our breath dreading the news.

"Drew died. He had cerebral edema. Husky was with him."

The shock felt more biting than any frigid air we had experienced in the depth of our freezing nights.

"He collapsed, went into a coma and died quickly. There were other guides up there, they knew he was in critical condition, but there was no time to get him down to a lower altitude or do anything, " Samuel said.

"Where's Husky?" I asked.

"They took him down quickly, he was so upset," Samuel said.

"You mean the guy actually has a heart?"

"This is what happens on the mountain."

Samuel went off to his tent while I sat down on one of the rocks, trying to put my thoughts together.

So Kili was the metaphorical mountain of life. The euphoria of attaining the summit of Africa's highest peak, and then death stealing someone away again, both on the same day.

My fellow climbers said that reaching the summit amounted to the hardest thing they'd ever done. Not for me. It felt like a piece of cake compared to living on a cancer ward with Jake. I had a choice about doing Kili. And I got to push myself physically further than I thought possible. But this time finding how much resilience I had was for a good reason.

Unlike so many of the books I'd read about Kili, my story didn't include throwing up, severe headaches, disorientation and stomachaches. I got lucky that way. This time ascending Kili had been about being strong. We climbed a beautiful mountain in Africa and I'd loved every minute of it until Samuel spoke those words.

Picking up a small rock and putting it in my pocket, I knew that every time I looked at it, that rock would be a symbol to me of Kilimanjaro. The glory and the toll of climbing this mountain, our mountain of life.

■ ■ ■

We gathered at the base of the mountain the next day for the traditional celebratory lunch after our descent. Exhausted, filthy, and encumbered by sadness from Drew's death, we knew something bigger than any of us erupted out of that dormant volcano.

Samuel gave each of us an official certificate, our diploma. We had reached Uhuru. It definitely said Uhuru. Proof of our success.

I had no idea if I'd ever attempt another mountain. Climbing Kilimanjaro felt extremely exhilarating but ridiculously exhausting and for the moment I vowed to never even go to a gym again. Our oxygen and sleep deprivation would take a while to recover from and I longed for my children, my bathtub and bed at home.

The flight home through Amsterdam lasted sixteen hours. We embraced each other, our newfound strength, and how different we were going home. Finally, we were forced to say goodbye at the airport in New York, but we lingered for a few moments longer. Our families, our homes beckoned but for one more moment we savored our trip together. Whomever I might have been a year before, that person didn't climb Kilimanjaro. The woman who reached the summit emerged onto the cab line at JFK.

As the cab slowly made its way through the traffic of Queens, my thoughts returned to Janet's words. I had accomplished exactly what I intended. But what had been revealed that lay dormant within me? In the midst of the traffic, horns and the dreary expressway, I thought of standing on the summit.

In the context of a greater universe filled with mountains and stars that endured for thousands of year, my life meant so little. The meaning of my life though was not to be found on that mountain, but within me. It is framed by choices to have the strength to keep going and to aim for the top.

I thought of what Sir Edmund Hillary, the first man to reach the summit of Mount Everest, said "It's not the mountain we conquer, but ourselves". Now I knew what mountain in life I wanted to climb and where the top lie. The shallow world of a Len, once at the heights of Wall Street, felt meaningless on that mountain. Uhuru is the word for freedom in Swahili. And I finally felt free. Knowing what I experienced training, what it took to get to the top, and what I did with it, would define me from then on. I had reached Uhuru. On top, at last.

SPRING 1999

EPILOGUE

June

I knew that my heart had opened up again when I noticed this guy at work one day. I felt it jump whenever I saw him. Not a minor skip like when you get a refund check from your health insurer and now you can buy something else you might or might not need, but a real one. Any cardiologist could easily have documented it if they had bothered hooking me up to an EKG at work.

He looked tall, about six foot two with an athletic build and short salt and pepper hair. A handsome man but that wasn't the point. His broad smile and large warm green eyes reminded me of better times. After watching him for about a month, I longed for him in the way they purportedly describe in romance novels, although I had never bothered reading one.

There were times when I intentionally avoided him. The chemistry he stirred up scared me. Was he thinking of me? Once, I saw him down the hall in a glass-walled conference room as I spoke to my boss in the hallway. Leaning against the wall, he kept staring at me, intentionally staring. He wanted me to know it. This went on for at least fifteen minutes. I didn't listen to a word my overbearing boss said.

The next day I walked into the large, crowded cafeteria at work and dropped my tray on one of the numerous, long, faux-walnut laminated tables. I hadn't noticed him but he walked over from the doorway nearby and straddled the yellow plastic chair next to me. He glanced at me sideways and then straightened out to face me on his chair. And so we began.

"Hi," he said.

I gave him a sort of half smile.

"I'm Alex. You're Kate?"

This time I nodded, another half smile.

"I started here about six months ago," he said.

"What area are you in?"

"I'm working on the clinical side. My team is responsible for evaluating programs that are designed to improve patient outcomes. My PhD is in Epidemiology," he said.

"It's so good to hear you haven't crossed over to 'the dark side' and you're actually trying to help patients. Too many people in healthcare are in it for the money."

"I've already encountered some folks here making decisions based on cost rather than what's in the best interest of the patient. My department doesn't generate any revenue so it's going to be an interesting battle," Alex said.

"Welcome to my world. Where were you before this?"

"I used to work at the CDC. I ran a similar program evaluating cancer prevention programs. We developed a prototype for a national reporting system for breast and cervical cancer based on funded state and local health department reporting. The CDC, when it gives money to state and local health departments, supports activities for better screening, especially for underserved population."

"My husband died of cancer," I said.

Alex closed his eyes for just a moment and shook his head.

"What kind?"

"Non-Hodgkin's lymphoma."

"I'm so sorry."

He leaned closer.

"Listen, I can't talk for long. I have a meeting in ten minutes. I know this is fast but would you have dinner with me?" Alex asked.

"Dinner would be lovely."

"Friday? 7:30? How about Gramercy Tavern? One of my favorite restaurants. In the front room we won't need reservations like the dining room. See you then?"

"See you then."

Work became an obstacle as I waited for the week to end. It wasn't until I walked into Gramercy Tavern on Friday evening and saw Alex anticipating my arrival did my body relax. He looked striking in his black jacket, black slacks and tan cotton button down shirt. I wore a tight navy blue knit dress and three inch heels. He seemed to like what he saw.

After we were seated at a table, Alex put our menus to the side, clearly indicating to the waiter that we'd be there for a while, needed lots of time to talk and don't bother asking us what we'd like until we've made it known we were ready.

"I did what I could to learn who this pretty woman was who I couldn't take my eyes off of. When people at work talk about you the words they use the most are genuine, passionate, compassionate, fun," Alex said.

"You can fool some of the people....But seriously, I don't know much about you. Please tell me."

"I'm divorced, for four years now, and have three great kids. Olivia is twenty-two, Scott is twenty and Sophia is sixteen. The divorce proceeded quickly and amicably so little damage remains in its wake. We met in high school and married too young, right out of college, and eventually grew apart. And now we both want the best for the kids so we've agreed to put their interests first."

"Then you're a lucky man."

"I think I'm a lucky man since I'm sitting here with you," he said with his large green eyes penetrating mine.

He looked at me with a confidence, but not the arrogance I had come to dread from certain men.

"Have you been dating?" I asked.

"I have. But we're both here hoping for the right one, aren't we?"

I sat there wondering if maybe this man could navigate his way into my heart.

"I hear we have a lot in common. We grew up near each other. I spent my childhood in Gramercy Park. And I hear you climbed Kilimanjaro and reached the summit last fall. I did too, about three years ago," he said.

Various men in the past year had not reacted well to my climb. And there was one who actually told me at dinner not to mention it again, that he did not exercise that hard and would never push himself like that. He thought that my climb was very off-putting to men and felt it emasculating.

"Other than having my kids, Kili was definitely the most extraordinary experience of my life. It felt magical. When I stood on the summit, it gave me a sense of the planet and where I belong on it. It certainly puts your life in perspective. How'd you decide to do it?" I asked.

"I've been climbing for years. I actually did Kili with Olivia, my daughter who was nineteen at the time. What an experience to watch her make it at that age."

Alex looked very relaxed. Whatever may be the mystery of why two people fall for each other, his face spoke to me as much as the words coming from his mouth.

"Interested in doing another mountain?" he asked.

"Maybe. I could handle the daytime but the freezing nights alone in the tent seemed endless."

"If you do it with someone, it won't be quite so freezing," Alex said.

I thought of climbing with Alex, sharing a tent. He was flirting with an idea that I might consider...one day. I had a lot to learn about this man but so far a red flag appeared nowhere in sight.

"Tell me the story of Kate," Alex said.

"I've had a very different ride. You really want to hear?"

"I want to get to know you. And I want you to know me."

"I'd love to hear about you. The ride people are on intrigues me since mine has been so unpredictable. I married young, thought my road ahead would be a straight one – love, marriage, children. Instead, it turned out to also include death, dating and finding myself. What a mercurial, but lately exciting, journey it's been so far," I said.

"I like your attitude. And as they say, 'your attitude determines your altitude.'"

That feeling of a gentle man had enveloped me when I had met Jake. But the fall I had taken with Len after Jake's death had been as harrowing as falling off a mountain.

It was way too soon to burden Alex with the story of Len, but Jake, Jake might be a good place to start.

"I have two stories. Tonight, I'll share one," I said.

Alex sat waiting for me while I felt the floodgates begin

to open. I had never shared my journey with Jake on dates with other men. But Alex appeared to be that man who would listen with compassion and understanding. Our conversation did not resemble at all the ones I'd had with Len, with other dates, when we first met.

I felt drawn to Alex. The intimacy already between us was reflected in his smile glistening in the candlelight. My hand lay resting on the table and he reached across and held it. I looked at his soft, kind eyes and felt that maybe I could let down my guard at last. Parts of me, walled off after Len, felt free. Remembering that feeling, that freedom I had felt on the summit, meant letting go now of the past.

By telling him about my story with Jake, I could let Alex in. It was time to let him in.

Alex held my hand tightly and I began. We began.

ACKNOWLEDGEMENTS

To my editor Susan Leon who believed in me and my manuscript. Her comments were priceless.

And to my wonderful children who set a high bar for this book and pointed me in the right direction.

Special thanks to Charlie Klippel, Gail Agrawal and Ron Aubert.

Thanks to Cathy Walsh, Rachel Sawyer, Laurie Dittrich, Russell Teagarden and Steve Katz for the insights and unwavering support.